Young Savage
-by Rasheed-

-Profound Publishing-

Young Savage
©Copyright 2010
Profound Publishing

ALL RIGHTS RESERVED
No portion of this Book may be reproduced, stored in any electronic system, or transmitted in any form or by any means, electronic, mechanical, photocopy, recording, or otherwise, without written permission from the Author. Brief quotations may be used in literary reviews.

Cover Art by S. Quanaah/Rasheed
Written/Edited by Rasheed

Rasheedcarter15@yahoo.com

Dedicated to my Mother Betty & Auntie Sharon

Printed in
December 2010

Acknowledgements

First and foremost gratitude and appreciation to the creator for blessing me with a physical body to experience life. My mother Betty (The infamous) Mozell, the greatest mom ever! One day I will pay you back all the money that I owe you, until then I love you. Lol My brothers nothing would be possible or conceivable without all of you cats. Antonio Mozell, Harrison Mozell, and Percy (Nice,) Hilson, My sisters Ann marie, held me down when I had nothing, but hopes and dreams. Alvina, My baby sister and the cutest kid sister ever. My babies. Caleb (Cool-C) Carter, Ron-C, Sariah, Ma'rya, and Ta'shya, Carter, My dad Ron (proud ass) Carter, My auntie Sharon, thanks a million for all the encouragement and reassurance, that things would get better when I felt like my shoulders would buckle beneath the pressures of change. Both of my grandmother's, Margaret King, and Mona Lomax, Grandma I could never celebrate you enough to compensate for all the love, care, and concern you have provided for me throughout my life. My homegirl Ebony Harris, Kimberly Burnside, keeping me up all night on the phone and teaching me the true definition of long range love lol. April, gave me a place to stay when I needed it the most. Gotta, (J.C. Lowe,) Duke, Carmella, Uncle Larry, (Love you Big Dog.) Uncle Alvin, got my game from you. Auntie Ann and Uncle Arron, Savon (George) Lowe, Larry King, my cousin can't wait to get to V.A. baby. Pookie, Mano, Ral, Chris, (keep your ass out of jail) means. Quan, and everybody on that side. Nefesha Wallace, you are so beautiful to me. All my nieces and nephews New-New, De'asia, La'nasia, and Chardeezy, crazy crazy crazy. Nuk-Nuk, Harry, with your big head ass. Dada, Muka, Ny-Ny, Dalilah, and my YaYa, my other niece forgive me I'm bad with names. Keith, Can't forget about my baby mother's both of them. It was each of our experiences that helped me develop the drive I needed.

My other peoples Raheem (Skeem) Booker, Mark (Ghost) Carrero, Kwame Booker, Leon Stitt, My brother from another mother. You faked a move on me kid, but love is love sucka m.c.

lol. Frank Demauro, Jeffry Smith, the smartest white boy I know, his words Lol Panama, we fought, argued, challenged, and fought some more, but it only made our minds sharper. Thaxton (Malik) Hamlin, You have been a great inspiration and guide to me. I appreciate you as a mentor and brother. A special shout to Allah (Tank) Reese, you held me down I will never forget you. Too strong in the mind. Raynard (Riz) Swanns, we've been through a lot together and although you get on my nerves at times, I love you and appreciate the brotherhood. Dog, I'm not playing possum I'm biding my time. Lol. Sha-Sha, my girl from way back. George Stevens, Junie, you showed me the ropes when I was brand new to the East side good looking out. Officer Brian Peters, thanks to you and your terrible attitude I don't ever want to see the inside of a prison again. Saladin, thank you for all of your wisdom, help, encouragement, brotherhood, and friendship. May our relationship flourish and continue on in spirit when and wherever brothers meet and link up for a common cause. Shout out to the meanest believer in the world Anwar, the brother who checked me every chance he got. I loved the look on your face when you said Rasheed, this book doesn't make no damn sense. Lol. Phil Payne, my man when it counts the most. Jimmy (Black) Swanson, I love you kid and we are going to keep on living and enjoying the experience. Kourtney, (Murder) James, we've been through hell and back fighting from one side of town back to back until we made it home. Lavon Tabori. Cox, Time flew by and we grew in separate directions, yet the memories of our yesteryears hold the dearest moments. Javon Ridgeway, Willie Hilson, Mark Roundtree. To my peoples Matthew (Inf.) Humphry, our relationship has kept me in tune with my youth.

To anyone caught up in my madness when I ran the streets. Please forgive me a brother was truly living like a savage. Uncle Carl (Unc) Mcdonald. I appreciate you more than words could ever describe thanks a lot, for everything, and that's all I'm saying.

R.I.P Sandy Westbrook

Chapter 1
Beat down to the ground

Nobody ever loved him. Not in this life did he expect to get a break. Born into the wrong family, situated alongside negativity, and unjustly rewarded for being naïve and ignorant.

He never knew his father, his daddy's identity was a mystery, something like an invisible force impregnating a young girl with the mind of a virgin. His mother was an enigma of confusion. A puzzle; layers of domestic violence heaped on top of alcoholism, mixed with drug addiction, and a mind ripe for deception easily disillusioned with reality.

Mother nature visited him prematurely, stalked his bedroom with the intentions of a predator. Took his youth and replaced it with readiness. Stretched out his manhood until it swung heavily and hung dangerously low. The hands of times fashioned his follicles until hair covered his genitals and sprouted through the pores on his chest and gave him the appearance of a man before he could actually think like one.

The first slap took his face by surprise and viciously penetrated his face, pushing it upward. His body spiraled around and rotated just in time to meet the second slap. The one that drowned out his reasoning with a sharp pain. It rung inside his ears. He scurried for safety only to find himself trapped between a locked door and a drunken mother.

A lady who spent most of her days sleeping away poverty as she waited for her welfare check. Her spare time was squandered on stoops, hanging out in front of liquor stores, laying across filthy mattresses in crack houses, turning tricks, and using her misery as an excuse to beat her son for less than nothing.

The onslaught of torture came out of the blue. Unexpected violence exploded into the boy's face. He never saw it coming. He sat at the kitchen table spreading peanut butter across two end pieces of bread. His eyes were fixated on the bravery of the group of roaches that crawled around daring someone to mess with them.

He made his sandwich, licked one side of the butter knife clean, and prepared to do the same to the other side with his tongue.

Janet, his mother, and the ball of cross addicted confusion staggered into the front door. Her eyes looked around the living room surveying the area. She saw the couch that rested in the corner. The white one with the red flowers etched into the cushions. The one that was for show and not sitting because it didn't have any springs underneath it. The cushions sat there held in place by being properly positioned against each other.

She walked further into the house and took a look at her small black and white t.v. the one with aluminum foil coiled around the antenna for better reception. Her breathing was heavy, ragged, labored, pressed between too much drinking, and mental paranoia. She looked at the walls inside her apartment.

They were tiny and dirty, they use to be white, but now they were beige, a combination of white paint stained with chunks of caked up dirt. She peered ahead taking in much of the view as her bloodshot eyes could interpret. Upon seeing Rodney, her son sitting at the table with his back to her moving his head up and down she approached him. Her movements were slow, uncalculated, and clumsy. He ate peanut butter satisfying his hunger, unaware of the unsuspected danger. She attacked him.

The first slap took his face by surprise and viciously penetrated his face, pushing it upward. His body spiraled around and rotated just in time to meet the second slap. The blow that drowned out his reasoning and forced him to scurry away from his mother in search of safety. He was unable to find it. His young hands wrapped around the backdoor to the apartment, but found it locked. He reached up to unlock the door, but felt uncoordinated hands closing around his neck and dragging him down. His fingers slowly lost their grip on the brass lock. Finally they slipped from the door and ended up wherever his body was flung.

First he landed against the refrigerator. His eyes blinked rapidly wondering would this night be his last one on earth, or would this beating last as long as the others. His heart beat frantically while he held onto every thread of his life. The life his, own mother put in jeopardy whenever she felt the need to.

His body hit the floor and his mother rolled on top of him. She rested across his back. He screamed out in pain hoping to convince her to let him go, but she didn't. She took the back of his head and rammed it forward smashing his face into the floor.

Blood crept out from where the boy lay. The stains on the floor weren't enough to lessen the arrangements of her anger. Once she became tired she released him. His head stumbled from her hands. She stood up and over his limp body, prepared to leave, but stopped, took a step backward, and stomped her foot down into his back.

"Get your ass up off my floor and clean this shit up!" Her voice was nasty, spiteful, vindictive, and in the exact same vernacular that all drunks use when delusional. "Do you hear me!" She demanded and needed an immediate answer.

"Yes." The boy spoke weakly and broken down.

"Now!" The wicked woman who was influenced by hard drugs, cheap booze, and a lifetime of misplaced failure yelled. She used her strength, yanked him up by his neck, and tossed his body side to side while swinging punches at him. "Get the mop, get it!" She yelled as she moved behind the crying child.

His hands quickly maneuvered around the wooden handle of the mop as he fearfully swooshed the mop across the floor. Blood dripped from his nose and mouth.

"Fix your damn face!" Another slap came from his mother.

The boy used one hand to mop and the other to wipe his face clean with his shirt.

"That's what you get. You make me so damn sick, looking like your no good ass father."

"I know." The boy said hoping to prevent anymore violence. He cleaned up the blood and walked off to his bedroom.

Chapter 2
Life for a shorty shouldn't be so rough

Rodney, stood in front of his mirror the one that was really a piece of broken plexy glass, which he used for a mirror. He checked his face squinting at the pain he felt when he touched his upper lip. There was a gash, one where blood oozed through the same way that liquid came out of a sponge being squeezed. He tucked his lip into his mouth and sucked on it. He sucked it gently nursing it back to normal. He felt around his teeth using his tongue as fingers feeling for damage. When he found it-it wiggled five teeth over from his front tooth.

He wiggled it around until it fell into his tongue. His eyes closed as anger translated into sadness. He spit his tooth out into his hand, blood covered the tooth, and leaked out the opening where the tooth once belonged. He looked at his face and studied it.

There was a mustache, a smooth and silky steam of hair that resembled a beard. He saw a sexy face. A mysterious look with a touch of cunningness merged together with subtle sneakiness, made him appealing. He was handsome, but still able to grow into a more beautiful creation. He was still a kid, just a kid, a ten year old kid, and built like a man. Mother nature visited him prematurely, stalked his bedroom with the intentions of a predator. Took his youth and replaced it with readiness.

He climbed into his version of a bed. An air mattress covered with a sheet. His bedroom didn't have the typical bedroom furniture. It only contained a few garbage bags which he kept his clothes in. It didn't matter if they were clean or not, this was what he used for a dresser. The walls were bare, he had no curtains, and nor did he have any privacy.

He snuggled in as much as he could under his sheet and prepared to fall asleep. A short time later he tossed and turned, then became annoyed by his mother and the company that she kept. Alcoholics and drug users, people like her, all crowded inside the living room partying the night away.

Sleep took over him and carried him along the rhythm of a dream. In this world he was safe. He was free to be a kid and live the life of a kid. In this dream he found peace, held it in his hand, and in this place he had a mother and father. His beatings were replaced with conversations and reassurance of love. His lips smiled unconsciously. He felt the appreciation of gratitude as he hugged his imaginary father. He loved this man who guided him through life's hardship, and taught him to stand tall and face all adversity with courage and the will to get up and try again. The man laughed, giggled like a woman, shriveled up until he shrunk into a red bunny rabbit and hopped away.

Rodney's, eyes opened and blinked repeatedly as sleep subsided from his face. He stood up and walked out of his room, paused, backed up, and snuck a look at his face. The bump on his lip had increased in size and took on a disfigured color. He sighed out in disappointment and pain. He swallowed it down and moved forward until he was walking down the hallway that led into his living room.

He stood there in the living room inhaling the stench of several odors combined. The first smell the he recognized was beer, a cheap natural ice sort of beer, and the second scent to hit his nose was mackerel, a fishy odor of funk. He looked down and saw the elements responsible for making the smell.

His mother lay face down on the floor. She was completely naked. The bones in her frail body poked out showing the structure of her rib cage. Her back bones protruded out and her butt was tan and tiny to match her skinny body. The body that too much partying had, disintegrated into a smaller size, of its normal look. A man, one to new to be considered her man, but the man who was with her lay beside her equally naked.

Rodney's, eyes tilted upward, he turned around and went into her bedroom, and returned carrying a ragged cloth long enough to be considered a blanket, but thin enough to be used as a sheet. He covered his mother with it and left.

Outside in front of his house he sat around watching life as reality unfolded around him. The first sign of it flew pass flapping its tiny wings as it soared higher into the sky. The second sign was two dogs running side by side with each other. They stopped at different garbage bags, sniffed at them, and took off running in opposite directions.

He began walking and looking for something to get into. He pulled his shirt off and stuffed it in his back pocket. The air was warm, soggy, and filled with humidity. His body temperature increased, sweat developed, and fell down his body; especially his armpits.

Rodney, didn't have many friends and the ones he did have weren't friends at all. They were just people who he knew due to them living next door, across the street, and down the block.

He was a talented kid with unlimited potential. He could slide a pencil across paper and keep it in motion until shapes appeared into images of creative art. His mind was active, keen, alert, and able to retain and process information into categories of organized thoughts at a rapid pace.

The other kids nick named him Savage, They blamed the musty scent that produced under his arms, the shabby clothes that ill fit him, and looked like something that a mechanic would wear. They called his unkempt appearance pure savagery. They taunted him, teased him, made fun of him, and picked apart his sense of self worth with thoughtless words.

He was walking down the street when he saw a group of girls. One he remembered from school. Her name was Dena, She was with her friends. They all looked nice, but Dena, stood out. She wore a plaid skirt with a white shirt covered with a blue sweater that matched the dominant color in her skirt. The other two girls were white and black and dressed regular. The girls were walking and talking when Dena, noticed him and waved.

His eyes snapped lively then filled with spirit and amazement. He waved back quickly and maintained his gaze. One of her friends noticed his admiration and frowned at him in contempt. Her eyes bulged as she gave him a funny look, lifted her arms, pointed at her armpits, and squeezed her nose like something stunk and harmed her nostrils. The white girl looked at the black girl and giggled before shaking her head side to side.

"Karen, that's not nice." Dena, grabbed her friend playfully by the arm.

"No." There was a pause then more words came. "He doesn't smell nice." Her friend responded to her and looked away like his funk began on his own body and he had to know that he smelled. The girls giggled and walked away. Dena, walked away, yet continued to glance over her shoulder looking at him. One second later she disappeared with her friends.

Rodney, walked along the street looking for an odd job or some other opportunity to line his pocket with a few dollars. He liked when people called him a good worker, a strong kid, and things like he had a bright future ahead of him.

He enjoyed working for Mr. Shattergate, the old man who owned the fruit wagon. He would package up the cucumbers, apples, and other fruits, and vegetables in a brown paper bag then hand them to the customers. Shattergate, handled the money. He would reward the boy's efforts with a few dollars and a sweet fruit. An orange, apple, or a half of watermelon.

He walked around looking for something to get into, but he didn't find it so he walked around until he saw an elderly lady standing out in the hot sun. She pulled her hat off, wiped sweat from her forehead, and placed her hat back on her head.

"Excuse me Ms. I can do that for you. It will only cost one dollar." Rodney, squatted down and began scooping up the trash in her front yard. He placed it in a large bag that was laying on the ground.

"I guess I can afford it." The lady looked over at the boy and his pauper appearance. He smiled a polite smile and kept working. In a short time he had finished and was knocking on the door.

"Are you done already?" The lady handed him a dollar. She looked around her yard feeling happy as satisfaction entered her heart. He pocketed the dollar and spoke to her using care and humility. He walked away in pursuit of more opportunities.

Rodney, found twenty more odd jobs throughout the day. He earned thirty five dollars and a plate of food. On his way home he stopped by the store and brought a stick of deodorant, a loaf of bread, and three dollars worth of lunch meat.

Chapter 3
Fell in love with the allure

Rodney, stood at the corner waiting for the light to change. He noticed a brown puppy, the light changing colors, and a chance to cross the street. He jogged through the intersection. He looked over his shoulder and noticed that the dog was following him. He opened his bag and dropped pieces of meat on the ground. The dog ate it then licked the cement. He walked away and the dog followed.

When Rodney, made it home, his house was empty as usual. He picked up the puppy and carried it into the house and took it to his room. He sat on his bed playing with the puppy. He rubbed on it as it leapt around barking. The dog lowered its head toward the ground, laid its ears on the floor, and jolted forward. The boy stepped back and stepped forward causing the dog to leap around in excitement. He ran away and barked. The boy laughed and got down on his hands and knees, barked at the dog, and scooped the dog up in his arms and hugged it. The dog licked his face. Rodney, smiled experiencing being loved for the first time.

Ten minutes later Rodney, was in the bathtub washing up with his dog. He used the same washcloth to clean him and the dog. He ran his hand over the dog's head just then it jumped from the bathtub and ran. The boy ran after him laughing as he ran in his dingy underwear chasing his new friend.

That night Rodney, slept with his dog under the same blanket. His mother came home knocking things around as she held onto her new boy friend's hand or the guy who she was loving for the moment. Rodney, got scared and pulled the blanket over his dog and went to sleep.

Early in the morning the sounds of lovemaking were still coming from behind his mother's bedroom door. He used that time to sneak out the house with his dog. He took his dog to the flea market and brought a leash in order to take the dog for walks. He looked down at his dog with a brand new collar and named him Bam,

A few days after finding the dog the boy sat in the park training the dog. He unleashed him and taught him how to obey. While in the park he saw activity, commotion, and interactions. Hands moved swiftly, reaching for something that was kept under a bush, handing it to other people, pocketing something. They did it all day long. He kept watching the guys as they moved along. He saw different cars pull up and slow down. He saw pretty girls, groups of them, standing around, and hanging beside the guys. He noticed their natural reaction to the guys. He saw one of them grab one of the girls and pull her close to him.

Desire burned inside the boy as his eyes gravitated toward the activity. He rubbed on his dog that lay at his feet breathing hard from running around the park following the instructions that Rodney, yelled to him. The boy played with his dog, yet his eyes constantly followed the activity. One boy in particular caught his attention. He sat on the park bench. He wore a blue and white shirt, a pair of navy blue shorts that were long enough to be pants, but they weren't and a pair of blue and white sneakers. The girls seemed to pay him the most attention. The other guys appeared to submit to him. The commotion of the activity gave off the suggestion that it existed due to him being there.

The boy's hair was shiny black with waves deeply ingrained in a circular pattern around his head. He sat back with his arms out stretched, his legs were spread apart, and he looked like nothing mattered to him, nothing at all.

"I'm saying though that thing looked delicious, bald, and all that." His eyes fumbled around as the memory of what he was talking about lingered across his brain cells. He retold the story full of animation including each and every detail. His thoughts shifted his pupils rightward, brought a smile to his lips, and pressed on his ego until it dripped out of his mouth. "It was like – it was like." He spoke while semi rotating his head with each phrase that he spoke. His right arm moved like he was conducting a symphony. "Yo, it was bald, neatly shaved, and looking real pretty. It had a few cute little razor bumps on it." He tucked his lower lip into his mouth and sucked on it.

"You ate that huh?" His friend asked staring at him in mockery. His interruption silenced his words while daring him to lie his way out of the situation.

Tranquility surrounded the area, quietness covered the park, and everyone waited for his answer. A few birds that pecked at the ground nearby, stopped their movements, ruffled their feathers, and glanced in their direction giving off the impression that they understood the contents of the conversation.

"That's how I give it up, she smelled fresh, cute little razor bumps, and I ate that off top." The boy answered arrogantly assuming his friends shared and understood his logic.

"So you just ate up some herpes bumps?" His friend asked. He shrugged his shoulders and made a face that could have easily followed the phrase humor me. He looked at his friend with a straight face.

"Fuck out of here!" The boy's hand waved dismissingly at his peers in disappointment.

"How do you know?" the chubby boy who was responsible for the intense questioning asked standing up and walking closer toward the boy in the red and white shirt who confessed to eating the cute little bumps. He winked his eye at the other boys and pressed down on his eyes and asked his question again.

"They wasn't herpes bumps, just cute little razor bumps." The boy spoke while shaking his head side to side rapidly. His frowned moved in union with his eyes as they squinted as reassurance that he was sure.

"Again my dude how do you know what kind of bumps they was?"

"I'm saying they wasn't bleeding with pus coming out of them and all that." His words came hurriedly and forced as he defended himself.

The boy on the bench, the dark skin one, with the wavy hair, the one who wore the long shorts that looked like pants, but weren't; the one responsible for all the activity and noise surrounding the guys who hung out in the park. He stretched his leg out and extended it, then readjusted his body on the bench. He ran his hand smoothly over the top of his hair.

A heavy set boy, borderline fat, boy not the disgustingly obese sort of fat, that it made it hard for him to wipe his ass, but big enough to be chunky, somewhat stocky. He carried most of his weight in his stomach. He walked over joining in on the joke and implemented his own sense of humor.

"That's fucked up we can't even smoke together." He shook his head. "Umm-mmm-mmm, oh nasty mutha fucka damn!"

Everyone laughed including Rodney, he laughed from where he kneeled down at. He was a few feet away rubbing on his dog. He was rewarding him for following instructions with affection and doggy biscuits.

"Man fuck yall!" The boy said unhappy to have been humiliated over his decisions. He looked over toward Rodney, "Fuck you laughing at dirt bomb ass nigga?" he scowled at Rodney,

Rodney, looked away pretending to laugh at something else a little ways off.

"Look at this nigga." The heavy set boy said to his friends. "He wasn't there he didn't make you eat bumps." The laughter continued, grew louder, came from every direction. Different vocal cords sung out creating a symphony of ha ha's, agghs, and cah cah's, Laughter was plentiful and everyone enjoyed a piece of it, all except Rodney, He no longer laughed. The boy's words reminded him of his lot in life.

Chapter 4
No way out

Torment and torture came suddenly, rapidly, and too got damn often. Rodney, walked the streets playing with his dog until he reached his front door. The first sound to greet him was voices. Hostility roared at high volumes as his mother and her latest lover argued and degraded each other with statements of hatred.

He entered the front door with caution, easily stepping into the house as if to avoid stepping on a land mine.

"Where the fuck have you been mutha fucka!" His mother yelled at him. His eyes prickled with fear and nervousness.

"I was taking my dog for a walk."

"Where the fuck did you get a dog from?" She walked toward him. Her presence was menacing and terrifying. He backed up slowly raising his hands to catch the blow that would eventually come. He looked at her as she walked closer toward him.

"Bitch don't try to change the subject-who the fuck was that nigga you was all hugged up with?" A man, her latest lover asked. He stood there fuming puffing hot air through the openings on the end of his nose. He wore a pair of slacks, wool knitted cheap looking pants, and a striped shirt that looked even cheaper. His shoes resembled the gardener snake that was used to make them. His face was unattractive. A clear result of too much booze, too little sleep, and one hit too many.

"Mutha fucka I already told you that was Benny, and don't nobody want no got damn Benny!" She shouted back at him.

"Could of fooled me, you was all hugged up with him, and drinking out of his bottle with your drunk ass!"

"All man fuck you!" Her words created the movements that followed. The man ran toward her and slapped her. Her face twirled around and stumbled in place as she attempted to shrug off the blow. The man raised his hand to hit her again, but felt the tip of her razor blade slicing across his chest and sliding down his stomach.

"Bitch are you crazy, cutting on me like that?" His voice weakened as he looked down at his body. Janet, was beyond words her adrenalin mixed with her intoxication instigated the second slice, the one that cut across his face and stopped along his neck. The man backed up as she moved forward swinging her arms fluently using them to speak her mind.

Rodney, watched his mother land on top of the man as he stumbled to the ground. He grabbed her wrists attempting to block her frantic behavior. Somehow the episode ended with her standing over the man as he lay on the bathroom floor.

"Bitch call a cab and take me to the hospital!" The man yelled as he pulled himself up alongside the sink. Bloody finger prints and an open palm rested on the sink. The area inside the palm print contained more blood due to him applying pressure to the sink as he pulled himself up from the ground.

"Don't be yelling at me mutha fucka!" Janet, looked over to Rodney, "Call a cab!" He raced out the front door and over to his neighbor Terry's, house.

He waited on his neighbor's porch until the cab arrived. Once it did his mother and her latest lover came out the front door together. He limped toward the cab holding his arm around Janet,

Rodney, decided to go back to the park. On his way to the park he was thinking of ways to get out of his house. He couldn't keep living like that. It was too much pressure. The constant annoyance of being the son of Janet, made him dislike being at home. He wanted to stay out in the streets and roam.

Anywhere was better than living in his house. It was at that moment that he decided he was going to make a change if he could help it.

When he got to the park he saw a few cars parked up on the grass with all four doors open. He walked closer to the activity. He saw the boy who he looked up to, pressed faced down on the hood of one of the cars. A few of his buddies were also being slammed on top of cars, the grass, and some were laid out on the cement. White men in tight blue jeans, carrying hand held radios, walked around and flipped over pieces of paper, and anything else that they thought something was hid under.

"I thought you were one of the smart monkeys Pookie." One of the cops said while squeezing his hand around the back of the neck of the boy who wore the long shorts. He spun him around to face him. "I'm watching you and keeping a close eye on you. I want you to fuck up, so I can lock your ass up, send you to be with your brother."

"Do what you do." The boy said staring directly into the cop's face.

"Tough guy?" the cop spun him back around and banged his head into the hood of the car. He reached inside his pocket and dug around for a short time. "Where's the drugs. I came out here looking to lock a nigger's ass up." He laughed at his own joke. "By the way Pookie, how are those kilos looking nowadays?"

"They still come compressed." The boy mumbled from the hood of the car. The police tossed everyone down on the ground and sat them next to each other.

"The next time I come out here. I'm locking somebody the fuck up for loitering do you hear me?" He threw a wallet to one of the boys who sat on the ground. When the undercover officer turned to leave his drug unit followed close behind him. One cop stopped and looked at the boy who picked up his wallet.

"Next time you might not be so lucky." He slapped his hand hard into his back then pounded into it. The cops got into their cars and pulled off and everyone stood up from the ground.

"Man fuck them sucker ass cops." The fat boy who carried it mostly in his stomach said wiping his hand over his clothes and swiping away the dirt; that had gathered on him as he lay on the grass.

"It comes with the job." The boy who the police called Pookie, said. He dusted himself off and walked back over to the bench and sat down.

Rodney, walked over toward the boys and looked around then walked up to Pookie, The boy looked up at him unconcerned who he was, or what he wanted, nor who sent him; all he knew was that this little dirty mutha fucka better had got out of his face and fast.

"What's up?" Pookie, asked staring at Rodney, giving him the impression that he could and would hurt him.

"Are you alright?" Rodney's, words came unexpected, yet his concern was sincere. The compassion in his voice softened Pookie's, answer.

"Yeah I'm good, that's what it do out here." Pookie, sat back and looked around. He noticed a few people coming up and speaking to his crew. He shook his head no and the boys turned the people away.

"My name is Rodney," He stuck his hand out and waited for it to be shook. Pookie, looked at him for a second then shook his hand.

"Pookie," He let Rodney's, hand drop out of his.

"If you want to I could clean your park up for you." Rodney, spoke without thinking. He just wanted to be away from his life at home and thought that Pookie, could make that happen for him.

"What?" Pookie, looked at him in disbelief.

"I can clean this for you." He turned around toward the park.

"This aint my park." He smirked realizing what was happening. "Sit down, it don't take all of that to talk to me." Rodney, walked toward the bench feeling embarrassed. He sat down beside Pookie, who scooted down and looked at him with a look of displeasure.

"Thank you." Rodney, said doing his best not to offend him.

"How old are you?" Pookie, looked over at him while he looked away then back over to him.

"I'm eleven." Rodney, lied assuming that the one year difference gave him more credibility. The boy laughed at him.

"What are you doing out here this late?"

"It's not late." Rodney, answered.

"Where are you from?"

"I'm from here." Rodney, rubbed away his nervousness by stroking his dog's ears.

"From here huh?" Pookie, thought for a second then looked ahead as he spoke. "I see you out here everyday playing with your dog at least pretending to, but your real focus is watching what's going on around here." Rodney's, eyes came alive as guilt crawled up his small intestines and cradled up in his chest. "What are you up too?"

"I was." Pookie, held up his hand and held it before his face.

"Don't bullshit me. Come correct or don't come at all." He looked at Rodney, and maintained his glare.

"I wanted to see what you do out here." Rodney, spoke truthfully.

"Why?"

"Because I like you. Your cool and people don't mess with you." His eyes shifted toward the ground. "Like they do me." His words were low enough to be ignored by an ant, but Pookie, heard him. He didn't respond to him he just looked at him.

"How do they mess with you?"

They call me Savage, tell me that I stink smell like funky draws, and they don't talk to me unless." He fell silent. He was afraid to repeat his reality out of fear that it would remain that way for the remainder of his life.

"And what did you learn from being out here watching us?" Pookie, changed the subject being that he understood Rodney's, history. He shared a troubled past along with him. Growing up he was in a special education class, his mother was really his aunt, his maternal mother's older sister. She was twelve when she had him and didn't know what to do with him so she gave him to her sister. His father was as much of part of his life as the man on his back getting a piggy back ride, and there wasn't a man on his back. The only thing he got from his father was an older brother. He also was a dirty little kid who grew up and started selling drugs.

"I know that you sell stuff and you use those other guys to sell it." He pointed over to the fat boy with the stomach weight. "Antwon, is the one who looks out for the police." He swerved his arm right and pointed at a dark skin kid, who talked on a cell phone. "Juice, and those other three boys stand over there waiting to do something." He looked over at him then pointed at the rest of the boys. "They run around selling stuff, they take the money up in that building right there." Pookie, grabbed his arm and pulled it down.

"Where is your mother?"

"I don't have a mother." Rodney, told him.

"Oh I didn't know that. I thought that you were Janet's, son the little boy from over there." He pointed across the park and over a few buildings were Rodney's, street was. " But now I see that's not you, you're not the same Rodney, who goes around doing odd jobs and charging people a dollar here and there, always helping out with the fruit cart, but I guess I was wrong because that's not you." Pookie, sat back on the bench and looked around. Rodney, didn't say anything either he eased back on the bench.

"Do you want me to do something for you? I could work for you if you wanted me to." Rodney, said.

"Do what?"

"I don't know anything." Rodney's, eyes beamed with optimism. Pookie, reached into his pocket and dug around until he had some money in his hand. He pulled it out and held it in front of Rodney,

"If you want, you'll get, and I'll be watching." Pookie, handed him the money and shook his hand. He stood up and walked away. He yelled for his friends and they all walked away and got into a few different cars and pulled off.

Rodney, walked away feeling good. He kept saying over and over if you want it, you'll get it, and I'll be watching. He walked up the street playing with his dog. He counted his money and saw that it was eighty eight dollars. He smiled to himself. He looked at his dog and took off running . The puppy ran behind him barking a tiny puppy growl.

When he got home his mother and her latest lover the one she cut from asshole to appetite, were sitting on the couch snuggled up with each other. They were toasting, tapping their glasses against each other's, and kissing, acting like the incident earlier in the day didn't happen. He walked in his room as his puppy followed behind him.

In his room he sat on the edge of his bed looking around playing with his dog. He lowered down on the ground and sat in front of his dog.

Chapter 5
So you want to be a Gangster

    Feet slashed against puddles bringing rain drops upward from the ground and soaking his socks as he ran. Pookie, was running, running hard as he could. He ran through a yard, hopped a fence, he kept running, his arms swung wide and voraciously.

    The police car sped in pursuit. The driver drove across the surface of the street. The tires rotated round and round keeping the tip of the car aimed at his back. The officer spoke into his radio. He gave the description of Pookie,

    Rodney, pushed a lawn mower along the sidewalk looking for a way to earn a few dollars. His dog jogged behind. His tongue hung out of his partially opened mouth as he let out sounds that resembled a winded runner after sprinting for one hundred yards.

    Pookie, spotted him and ran toward him.

    "Put this in your pocket and keep walking." Pookie, spoke loud as a tired man could. Two police cars turned the corner as he turned away from Rodney, the boy kept pushing his lawn mower. He looked over his shoulder staring at the excitement. The look the older boy gave him was enough to convince him to keep walking.

    "On the ground asshole!" A cop yelled mid way through the process of jumping out of a moving car, tackling the boy down to the ground, and handcuffing him. Another cop drove the car up on the curb and almost ran over Pookie,

    "What kind of shit is that?" A lady wearing a pair of shorts that stopped beneath her front pockets said. Her chest stood upright aiming at the sky. They were tightly contained inside her fitted t-shirt.

    "Get his ass up here." The cop who almost ran him over said. His partner lifted Pookie, up from the ground and slammed his unprotected face into the hood of the squad car.

"Fuck you!" Pookie, kicked his leg backward just missing the cop by a few inches.

"Did he hit you?" His partner asked walking around the car. The guy shook his head no, but his partner responded as if he said yes. He punched Pookie, in the face, then he did it again, and three more times.

"Fuck the police!" A single voice yelled out of the developing crowd.

"Fuck you too!" A cop with a short temper yelled at the crowd.

"Punk ass mutha fucking white boy!" A big black guy wearing a black do rag with the strings hanging down the sides of his face yelled. The cop pulled out his gun and cocked it. He aimed at the man. His eyes revealed hatred, racism, and the thought give me a reason.

"Shut your black ass up and step the fuck back!" The cop said aiming his weapon. A moment later two more squad cars came cruising up the street. When the cars stopped six more officers hopped out of the cars.

"Did you find the dope?" The blond haired over muscled cop asked.

"Not yet, you know how these jigs are into hiding shit up their asses." The cop who held Pookie's, head in place against the car responded.

"Why did you run Pookie," A black cop asked expecting an answer. When it didn't come he opened the backdoor to the squad car and assisted the other cop in forcing the boy into the backseat of the car.

Rodney, pushed his lawn mower up the street. His heart beat against his chest like a bully's fist. The shape of the package of cocaine in his pocket bulged outward, noticeably visible. Every time his leg rose and fell the package switched angles and protruded outward. He walked until he reached his front door. He hurried inside his house and rushed to his bedroom.

Along the way he heard his mother's bed bouncing as a few giggles and some short grunts escaped through the wall. He shut his bedroom door. In his excitement he left his puppy outside in the hallway. The small bark startled him. He turned around and let the dog inside the bedroom.

The boy sat down and pulled the package out of his pocket. He looked at it. Huge pieces of a tan substance glittered and shone brighter than crystal.

"Oh shit." Rodney, mumbled softly. The dog barked like he had something to say. The boy stuffed the drugs deeper into his pocket and barricaded his bedroom door shut using his dresser as re-enforcements. He sat down on the bed and waited on Pookie, to come and pick up his drugs.

One hour later Rodney, stepped from behind his bedroom door. He peeked out searching the hallway for a sign of his mother. When he didn't see any he crept out of his room. Bam, his puppy lifted his head up as his ears perked up. The dog stood and followed behind the boy.

Out in the hallway he walked carefully down the hallway. He stopped short of his mother's bedroom door. A bright light shone out of her open door. He sighed in disappointment before taking a few more steps down the hallway.

On the way pass his mother's open door he paused, he had to, something caught his attention. A man, a different one form the one she slashed up lay across her bed completely naked. His puny body rested across her bed his curl dripped dried activator and sweat. Tiny balls of hair napped up in the center of his chest. The boy's eyes followed the length of his body where they stopped. A pair of dark brown dress socks ran up his ankles and stopped just below his calf muscles. The man motioned his hand in a half circle giving the boy a friendly wave. Rodney, walked away ignoring him.

He walked until he reached the bathroom where he saw his mother. She was half way cocked over the tub. Her hands held her shirt by the sides as she kept them out of the way while she peed in the tub.

"Where are you going mutha fucka!" Her voice was sharp and direct.

"I was going to go out for a walk and get my dog some fresh air." He looked at her hoping she didn't read in between his lie.

"You got some money?" she asked looking at him while she relieved herself.

"Not really."

"Well how much money is not really?" Her eyes focused on his hands as if money would grow out of them.

"I got about three dollars."

"Broke ass mutha fucka. What are you good for?" She lifted up from the side of the tub.

"Nothing." He lowered his head to add meaning to his words.

"Got damn right." She walked pass him, stopped, stared at him, then finally passed him. Her t-shirt was small and did a poor job of covering her nudity. He walked until he reached the front door then left through it.

Outside he walked with his dog. The two of them moved along in silence. The sounds of people speaking to each other rolled through the air as he passed a front porch. Loud music blared out of cars that waited at a stop sign for other cars to go, and faded out when the cars disappeared further up the street.

When the boy approached the park he saw the usual faces standing around. He walked up carefully, paranoid that others knew about the package secretly tucked in his front pocket.

"Did anybody see Pookie?" Rodney, asked fearfully.

"What do you want with Pookie?" The boy with the beer keg belly asked standing in front of him.

He..I...well." His mind raced as he considered telling the boy about the stuff inside his pocket. Then he thought against it, what if the boy took it from him and said that he never came back with it. "He was supposed to take me to get a haircut today." Rodney, spoke quickly defending what he was entrusted with.

"He's in jail." The boy looked down at Rodney, he maintained a firm appearance as he waited for him to respond.

"Dang." He said pretending to be saddened by the misfortune. He looked around with droopy eyes. "I'm never going to get a haircut." Rodney, spoke slowly allowing disappointment to roll of his tongue.

"That's fucked up, but hey shit happens." The bigger boy turned his back and walked away from him. Rodney, turned around and walked a few feet and played with his dog. He ran alongside his dog, then stopped, faked a kick at the puppy, and ran. The dog jumped forward and kept snapping at his foot.

Rodney, walked with his dog while witnessing a man walk up wearing a tight blue jean jacket. The coat flapped opened because it didn't have any buttons on it. He had on a green shirt that advertised a brand of cigarettes, a pair of gray sweat pants, and a yellow hat that looked like it belong to a person riding a ten speed bicycle in a marathon. The hat was drawn down over his eyes. The man walked up to the boy who sat on the bench talking on his cell phone.

The boy looked up at the man, frowned, then stuck his finger forcefully to his right, and went back to talking on his phone. He never looked up again. The boy with the biggest stomach looked around scanning the entire area before taking the money from the man. The guy handed over his money, walked a few feet over to another boy who handed him something and walked away. He walked up to a couple of the guys and continued to have the conversation that he was having before the fat boy flipped up four fingers two times.

Rodney, watched and waited. Hours went by before a shadow of a man came walking down a side street that led directly into the park. The person walked smoothly through the street holding his hands in his pockets. He walked up until he ended up in the park.

Upon his arrival all the movement ceased. The boys turned their attention toward him, and closed in on the area where he stood. Rodney, sat back focusing his eyes to see who the face belonged to. The boy sat down on the bench and spread his legs and rested his arms along the back of the bench.

"Yo, what the fuck happened?" A light skin boy with curly hair, but bad skin asked.

I got rolled on." Pookie, sniffed through his nostrils. "They didn't get shit, took me down town for obstruction of governmental administration and resisting arrest.

"I know they mad, thought they had one, and came up empty handed." The boy said rubbing his hands together excitedly. "Faggot mutha fuckas." He added the insult to prove his loyalty to Pookie,

"What's up?" Rodney, walked up appearing to be one of the crew members. He stuck his hand out and nodded his head up and down. His hand stood in mid air extended waiting for it to be acknowledged.

"Look at this little mutha fucka right here." The boy with all the stomach mass said.

"Chill that's my dude right there." Pookie, leaned back against the bench. Rodney, lit up with thrill and delight. He thought over the words he had just heard and felt happiness dripping down his insides. He wanted to run, jump, shout, and say hell yeah. Pookie, extended his hand and embraced Rodney's,

"I still." He looked at Pookie, wondering if he should speak in front of everybody. Pookie, waved his hand forward. Rodney, looked around before digging into his pocket.

"What the fuck?" The boy with the bulge in front of his body reached into his jacket.

"Its good that's my dude." Pookie, said calming the situation down. The boy eased back as Rodney, pulled a huge bag of cocaine out of his pocket. He attempted to hand it to Pookie,

"Loop," Pookie, said never once reaching out for the package. The boy with the fat stomach took it from Rodney's hand. The younger boy jumped forward assuming he was being tested. Laughter followed his movements.

"Loop, you saw that little man was about to do you dirty." The boy with bad skin spoke, instigating the situation. He laughed.

"Main, shut the fuck up." Loop, said walking away. He handed the stuff to a boy who was about Rodney's, age and told him to tell Tiffany to bag that up. The boy ran across the street and disappeared in between two buildings.

Rodney, sat down on the bench beside Pookie, the boy looked over at Rodney, and slid down. Everybody stood around watching his interaction with Rodney,

"What's up coke sell itself now?" Pookie, spoke to no one in particular, but everyone responded like his words were directed specifically for their ears. People walked back to their posts and continued to work the way they were prior to Pookie, showing up.

"Good looking out I needed that earlier today."

"I got you." Rodney, said trying to impress Pookie,

"You got me?" Pookie, broke out into a roaring laugh that rippled out of his mouth like it comforted some unseen ache that needed soothing. "That's peace. I appreciate that." He laughed again. "My man Rodney," He paused and took another look at the boy. "Or Savage, which one do you like?"

"Which one is the coolest one?" Rodney, said trying to look cool. He slumped on the bench the way he saw Pookie, sit countless times.

"Savage, is hot, that sound like a nigga is about his business, and he's going to do any and everything to get that paper."

"That's what I thought too. You can call me Savage," Rodney, nodded his head up and down.

"Game tight huh." Pookie, laughed some more. He looked over at the boy one more time.

Rodney, became a regular around the park. He sat around watching everything and ran a few errands for Pookie, who just sent him on meaningless tasks. He could have easily done the things himself, but he wanted an excuse to give the boy some money. Pookie, didn't mind giving it to him because the boy used it to buy clothes and sneakers. Since hanging around Pookie, the boy took pride in his appearance. He brushed his hair, his teeth, and washed up everyday, well the best he could, his mother didn't always have hot water.

Tiffany, came out from in between the buildings switching and swaying her hips side to side. Her movements defied gravity she barely touched the ground when she walked, nor did her hips stop shaking and rolling while she moved forward. She crossed the street and walked into the park and walked up in front of Pookie,

"He's here." She smiled then turned and waved to a few more people and smiled some more. She stood around for a split second before turning around and walking toward the buildings she just came out of.

Rodney, sat a few feet away staring at Tiffany, his eyes stretched upward, sideways, and downward all at the same time. His eyes concentrated on her picking up every detail of her facial design. She was brown skin, long hair that wrapped around into a huge bun in the back of her head. Her body was squiggly, wiggled around into a sculpted frame of irresistible beefiness. Rodney, looked at her unable to breath. His air maintained its position inside his mouth and refused to move.

His eyes turned with her head as she looked to the side and waved He followed the length of her arm down to her finger tips that were neatly manicured. He followed the skin around her mouth as it went backward and sunk into her cheeks where dimples formed in her face. The sound of her voice giggling drowned out his senses and impaired his hearing. He watched her walk across the street focusing on her nimbleness. The grace that she moved with lured his attention and kept it attached to her until she disappeared from his eyesight.

When his mind returned to its natural state he noticed that Pookie, was no longer in the park. None of his boys were around. Rodney, was all alone with his dog he reached down and rubbed on it and thought about Tiffany.

Chapter 6
It's about to get ugly

Rodney, was at the park when it happened. The commotion was constant. The incident that created the atmosphere for the boy to get shot in the face. It happened right in front of him.

The park was crowded with people who hung around Pookie, and his crew. Other people were in the park enjoying the weather. Some people played basketball, females flirted with guys, and little kids slid down the slides and swung on the swings.

There was a girl a light skin pretty one, who had on a tight skirt. It rose up to the bottom of her panties and made her camel toe visible. She walked around acting pretty. She bopped and swayed her hips side to side. From the looks of things she wanted to get Pookie's attention, but he didn't want to give it to her. She became loud, looking for a reason to say something to him. It never came he stood up and walked away disappearing in between the buildings.

A man pulled up in a metallic blue car. The wheels on the car kept spinning when the boy hopped out of the car. He walked up to the girl and yanked at her arm. She pulled away.

"What the fuck are you doing over?" He asked fuming with anger.

"I don't have to explain myself to you." She spun away from him and prepared to walk away. The boy grabbed her and slapped her hard, so hard she stumbled two feet to the side and shifted all of her body weight on her left foot. She would have caught her balance had he not slapped her again. She hit the ground and stayed there. He kicked her in the ass.

"Bitch get up and take your ass home and get my mutha fucking son!" He stood over her looking down with pure hatred.

"Come on dude you're making it hot around here." Loop, looked away from the man careful not to stare him directly in the face.

"Oh you fucking her?" The man's eyes lit up with fury. His dark face darkened as he began to take on the appearance of a monster. He rose up, swelled up in the chest, and stepped closer to Loop,

"Come on with that bullshit." Loop, spoke softly defusing the situation. He wanted to anyway, but the guy wanted more reasons to get stupid. He punched Loop, in the face. Blood followed the movement, pieces of his lip separated and split. The punch was powerful. Loop, fell down where three punches met him head on. Rodney, looked around searching for more of the crew, but they weren't available. They were nowhere to be found. Rodney, looked on as his eyes beamed with fear.

The man took his anger out on Loop, and his baby mother at the same time. He took turns kicking each one of them. Rodney, stood there until he leapt forward with a sharp kick that landed square in the center of the man's crotch. His nuts smushed inward against the tip of Rodney's, sneaker. The man's eye's looked around in pain and confusion. He grabbed his nuts and squeezed them to massage out the sting.

"I'm fucking you up!" He charged toward Rodney, the boy turned and ran, his dog ran alongside him. The, man chased after him and his dog. The dog ran and looked over its shoulder and barked a little bark, but kept running away from the danger.

Rodney, ran until he felt the first punch hit his back and knocked him over. He rolled on the ground attempted to get up, but felt more anger falling into his back. The man stood over Rodney, punching into his back like he was hitting another grown man. The boy's face stretched out in pain as the man issued him a level of hurt his mother could never give him.

When the man finished satisfying his anger he stood up, walked over to Loop, stomped on his face, snatched the girl up by the face, and tossed her into the car. He went back to kick Loop,

Rodney, felt someone picking him up and placing something in his hand.

"Fuck that Rodney, let that nigga know." Main, stood beside Rodney, scared to do what he was suppose to do. Therefore he put Rodney, up to do it. Rodney, thought about it, but the pressure from Main, yelling at him and telling him to do it. "Hurry up before he gets away."

Main, placed a shaking hand against the boy's back. He nudged him forward.

"Don't even think about it, just run up, and squeeze." He pushed the boy forward. Still in pain Rodney, ran forward. He lifted his hand up revealing a chrome thirty eight. A six shot revolver. He ran up after the boy. The man watched as Rodney, approached him, but didn't bother to run he stood there waiting for him. To people standing around witnessing everything he looked crazy and in the mood to die, but the truth of the matter was he didn't see what the boy was carrying, plus in his mind the kid didn't move as a threat.

Rodney, moved clumsily stumbling around until he stood in front of the man.

The first shot crackled then echoed, the fourth, fifth, and sixth shot went into the car, smashed the window, hit the girl in the arm, hand, and thigh. A few screams followed behind a high-pitched scream, the sound of feet stampeding forward fleeing trouble sounded in the background.

Rodney, looked around and saw everyone running and getting out of the way. He looked at the ground where the man lay groaning in pain. He rolled around holding his face. Blood poured out of his face like water leaving an overturned bucket. The girl sat in the car breathing hard and holding onto her chest. Rodney, looked up in time to see Pookie, coming from in between the buildings.

"What the fuck?" Pookie, said walking across the street. He looked around as the police cars moved forward rushing the crime scene. Rodney, stood there holding the gun not sure what to do. He just stood there looking lost. Loop, stood up off the ground and walked over to the boy and told him to run.

"Run nigga they coming for you." Fear seized Rodney, as his choice closed in on him. He turned and stood in place looking puzzled. The cops approached him.

"Drop it!" One cop yelled.

"Put it down, it's not worth it kid!" Another cop added aiming his own weapon at the boy. Rodney, looked at the cops, turned, and began running. He ran fast as he could, carrying the gun in his hand as his arm swung up and down from the weight of the gun.

The police ran after him yelling freeze. Pookie, and everybody else wasn't there to help when the fight first jumped off were all running behind the police yelling run Rodney, run.

Rodney, ran, but still held onto the gun. He looked over his shoulders periodically to see how close the police was to him. He was inexperienced and new at crime. He didn't know where to run to; so he ran home, still carrying the pistol. He ran fast as he could. The police were still close behind him and Pookie, and everyone else was right behind them.

Rodney, made it home and ran in his front door. He ran into his mother's room where she lay drunk and fast asleep. He shook her repeatedly, but her body just moved with his force. He stuffed the gun under her mattress.

The sound of the front door crashing in didn't wake his mother up.

"Ma, get up the police are here!" the boy yelled over and over until the woman's eyes flickered, stared at him, and drifted off. The first cop to reach the bedroom shoved Rodney, down to the floor and handcuffed him. "Ma!" Tears fell down the boy's face while he screamed for his mother. "Ma, help me, ma get up!" His voice broke down into tiny syllables as he cried. His mother still lay fast asleep on the bed.

When the police brought Rodney, out of his house a crowd had gathered. People stood around looking at him. The kids who teased him looked on in horror as scores of police cars pulled up in front of the house. Terry, the next door neighbor hobbled outside to see what was going on.

"What are you doing treating that kid like that?" He asked.

"Terry," The boy said weakly.

"Backup." The cop who held onto the back of Rodney's, wrists said.

"That's my nephew." Terry, lied to the police.

"Well your nephew just killed somebody." The cop said walking the boy to the car.

"What? Are you sure, this boy wouldn't hurt a fly." Terry, walked beside the police.

"Well he just hurt a human." One cop said holding up the gun that he pulled from underneath the mattress. Terry, ran in the house. Where three police officers were attempting to wake Janet,

"Bitch get up." Terry, yelled at her face as he smacked it. The cop turned away to block his smirk. "Bitch your son just killed somebody get your drunk ass up!"

"Terry?" Janet, asked partially waking up. She looked like she wanted to lay back down, but Terry pulled her up out of the bed praying that she had clothes on.

"Terry, put me down." Janet, said finally getting up. She yanked away from her neighbor.

"What the hell is all you doing in my mutha fucking house?" Janet, looked at the police.

"Rodney, killed somebody." Terry, looked at directly in her face.

"Well lock his ass up and don't be coming in here fucking with me!" Janet, laid down and climbed back under her sheet. The police took turns looking at each other, at Terry, who told them that he would go with them.

Chapter 7
Indentured Servant (DFY)

    Love was a scarce commodity, Especially for Rodney, after four months in a boy's home no one came to visit him. He thought about his mother her craziness despite all of her alcoholism and unpredictable mood swings he missed her. He lay in his bunk daydreaming about the park. He saw himself plastered across the park bench sitting next to Pookie, except in his fantasy he was the one running the area, controlling the activity, and falling in love with Tiffany,

    His mind wondered about her, his desire craved her attention, wanted to touch her. He sat up on his bunk and looked at the Hip-Hop magazines that were given to him by one of the other kids at the facility who went home. He didn't' have many friends in the boys home, but the one he did have he was the one he liked the most. His name was Abdul Muhammad, but all the other kids called him Dooski,

    Dooski, was a dark skin guy who was six years older than Rodney, He had been locked up since he was fourteen. He had rough looking features that made up his face. His hair was wavy. He only stood five feet tall, but his mouth was loud and flamboyant. He was from Harlem, every word out of his mouth was 126th and Lennox avenue. He was locked up for getting caught with a kilo of cocaine. He took a liking to Rodney, due to his laid back and quiet demeanor.

    The day that they met Dooski, just walked up and stuck out his hand and introduced himself as Harlem's finest. Since then they were hanging together. Rodney, learned a lot from being around Doooski, the older boy taught him how to correctly brush his hair in order for it to curl up into waves. The two flipped through the card deck doing pushups together, talked about their lives until they got arrested and shared stories about girls. Dooski, did most of the talking Rodney, did all of the listening.

Rodney, looked at the pictures of all the rappers and their jewelry, he noticed the girls standing beside them looking like they got paid to look pretty, and he looked at the cars. He liked the girls more than anything else in the pictures. He flipped through the pages studying each one like it was a lesson in a text book.

He looked through the book and saw pictures of things he could never own unless Pookie, gave it to him. He sat on his bunk overlooking or ignoring everything else around him. The area around him was a dorm area. It contained thirty beds all doubled bunked. The beds were positioned alongside the walls. In the center of the dorm was a desk where the staff members swat. They were the ones responsible for babysitting unruly boys.

The rules of the facility were easy for Rodney, to follow. They were no lending and borrowing without permission. This prevented people from stealing other peoples' clothes. There were no loud noises, no war stories, or reminiscing about the past if it contained violence and drugs. Of course fighting wasn't allowed. Those were the ones Rodney, paid attention too. The others were too many to name or remember therefore he did whatever he had to do to keep out of trouble.

The food was disgusting to some of the boys, but to Rodney, he couldn't complain due to not eating like that at home. He did what he had to do and excelled at all of the vocational training, schooling, and athletic sports. He didn't worry about much the facility took care of all his needs. He didn't get mail, but it didn't matter he was use to not meaning nothing to nobody.

"Yo, B, you don't hear that man calling you?" Dooski, stood beside Rodney, holding his hands on his hips and looking down at him like he couldn't believe him. He let out a quick sigh and walked away.

"Who?" Rodney, looked around. Dooski, pointed to Bruiser, the staff member in charge of their unit for the day.

"Adams, you don't want this mail?" Bruiser, held up two letters. Rodney's, eyes lit up and swirled in disbelief. He got off his bunk and walked over to the desk. He grabbed the letters and walked back to his bunk. The other kids clapped as he walked back to his bunk. Some did it out of fun, others did it because everyone else did, and the people who knew his situation did it because this was the first time he had ever received any mail.

"Noise level!" Bruiser, said rubbing his hand across his face to block his mouth which contained a smile. Bruiser, was a short black man who looked like a retarted dolphin with wavy hair. He always came to work wearing the latest jerseys and talked in the language that the younger kids used. He like Rodney, and showed it by not letting the other kids pick on him, he restrained an older kid and almost broken his arm. The kid was teasing Rodney, by calling him a bum, telling him that he wasn't never going to get out, and he should fuck him in the ass. Bruiser, broke up the confusion, but kept the idea of teaching the older kid a lesson in the back of his mind.

His chance came when the older kid received a bad letter from home. Melvin, the boy who got the bad news walked around the dorm saying fuck this, fuck that, and that everyone could suck his dick. Bruiser, watched him, kept his eyes glued to the boy's back while he walked around punching the wooden locker that the boys used to store their belongings.

Bruiser, told him to calm down, but he wouldn't. Bruiser, moved concisely charging directly at his target. He ducked low and drove his shoulder into the boy's mid section, wrapped his arms around his legs and lifted him up. The boy fell back first into the carpeted floor, where he was flipped around on his stomach. Each one of his arms folded neatly behind his back like the flaps on an envelope. He yelled out in pain, but the restrainer didn't' loosen his grip, take pity on, nor care that the boy was in tremendous pain.

Rodney, sat down on his bed and read over the names on the letters. The first one read Dena Cooper, he smiled to himself and sniffed the letter. It smelt of roses and perfume. He could pick up on sensitive details due to not being around them. He looked at the second letter. The name said Marcus Cunningham,

His eyes circle around in confusion as he wondered who this person was . he looked at it then reached in the slit and pulled out the piece of paper.

His eyes raced over the words which he read.

Peace, what up? I hope you're not letting those niggas take shit from you. (Smile.) Yo, its good out here everything is still moving, but the park aint the same without you. I miss you. Everybody else misses you too. Loop, appreciates what you did, but I still wonder what the fuck were you thinking about, shooting that nigga in broad daylight, in front of all of those people, then you stood there, and finally you ran with exhibit A. (Smile.)

One some real shit stay strong and hold your head. Four years will go by so fast that you won't even miss it. While you're in there get your mind right. Read, read, read, and keep on mutha fucking reading. Open your mind the world is bigger than the park. I sent you three hundred dollars and Loop, sent you three hundred, and we was wondering if you can get packages in there? If you can make a list and let me know. I will make it happen.

Well kid I'm about to get back to what I do, but in the mean time stay sucker free, shake fake ass niggas to the left, and keep your mind on the future. They can't break you unless you let them. Pain is suffering and weakness leaving the body. Peace.

P.S. I got your dog. May bad for not getting in touch with you, but I didn't know your name. Now I got your whole government. Rodney Adams, Remember if you want it, you'll get, and I'll be watching.

Rodney, folded the letter easily and gently valuing it as if it fell from heaven and held the solution to all of humanities ills. He stared ahead lost in his mind envisioning the park, the bench Pookie, him, and Tiffany,

Rodney, looked up to see Dooki, hulking over him reading his letter along with him.

"Savage, what were you doing in those streets?" Dooski, asked looking down at his friend.

"Nothing really." Rodney, shrugged his shoulders.

"Who is the other one from?" Dooski, reached for the letter. Rodney, pulled back keeping his letter out of reach.

"Can I read it?" He asked playfully.

"Hurry up B, see what's good cuz-o." He ran his brush over his waves as he looked at Rodney,

The second letter was from Dena, the girl who was nice to him when he was home doing odd jobs and ignoring the other kids who teased him.

"Dear Rodney," Dooski, said reading out loud.

"Dooski," Rodney, was slightly irritated.

"Come on B, read that shit." Dooski, laughed at himself and took a few steps back.

Rodney, read the letter along with Dooski, the letter said.

Dear Rodney, how are you doing? I was meaning to write you, but I was scared at first. I mean we weren't exactly friends, but I still was sad to hear about what happened to you. I was a little shocked I couldn't actually believe that you really shot someone in the face, then the girl. She could have died. How did you feel when you shot them? Everyone at school was surprised as well. You are sort of like a celebrity. I can't wait until you come home and I will write to you again when I get a chance to.

Love always your good friend Dena,

Rodney, smiled and folded the letter up and put it next to the one from Pookie, and slid them under his pillow where his hand bumped into his bible. He pulled out the bible and placed the two letters inside the pages as he opened them. He closed it and put it back under his pillow.

"Yo, B, that's your girl?" Dooski, asked still brushing his hair. He counted silently to himself as he brushed fifty times to the front, then to the back, and then he did same to both sides of his head.

"You read the letter with me. It said good friend, not girlfriend."

"Bitches always say friend. I got friends, broads I be fucking."

"I didn't do nothing with her." Rodney, confessed truthfully.

"Who is Pookie?"

"The guy who I told you about."

"The nigga who got his ass whooped or the one who gassed you up?"

"Didn't nobody gassed me up." Rodney, became defensive.

"I'm saying B, niggas," The sound of Bruiser, alerting the boys that it was time to return to their cubes and be counted silenced Dooski's, words. The boy walked over to his cube.

Chapter 8
The Student becomes The Teacher

"Bitch ass nigga, you bitch ass nigga." Beast, spoke viciously as his foot stomped downward smashing into some boy's face. The boy lay on the ground receiving the stomps as they jumped at his face.

The boy lay on the ground staring straight ahead, looking at nothing in this world. His mind was numb, separated from his body, and unable to process the pain of being fucked up.

It happened fast, started over some bullshit, and led into some serious shit. They were all sitting around in the day room watching t.v. A re-run of Martin, the boys were laughing, eating popcorn, and arguing over who looked better between Gina, and Pam,

A conversation erupted in the back. One where Beast, a kid who earned his name by being built and physically strong as an ox. He worked out all the time, lifted most of all the weights in the weight room, although he could and did didn't matter. He was one of the nicest people who respected everyone regardless if he could beat them or not. He pointed in the boy's face and told him to stop playing with him. He got up to walk away. The other guy, didn't stand a chance, didn't possess the will to out fight his opponent, but allowed the presence of everyone else to determine his decision.

He stood up and ran behind Beast, and swung two right hooks from behind. Both punches landed in Beast's, face. The punches were all that he had, all of his might gathered up, and exhausted with the force of two flies crashing into the front of an eighteen wheeler. Beast, swung around with his arms extended outward and grabbed him by the shirt. The motion was quick and easy as he sucked the boy into him like a whirlpool. He lifted him high up into the air and slammed his body down. He grabbed the boy's shirt and swung bone crushing punches. Each punch sounded like something collapsing underneath something else.

The power and force that attacked the boy brought fear into Rodney's, chest. He felt scared for Beast, he thought something bad was about to happen, in fact he wanted to jump up and break it up.

"Dooski, we have to stop that." Rodney, looked around in fear watching the boy get pulverized and beaten to a bloody mess.

"Mind your business B, that's not me and it's not you, we good." Dooski, sat there on the couch eating his candy bar taking small and calculated bites out of it.

The sound of a whistle blew and the staff came running up the hallway. They ordered everyone to return to the dorm. They grabbed Beast, but couldn't restrain him. He pulled away and stomped down on his head. Two staff members jumped on his back and two more grabbed his legs. They tussled with him and still couldn't stop him. Finally after he calmed down he allowed the staff to escort him down the hallway.

The next fight happened during major clean up. That was a routine that happened once a week. Each kid was assigned a work detail. The tasks ranged from all sorts of job descriptions. One was toilet and sinks. Another was dusting, and shower walls and floors.

Dooskie, was the one who gave out the jobs being that he had been living in the cottage the longest. Being that Rodney, was his man he gave him an easy job like dusting. Everything was going according to plan until a light skin boy. Ellis Wilson, a trouble maker who stayed in trouble. He got into so much trouble that he ended up not being able to do anything except sit in a chair facing the wall.

He went and told the staff that Muhammad, was taking people's side and giving Adams, an easy hob. The staff went and got the clip board and looked over the charts, pulled out a pen, and rearranged the jobs. He gave te paper to Muhammad, and told him to issue out the jobs.

Inside the bathroom Rodney, fumed as he poured cleaning powder inside the toilets. The terrible job that he got stuck with since Wilson, opened his mouth to the staff. Rodney, was mumbling to himself.

"Are you talking about me?" Wilson, stood behind him doing his best to look intimidating. The whole incident caught Rodney, off guard. Wilson, was the biggest punk in the whole dorm, yet he had the courage to get up in Rodney's, face.

"Why did you tell B,?" Rodney, looked at him wanting to know his line of reasoning. "Look you still got same job that you were going to get anyway, but you fucked me around in the process." Rodney, spoke to him in an aggravated tone.

"That doesn't matter, but I'm saying Dooski, has to keep it fair, he can't just give you jobs because you're his man."

"Fuck you." Rodney, turned his back on him. The punch stole into the back of his head. Rodney, swung around as butterflies sprinted across the lining of his chest. He backed up into the stall. Ellis, stood in the doorway frowning hard doing his best to scare Rodney, who did feel fear sneaking around his body. A surge of energy motivated him. He rushed forward swinging wild and hard. The punch hit his lip, not fully hit it, but touched it good enough to incite fear in Wilson, The boy backed up until his back landed against the sink. He lifted his foot up to block the punches that Rodney, threw hard and wildly.

Ellis, backed up and ran backward. He started jumping around.

"Yo, watch out for staff I'm about to hurt this bitch ass nigga." Ellis, jumped around and Rodney, did the same. Rodney, looked at his face and threw a punch that grazed his nose with ends of his knuckles. A few boys stood around watching the fight, but pretending to be doing work details.

Ellis, rushed Rodney, and grabbed him. The two boys locked their arms around each other and tussled. Rodney, having the advantage dipped down low and scooped slammed Ellis, then climbed over him and punched into his face and his hands as he held open palms trying to block his face.

"Break it up-break it up somebody is coming." One of the boy's said pulling Rodney, off Ellis, Rodney, walked over to the toilets. Ellis, got up and rushed him. He grabbed the toilet brush and ran after Rodney, he swung a nasty brush, one used to get shit stains out of the sides of toilet bowls. He missed, but the water from the brush flew forward and landed on Rodney's, face.

Disgust, anger, and the desire to kill burst throughout his body. Ellis, saw the potential terror and dropped the brush and ran. Rodney, ran behind him, but ran into a staff member who asked him what was going on.

"Whoa-whoa-whoa, what's going on?" Mr. Statchet, asked holding onto Rodney's, arm.

"Nothing." Rodney, lied.

"It didn't look nothing was happening it looked you were seconds away from slugging it out with Wilson,"

"No that wasn't it." Rodney, smiled a fake smile and pretended that it was nothing.

"Well according to my eyes I guess I'm going to have to write you two up for challenging each other, maybe that way you can learn to take responsibility for your actions." The staff member walked away and went to get the papers to write them up.

Rodney, took off running into the dorm where Ellis, sat in his chair facing the wall like he had been there all along. Rodney, ran up behind him and punched hard into the side of his face. The chair tipped over and Ellis, fell to the floor. Rodney, squatted over the boy and punched into his face and kept punching. Once his arms became tired he scratched into his face and dug his nails into his face. When the staff came to break it up Rodney, was gone out of his mind. He lost his marbles somewhere in the cracks of insanity. He bit Ellis, and held onto his skin. He shook his face around like he was a dog.

When the staff manage to pull Rodney, off the boy he pulled away and slipped out of their hands and ran back over to Ellis, and stomped on his head and face. Ellis, stood up and backed up in the corner. The staff got a hold of Rodney, and pulled him back. Overly excited and angry Rodney, pulled back and leapt forward, but remained in place. Two staff members held his arms.

Rodney, yelled , cursed, and threatened to kill Ellis, The staff slammed Rodney, on the ground and restrained him. One staff sat on his feet and another sat on his back holding his arms. Ellis, used this time to run up and kick him in the face.

Back up Ellis!" Bruiser, yelled as he held onto Rodney's, arms. Rodney, screamed and yelled moving and shaking attempting to get up. "Rodney, take it easy this is Bruiser!"

"You mother fucker!" Ellis, yelled while attempting to kick Rodney, again.

"I'm going to kill you mutha fucka!" Rodney, yelled loud and forcefully. Spit flew out of his mouth. Dooski, walked in the dorm. He saw his friend laid out on the ground being held down and Ellis, sneaking kicks on him. Dooski, ran toward him cocking his arm all the way back the whole time. When he got within striking distance he threw the hardest left cross that a person in the sixteen age bracket could.

The punch caught Ellis, off guard and knocked him to the floor. Dooski, threw more punches that connected with his face.

"Davis, go next door and get Redding, and Statchet, now!" Matthew, A stocky white boy ran to the other dorm unit to get help. When the other arrived Dooski, was standing over Ellis, punching down at him. Statchet, tackled him to the ground and restrained him. Parker, didn't' have to put his hands on Ellis, he told him to turn over and he did. Parker, placed the bottom of his foot on his state issued boots.

"Everybody is always messing with me. I didn't do nothing!" Ellis, yelled.

"Calm down Rodney, calm down." Bruiser, spoke into his ear, but it was useless the boy was angry and fully aware of his emotions.

"Chill B, I got that nigga for you." Dooski, said breathing heavy as he lay on the floor.

Twenty minutes later everyone had been let up from the floor, except for Rodney, he was still being held down to ensure that he had fully regained control of himself. Everyone sat around pretending to watch t.v. instead over their back, where the commotion was taking place. Rodney, lay on the floor looking over at Ellis, he wanted to kill him, break his fingers, shove his face in the toilet bowl, and make him lick the stains off it with his half breed ass tongue.

Chapter 9
Let me be your angel,
Let me be the one for you –ooooh!

Rodney, wrote letters to Pookie, and damn near everybody in the park. He wanted to ask about Tiffany, but didn't have the courage to. He told him about his fight, mentioned how the other kids started calling him Savage, and it wasn't for the same reasons that the other kids back home use to call him it. They called him out of respect and gave him a name to go by after he had savagely beaten the shit out of Ellis Wilson, He told him about learning how to type the home row keys on a type writer.

He wrote letters to Dena, talked about poems, stole lines out of them, and wrote beautiful letters to her. He included drawings in them. One drawing he made especially for her. He wrote to his mother, but she never wrote back. He wrote to Terry, who wrote back and told him that his mother had went to jail for shop lifting with David, one of her latest lovers. Terry, told him that his mother had been evicted and took the house three house down from him on the other side of the street. He said that since she had gotten out of jail she had some crazy ass nigga living with her, one that she cut up every other weekend.

Eighteen months had passed since Rodney, first stepped into the facility that plus the four months that he had to wait to get to the facility. He had a total of twenty two months. That meant that he had to do twenty six more to fulfill his four years. After that he would be free to explore the park and sit on the bench with Pookie,

There was a boy in the detention center, one in particular. He stood out from the rest. It was due to his oversized head. He had one finger, a fat irregular sized finger, it was a regular finger like the rest of his fingers, but this one looked swollen and injured. He was Panamanian, a fat ugly, secretly gay person who was going bald at an early age. He hung out in the showers a little bit too much. He would linger around sneaking glances in between the other boy's legs, looking for a fantasy.

None of the other kids liked him, they didn't trust him. He was one of the people who stood beside you pretending that your cause and his were one in the same, yet he was the one who would go along learn the information then turn it over to the staff, and get people in trouble.

Rumors speculated about his background. He claimed association with a well to do family who loved him enormously, but the other kids said that no one loved him. They called him a rapist, who called his crime a big mistake and a case of peer pressure.

He told on Dooski ,and Rodney, They had snuck off together and did the unthinkable. The facility was a co-ed facility. It housed troubled boys and girls. The only divider that stood in between them was a high barb wired gate that they weren't allowed near. They had to stay thirty feet away from the fence.

It served its purpose as far as creating lust, inciting desire, and sending a person to the hall. That was disciplinary dorm for the boy who couldn't behave or found it easy to break the rules.

Dooski, always stood in front of the fence brushing his hair pretending he was too cool to participate in the games like softball, football, and the re-lay races that they enjoyed as they killed time in the summer heat. He made sure that when he spoke his words and movements were exaggerated. He talked loud, mentioned Harlem, winked at the girls, and when though no one was looking he blew kisses through the fence.

One day all of his persistence paid off. One girl from Rochester, New York. A sixteen year old run away, high school drop-out, and fugitive from the Division for Youth until they caught her. Her body resembled the features of a grown woman. The clothes that she decorated her body with helped her disguise her youthfulness.

Dooski, loved her, had to have her, and he spent all of his time writing letters to her. He secretly dropped them alongside the gate whenever he found a moment. Finally after receiving ten letters, or sick and tired of being bored. She tossed a letter on the ground. She called his name, gave him a sneaky look, pointed at the ground, and walked away.

He smiled, looked around, and kept searching until he saw a staff member looking his hardest to act like he wasn't paying attention to him, but really was waiting for him to pick up the letter. Dooski, nodded his head up and down. He walked around as thought about his next move. He called Rodney, over to him. Rodney, ran over to him dripping from sweat. He was playing in the softball game. The front of his shirt contained a huge spot created by sweating too much.

"Yo, grab a catcher's mitt." Dooski, said smoothly as he picked up one of the gloves and put it on.

"I'm already playing." Rodney, was eager to rejoin the game.

"Later for that B, this some real shit, grown up people shit." Dooski, lifted up his chin and added base to his voice. He looked at his friend who picked up the other glove although he didn't want to. Dooski, threw the ball back and forth between him and Rodney, He motioned his finger toward the gate signaling for him to toss it near the fence. Rodney, squinted his eyes wondering what Dooski, was up to. He threw the ball anyway.

Dooski, jumped purposely missing the ball. He landed on the ground and rolled twenty two times more than he would have had he not been trying to get close to the fence. He rolled and kept adding speed and force to his roll until he bumped into the fence. He scooped up his letter, slipped it in the glove, and stood up brushing his pants.

"That's why I don't play sports B, shit like that." He looked disappointed while he turned and walked away. There were a few laughs from the girls who misunderstood his movements.

Later that night Dooski, read the letter and shared it with Rodney,

"Yo, I'm going to have her hook you up with one of her friends." Dooski, brushed his hair. He handed the letter to Rodney, "Yo, read it again B."

"We already read it ten times." Rodney, was annoyed and tired of reading the same thing over.

"That's how you get to know a person from the shit they say." Dooski, spoke like a love specialist with all the knowledge in the world.

"What if she's lying?"

"Then were even because I'm lying like a mutha fucka B." Dooski, smiled and took his letter and re-read it. He pointed at one line and read it out loud. "I see you everyday standing out back with that boy. The one you are with all the time, but I don't pay attention to him. I focus on you. I love an older man and I think I could enjoy being your girl." His lips widened as he read the words.

As time went by the boys had formed friendships with the girls. The girl who Dooski, talked to was Tamera, and her friend the one they hooked Rodney, up with was Heather, the boys wrote letters and compared their game. Rodney, read more and that gave him more of a lyrical edge over Dooski, His letters were more meaningful.

Dooski, just kept saying how good she looked, what he would do to her, and how much money was really up in Harlem. One night the boys had convinced the girls to sneak out and come to the gate and spend some time with them.

When the time came to sneak out and visit the girls. The boys had put together a plan and waited for the shift to change. Shift change came at eleven o'clock and the day shift went home leaving one man responsible for watching the boys while they slept.

Rodney, lay in bed feeling nervous his stomach churned over and rotted as he passed gas. He thought about getting caught, but then pushed the thought out of his mind and focused on Dooski,

Dooski, lay in his bed pretending to be sleep. He rolled over and moaned out saying nothing. He stretched out and did a good job at acting. Rodney, fell asleep in the process of waiting, but it wouldn't last long. Dooski, was at his bedside shaking him.

"What?" Rodney, asked rolling over facing the person responsible for shaking him.

"Shhh." Dooski, knelt down at his side pressing his finger tightly into his lips and squinting down hard as he could. "Come on." He tapped Rodney, and waved for him to follow him.

Rodney, rolled over and got out of bed. The two of them walked like bandits tip toeing pass the sleeping guard. Rodney, took his time moving slow, Dooski, pushed him forward. Rodney , turned around and mouthed the words stop pushing me. Dooski, mouthed the words go nigga and pushed him out of the dorm.

The boys snuck out of the door and crept toward the side door. They walked out the door and the cool air blew against them welcoming them into a fucked up situation.

"Come on." Dooski, walked off. "Yo, we don't got all night so you better be trying to get some pussy." He walked smoothly giving off the appearance that he wasn't scared. He looked at Rodney, stopped moving, and stuck his hands up. "Don't get scared on me now." Dooski, looked at him and gave him a quick look that meant don't be bullshitting.

The two boys walked alongside the gate careful to stay low to the ground. They crept around looking for the girls. A few minutes passed, then a few more minutes went by, and shortly after that twenty more minutes went by and the girls still hadn't shown up.

"I told you those bitches was fronting. I don't know how you got me out here bullshitting." Dooski, looked at Rodney, forgetting that the plan had begun and ended with him. "Let's get out of here B, your bitch probably got scared and scared my bitch into not coming.." He sighed out of disappointment. He turned to leave when he spotted something move. He looked carefully. "Oh shit somebody is coming."

Rodney, laughed out of nervousness. Dooski, looked at him aggressively. The boys were about to run until Heather, whispered out Savage,

"I told you that was my shorty B, she's in love with me. Word." Dooski, walked toward the gate like a celebrity being followed by a camera crew filming his own reality show. Rodney, looked away in disbelief. Before long they were all pressed against the fence holding hands through the gate. One thing led to another and fingers poked through the openings in the gate and pressed into titty nipples, darted repeatedly into mid sections, and felt on much of Rodney's, penis as she could get a hold of.

"Rodney, let me see you dick." Heather, spoke softly.

"Heather," Tamera, gasped. Dooski, looked over attempting to get a better view of what was happening a few feet away.

"That's what we are here for isn't it?"

"Yo, my man aint about to be doing all of that you got to show him some pussy or something." Dooski, involved himself in Rodney's, business. "Yo, let that nigga hit it from the back or something." Dooski, spoke up then looked at his own girlfriend. "Yo."

"Don't go there. I thought you had respect for me?" She gave him a small sample of her feisty attitude.

"Yeah you right. We are going to be together anyway so what's the rush?" Dooski, was upset that he snuck out the dorm just to hold hands, touch, and feel on her juicy body through a gate.

A slight moan hit the air and traveled like a faint grunt. More sounds came along with the clinging of metal being shook up and down.

"What are they doing?" Tamera, asked squinting her eyes in order to see in the dark. She looked for her friend who was no longer a few feet away from her.

"Yo, Savage, Savage." Dooski, called out for Rodney, but didn't get a response. He looked at his girlfriend who suggested that they go and find them. They moved slowly along the fence on opposite ends slowly creeping using each other as protection, from the unknown.

The closer they got to the end of the fence the clinging sound increased, the noises became clearer, and Rodney, stood on one side of the fence with his pants down around his ankles. His body leaned into the fence like he was trying to walk through it. His dick hung through one of the openings sliding in and out of Heather, he held onto the fence and pulled himself into it with force. A spaced out and confused look captivated his face

Mother nature visited him prematurely, stalked his bedroom like a sexual predator, and stretched his manhood until it hung low and swung heavily. He used it, wielded it like a knife jabbing at her rib cage. He stuck it all the way in her. His feet dug into the grass as he planted them and pushed hard as he could. His movements added pressure and caused the girl to cry out louder.

"Oh my god Heather," Tamera, spoke out in delight, shock, and amusement. She knew her friend liked Rodney, listened to her when she said that she was going to go for it, but still couldn't believe what she was seeing.

"Yo, B, you buggin." Dooski, laughed. He grabbed his mouth with his hands. He didn't want to get caught and get in trouble.

"Call me big daddy." Rodney, said wanting to impress his friend.

"Big daddy." Her words caused excitement in Dooski, who sat there side by side with his girlfriend separated by a gate. They both stood there watching their friends. Rodney, came and brought attention with him. He was shaking the fence hard as he could, it rattled loudly. A light came on, a voice shouted, and more lights came on.

Tamera's, eyes lit up with fear, she grabbed Heather, by the arm, and together they ran. Rodney, pulled his pants up. Dooski, turned and ran his laughter rippled through the air as he moved. Rodney, ran behind him. The sound of voices yelling for them to stop, accompanied by multiple sets of keys jingling up and down, and running feet encouraged the boys to run fast as they could. They ran toward another cottage that wasn't theirs. Dooski, led the way and Rodney, followed him. The staff ran after them with flashing lights. The boys hid behind a cottage. They waited a few seconds giving the men time to run pass them, then they came out of hiding and ran toward their own cottage.

"Over there!" One man shouted while pointing at the two boys.

"Oh shit." Dooski, laughed as he ran. The boys ran until they reached their dorm and snuck back inside. Rodney, ran down the hallway, slowed down upon entering the hallway that led to the dorm. He noticed that the lights weren't on. He walked into the dorm and quickly undressed. He got into bed and wiped the sweat off his body with his blanket and sheet.

Dooski, ran the other way toward the bathroom. He took off his clothes, tossed them in a corner inside the showers, and ran to the last stall. He pulled his underwear down and started jerking his man muscle up and down.

The sound of keys opening the door and people coming into the cottage woke up most of the dorm. The night watchman woke up, took his feet down from the desk, and looked around.

"Bowie, didn't anybody run in here!" Big John, a four hundred pound staff member asked breathing hard.

"I didn't see anybody come in here." The gray headed man responded sitting up to face his co-workers.

"Check the bathroom. I'm sure they ran in here." He stood still trying to look intimidating, but really he was catching his breath. "They either ran in here or one of the neighboring cottages."

A minute later a guy returned pulling Dooski, by the arm.

"This one was hiding in the bathroom." Rodney's, heart backed flipped around inside his chest. He was scared, pain trembled around his heart and the base of his penis. He took short breaths while he waited to see how Dooski was going to be punished.

"What's good B, a nigga can't get money no more, can't spank the monkey, can't get his nuts out the sand?" Laughter filled the dorm as the boys laughed. A few of the staff laughed too.

"What were you doing in the bathroom?" big John, asked staring down at Dooski, with fierce emotion.

"Ask this dude B, he interrupted me.: Dooski, pointed at the other staff who stood beside him holding onto him.

"Charlie, what was he doing?" Big John, looked at his friend.

"He was masturbating." His face reddened with embarrassment at finding a black kid pulling on a dick probably longer than his.

"Get in your bed." Big John, ordered him. Dooski, walked away looking disappointed at not being able to finish pleasing himself.

Sleep came and took over Rodney, setting him at ease. He got away, Scott free, and independent of any repercussion.

Chapter 10
Now, that's what you get, punk bitch!

The Panamanian boy. The fat ugly one with the enormously larger finger tip. The one who said he couldn't stand gay people, hated their guts, but spent all of his free time around them when no one else was around. He claimed that he was using them, but his action never acted out his words. He was either playing cards with them, engaging in long conversations, and just sitting up in their faces trying to look cute. One boy in particular was his favorite. His name was Brad, He was openly gay and the Panamanian boy was openly infatuated.

He overheard some of the boys talking about what happened the night before. He listened while they talked about a girl who had got hammered from the back and made so much noise that she alerted the staff. The other boys laughed and wondered how they could sneak out and get their own few minutes through the gate. Not the Panamanian boy. He was a jealous hearted, fat fingered freak who loved to push his finger inside of Brad,

One day he came around drinking a soft drink that couldn't be purchased inside the facility because they didn't carry that brand. It came from the street and he had to have gotten it from one of the staff.

A few minutes later Dooski, and Rodney, were called into the office to speak with the cottage's counselor.

The boys' denied everything, but still ended up on restrictions for suspicion, being that there wasn't any evidence; just hearsay.

"We should fuck him up." Rodney, said referring to the fat fingered boy.

"If we do that they are going to put two and two together and come up with us." Dooski, nodded his head up and down. "I got a better plan." He smiled at Savage, "Follow me." He smiled wickedly.

Later in the day when no one was around Dooski, broke into a white boy's locker, took out all of his personal belongings, and slipped them into the fat fingered boy's locker.

Next he broke into Brad's, locker and began taking things.

"Yo, B, watch out and hold me down." Dooski, looked through his locker and found his mail and began copying down his addresses. Rodney, looked around and watched over his shoulder seeing what his friend was doing. A second later they moved along the dorm and crept up into the dayroom.

They sat down at a table looking over the address.

"Here it is." Dooski, smiled as he held up a letter. He pulled out a piece of paper and a pencil. He began writing the letter with his left hand. He started the letter off pretending to be the Panamanian kid.

"Tell me some of that good shit to say." Dooski, looked at Rodney, who just started talking.

Hi Ms. Smith I'm your son's lover. My name is Earl P. Kopp, I'm gay and I have been plugging your son since he's been here in the facility. I want to thank you for birthing someone so special to make me happy. I love him so much and I love you too. I can't wait to meet you. I feel close to you and the rest of our family already.

Until next day stay sweet and remember I love your son. Don't be shallow because were not nasty and gay we are open minded and in love.

"That's fucked up." Rodney, snickered. He watched Dooski, lick the envelope and drop it in the mail slot. The two boys walked away feeling avenged.

Chapter 11
Lose a brother for his family to regain him

The stolen items in the big fingered kid's locker, and a call from Brad's, mother was enough to get the boy sent to a tougher facility where they kept sex offenders or people who commit crimes while they were locked up in the facility.

The wind blew casually cooling the dry air that stuck to his skin and wrapped around him until he was sticky from sweat. He stood around outside with Dooski, who looked though the gate staring at Tamera, he blew her kisses and watched her catch it and wipe her hands across her lips.

"Yo, I got her open B," Dooski, smiled as he nodded his head up and down. He turned to Rodney, "There goes Heather," Rodney, nodded his head acknowledging that he heard him.

"Dooski, the counselor wants you." Sticks said. Rodney, and Dooski, both looked at each other then over to the tall lanky Spanish kid.

"What does he want?" Dooski, asked half way terrified.

"I don't know he was just looking for you." Sticks, relayed the message and walked off.

"You think he know about us selling those things?" Rodney, asked. He knew when Dooski, first came to him with the idea that it wasn't a good one. Rodney, worked in the vocation building where he stole small plastic bags. Once he smuggled them back to the dorm. He passed them off to Dooski, who rolled them up in green state issued towels, stuffed them with the bags that he situated to fit like a tunnel. Then he put rubber bands around them and filled them with warm lotion that he kept heated by leaving them near the heater all night. He even put a small plastic glove tied into a knot in order to keep the water from spilling out. Once they were ready he sold them to the other kids in the dorm for five dollars.

The boys used them as a substitute for women. They took them in the bathroom stalls and fucked them. They held onto the sides of the towel and stroked away until they released their frustration.

"We got rid of all the evidence." Dooski, looked at him nervously.

"Shit." Rodney, looked equally nervous knowing that him and Dooski, are one in the same. If you saw one you saw the other lingering a few feet away. Dooski, walked over to the cottage and went through the door.

Twenty minutes later Dooski, came out the door walking cooler than ever. His legs stepped and reached harder as he walked. His arms swung in tune with his walk. He walked and looked around. He shouted out Harlem, U.S.A. baby. He walked up on Rodney, and hugged him.

"I go home next week B, they did a home assessment and everything checked out. I'm out B," His lips spread sideways into a huge smile. A fleeting sense of fear crossed over Rodney's, heart. He felt nervous.

"That's good...I mean...damn." Sadness echoed out of his mouth.

"I'm out of here!" Dooski, yelled out loud to no one in general. It seemed that way, but Rodney, knew it was solely for Tamera, who stood up, pouted, threw a lawn chair, and scared the other girls before walking away disappointed. "I got her B, that's my broad son." Dooski, smiled and laughed out a silly laugh.

"Yo, I'm going to miss you kid." Rodney, spoke up doing his best to conceal his brokenness. He wondered how he would feel without Dooski, it never crossed his mind that one day they would be separated.

"Yo, we are going to hook up in the streets B, that's real from the bottom of my heart. We are going to link up. I get money B,"

"I know." Rodney, didn't have the words to match his feeling so he said nothing more.

The next day came in and walked out fast as it came. Six more days left with Dooski, was all Rodney, had. He felt sad and out of place. He was happy that his friend was getting out and going home, but sad that he would never see him again.

Rodney, sat beside Dooski, on the edge of his bed. They were conspiring how to sneak drugs from Harlem, down to Niagara Falls, Where Rodney, was from.

"Yo, it's money out there B?" Dooski, looked at Rodney, who shook his head up and down. "I'm telling you when I come I'm bringing coke, pure fucking coke."

"Yo, its going to work." Rodney, didn't want to talk about drugs he wanted to hang out with Dooski, but all Dooski, wanted to do was find out would he need guns when he came to visit. He thought that because he was from Harlem, all the females in the town would want to sleep with him for that reason alone. He asked Rodney, did he have a place for him to stay while he in town.

"I told you I know this kid Pookie, he makes a lot of money and we could do what he does and get a lot of money too." Rodney's, voice was filled with excitement thinking about working side by side with Pookie, and Dooski,

"B, I keep telling you that we are too old to be hero worshipping. We got to get our own shit established." He looked at Rodney, like how many times must I remind you.

"I know, but Pookie,"

"Son, fuck Pookie, people are going to be talking about us like that." He wrapped his arm around Rodneys's shoulder. His hand went forward. "Picture this me and you, matching cars. My shit is Red and your shit is."

"Red." Rodney, said filling in his sentence.

"No-no can't do that niggas will think that you driving my shit B,"

"Alright then brown then."

"B, who the fuck you know that be rocking brown whips?" He took his arm from around Rodney, "You need some fly shit, shiny wheels, t.v.'s, basic essentials. You know nothing to flashy just something light to get the bitches open."

"What kind of cars?" Rodney, asked not caring one way or the other. He only cared about Dooski,

"I'm getting the new Range Rover, something light, but heavy enough to represent a couple of dollars." Rodney, smiled at the way the word came out of his Dooski's, mouth. He said dollars, but it sounded like daa- las. He was from Harlem, and had to represent that.

Chapter 12
Can't be scared, got to stand on your own two

When the day for Dooski, to leave he was up bright and early. He handed Rodney, a piece of paper with his home address and phone number on it. He slid him his walkman, his tapes, and all of the food that he hadn't eaten. He looked at Rodney, hugged him for a long time, a real long time. He gripped his friend like they were long lost brothers who recently found each other.

"Yo B, don't be bullshitting, getting out and falling in love and fucking up money and all that." He pulled away from Rodney, "Remember B, we are too old to be worshipping niggas. It's our time and them old school niggas got to move over B," Rodney, looked sad as his friend walked out the dorm unit. Dooski, turned around and stared at Rodney, "Money, is power and power is success. Cash everything around us B, big things popping my dude. I love you kid Harlem!!"

"I love you too B," Rodney, tapped his hand softly over his heart. He smiled watching Dooski, act a damn fool for the last damn time. He watched Dooski, climb into the red state van and slid the door shut. The van pulled off taking Dooski, closer to Harlem.

Later that night Rodney, slept like shit. He hadn't fell the sleep at all. He kept looking over at Dooski's, bed. The bed that was filled with another person. One hour after he had left. A white boy lay in bed tossing and turning periodically looking up to make sure no one was creeping over to his bed. His movements told everyone that he was a new jack. A person new to the system and afraid for nothing. In lock up people will try you, but if you mind your business, keep to yourself, and conduct yourself respectfully, you'll be alright. Rodney, rolled over and looked away from the bed and faced the wall.

The next day Rodney, walked around looking sad. His insides burned and rubbed raw. They created an anxious feeling inside of him. He didn't speak as much as he did when Dooski, was around. He didn't feel the need to these niggas wouldn't understand him anyway. They weren't from Harlem, and they damn sure weren't Dooski,

"Yo, Rodney, you look mad sad kid." Gizwhop, said truly concerned. Rodney, looked at him and understood why people named him the way they did. He looked like a cross between a two thousand year old man and the gremlin Gizmo.

"I'm chilling." Rodney, lied.

"Yo, you miss that nigga kid. That was your man, it be like that." Gizwhop, looked at him seriously.

"Yo, who is this." Dre, a brown skin kid stood up brushing his hair. "Forty nine-fifty." He walked arrogantly as he paced the floor. "Yo, B, I'm from Harlem." Dre, nodded his head up and down like he was listening to a beat. "Yall fly bum ass niggas gather around." Rodney, smiled at the sight of Dre, acting like Dooski, "Yo, you know where all the bad bitches at B?"

"Harlem," All the boys standing around chimed in.

"All the money is up in."

"Harlem." The boys said together.

"You know where all the best rappers from?" Dre, said brushing his hair.

"Brooklyn," Medina, added.

"Yo B, get this fly bum ass nigga out of here." Dre, sounded exactly like Dooski, and that made everyone burst out laughing.

"I'm saying kid when you get out. You can get in contact with him." Gizwhop, smiled at Rodney,

Six months later the counselor called Rodney, into his office. Rodney, walked into the office and took a seat. The counselor hung up the phone and stuck his hand across the desk.

"Good luck, wear a rubber, and take care of yourself. You go home tomorrow." Rodney, looked at the middle age white man like he was crazy. "Yes you go home tomorrow." The words hit Rodney, and took his breath out of his mouth and held it suspended in the air.

The next day found Rodney, fully dressed holding onto his bags, which contained letters from Dooski, Pookie, Heather, and Dena, He walked out the door and climbed into the van.

"Don't come back kid!" Gizwhop, yelled through a window.

"Gizwhop!" Rodney, waved at him without looking back to face him. He got into the van, sat back, and enjoyed the ride.

Hours went by with him getting out of one van and into another. The last van he got into contained a kid who was shackled.

"Yo, I'm on my way to Tryon. Where are you going kid?"

"I did mine. I'm going home B," Rodney, said sounding like Dooski,

"Oh word." The kid looked at Rodney, "That's what's up."

"Peace." Rodney, climbed out of the van and got into another van where boy just got out of and entered the van he just exited.

Before long Rodney ,was sitting in a tall building in Buffalo, New York. He sat around talking to a few people who told him that they were going to be his probation officers while he was out for the next year. He sat there patiently listening to them explain to him all the rules that he had to abide by.

Shortly after that Rodney, was put into a car and drove to Niagara Falls. Rodney, rode in the car until he passed the park and a wealth of feelings covered him as delight shone across his face.

"This is a heavy drug related area Rodney, and I don't want to see you around here." Fred, one of his probation officers said. Rodney, looked into his face, absorbed all of his whiteness, and nodded his head up and down. "I'll expect you to abide by your curfew and I will be calling and checking up on you." Rodney, nodded his head again.

When he pulled up in front of his house he saw his mother standing out front. She looked smaller than he remembered. Terry, was there too. He was holding a biracial baby. He rocked the baby around in his arms. Rodney, stepped out of the car and walked over to his mother. She gave him a tight hug.

"Look at you all muscular, with your wavy hair, and baby you look good." She smiled .

"What's up Rodney?" Terry, said. This is my youngest daughter Clara," Rodney, looked at the baby. "Donna, come out here and let Rodney, see you." A few seconds later a frail and ugly white girl came walking out of his front door. She had raggedy teeth that needed to be pulled and replaced with better ones real or false it didn't matter, anything was better than the ones she already had.

"She's eighteen." Terry, said proudly.

"And going on forty something." Janet, added looking at Donna, like Terry, could have chosen a better looking white girl than that.

Fred, and Janet, talked while Rodney, stood around watching everything around him. He looked up and down the street. He saw a group of girls who looked at him and smiled. He stared at them wondering did they remember him.

Soon as Fred, pulled off Rodney, walked over to the park. When he got there things had changed. A few new swings had replaced the older ones. A few more benches were seated at the other end of the park. A motorcycle rested on the grass. A group of people sat around smoking weed and sipping liquor out of a plastic cups.

Rodney, walked toward the benches. He looked for Pookie, wondering if he still looked the same, but he didn't see anybody who resembled him.

"Oh shit."A thin kid stepped up and walked a few feet forward. "Oh shit Rodney?" he smiled and ran over to the boy. Rodney, looked directly at the guy and readied him to fight. His fists positioned into jack hammers of violence.

The guy got within inches of Rodney, when familiarity settled across his Rodney's, face.

"Loop?" He questioned.

"Hell yeah. What's up boy-boy!" Loop, grabbed him and held onto him. He let him go and stepped back from him.

"Where did your body go?" Rodney, asked him. He stared at Loop, he looked at his face, then his head; which looked bigger without the extra meat that covered his face. He looked at his stomach and saw that it was flat as a desktop.

"I caught a case. They gave me a three to life bid. Sent a nigga to one of those boot camps, sir yes sir, and all that shit." Loop, looked at him smiling. "Pookie, should be here in a minute.' He smiled then turned around. "Main!" His voice yelled loud and carried across the park.

A boy down on his knees shooting dice looked up. Loop, waved him over to him. The boy jogged over to him. He stopped in front of them looking disappointed.

"Who is this?" Loop, smiled. Main, looked at Rodney, and shrugged his shoulders.

"You don't remember me?" Rodney, studied Main's, face and kept looking at him.

"Oh shit Savage, oh shit kid." He laughed and hugged him.

A car pulled up to the curb. The driver eased out smoothly and stood against the car. He had his hands crossed over each other, and kept them down by his private parts.

"uh oh there he go, shoot em up bang bang." Pookie, walked toward them. "Bang bang." He laughed. Upon seeing Pookie, Rodney, lit up with happiness and excitement.

Chapter 13
Ayo number one question is, "How can I be down?"

"Yo, I'm ready to get some of this money. I was locked up with this kid from Harlem. He was getting money, not like you, but he was around my age, and that got me to thinking like shit I can do it too." Rodney, sat in the passenger seat of Pookie's car. Pookie, listened to him without speaking he just drove the car.

"How many crack heads do you know?" Rodney, looked over at Pookie, and thought about what he just heard.

"None." He shook his head while he spoke.

"What's going on out here? Who got all the money? Who needs the money, and whose down with who? What parts of town are ripe for the picking?"

"I don't know." Rodney, admitted.

"Yet you ready to jump out here head first." He pulled up in front of the mall and parked. "What did you learn while you were locked up? Or did you waste time doing whatever it took to make the time go by?" Rodney, didn't answer because he didn't have one.

Rodney, and Pookie, got out of the car and walked around. Pookie, talked to Rodney, while they shopped. His words were more powerful and strategic in his ears than Dooski's, He brought Rodney, some clothes, three pair of sneakers, and put two thousand dollars in his pocket.

Before taking Rodney, home Pookie, rode around talking to him and showing him where everybody hung out at. When the ghetto tour was over Rodney, and Pookie, were shaking hands.

"Are you going to put me down so I can get this money?" Rodney, was ready to prove his worth.

"You just got out, go get some pussy, and get at me later." He pulled off, slowed down, backed up, and rolled his window down. "Savage," Rodney, turned around to see what he wanted. "Have some fun first." Pookie, nodded his head then pulled off.

Rodney, walked into his house and saw him mother sitting down watching t.v.

"What's in your bag?" She asked.

"Something for me." He said not looking at her. He walked pass her and into his room. Janet. Looked at her son hiding her smile. In her mind she had succeeded at raising her baby boy to be a man. A man who wouldn't take shit form nobody. She went back to watching her t.v. show.

The next day Rodney, walked down the street on his way to the park. Terry, pulled up alongside him.

"Rodney, where are you going do you need a ride?" Terry, spoke out of his passenger window. Donna, leaned back out of the way giving Terry, a better view to Rodney,

"I'm good I'm just going right there." He pointed toward the street a few blocks away.

"Alright." Terry, blew his horn then pulled off. Rodney, walked up the street where he ran into a few people who looked at him, made eye contact, and nodded their heads to him.

"Savage!" A voice came from across the street. Where a light skin boy stood among a group of other people. Rodney, noticed him and looked at his face wondering where did he know it from. He realized that he didn't know the boy, but still nodded his head to him. "Alright okay. That's what's up." The boy smiled and turned back to the people who he was with.

When Rodney, made it to the park, he looked around, but didn't' see anyone hanging out. He sat on the bench waiting for everyone else to arrive.

"Savage!" Main, yelled out of a top window. Rodney, looked up at him. "Come in the building!" He yelled down at the street. Rodney, approached the building and walked into it.

"What's up?" He shook Main's, hand.

"Aint shit. What are you doing out here on a Thursday?"

"Waiting on yall."

"Niggas don't do Tuesdays and Thursdays. The police be on shit. That's how Loop, got caught up." Main, walked up a few stairs with Rodney, moving behind him. They walked into an apartment and sat down. Main, lit up a blunt and passed it to one of the two girls who were sitting on the couch. Rodney, looked around his eyes scanned the room and checked for a threat. A habit he learned from being alone for all of those years. He had no one to watch his back and out of necessity he learned to depend on his intuition for personal safety. Sensing no danger he sat down.

"Smoking?" Main, held up a blunt and passed it to him. Rodney, took it although he didn't smoke. He put the weed against his lips and pulled inward bringing a cloud of smoke into his mouth. The girls sat around giggling and teasing each other, one looked at Rodney, and waved. He nodded his head, but remained focused and alert.

"Main, we need some more beer." One of the girls said. Rodney, looked at her. She was short and light skin, had a little bit of curves that expressed itself in her hips and rear end. She shook her head causing her hair to bounce around and tangle up into strawberry colored curls.

Her friend was mulatto, white and black or white and something else. She was more shapely than her friend. She was the one whose eyes roamed over Rodney, and assessed his body underneath his clothes.

"Ride with me." Main, tapped on Rodney's, leg to get his attention.

In the car they rode around in silence until Rodney, broke it.

"Who are those girls?"

"Some Canadian bitches. Cold freaks, I fucked both of them and I be taking their money." The sound of his words brought Dooski, to Rodney's, mind. All he heard was Yo, B, get the money, fuck everything else, and we are too old to be hero worshipping. Rodney, reached in his pocket and felt around. He only had a few dollars left over from what Pookie, had given him.

"Do you want to fuck one of those of bitches?" Main, looked at him and shrugged his shoulders. "After four years I would want to fuck one of them." Main, smiled.

Two hours went by with Main, Rodney, and the girls smoking and drinking. The girls giggled at each other and wanted to get a little cozy, Main, disappeared into the room with one of the girls. The mixed one. The other one was talking to Rodney, and doing her best to get his attention, but his mind was on something else. He thought about Dooski, and 126th and Lennox. He thought about how he had been home for a couple weeks and hadn't made one move that could indicate that he wanted some money.

"Do you want to smoke some more weed?" the girl asked. Rodney, didn't' say anything he just looked at her then away from her. She opened her purse and pulled out some more weed along with a blunt. Rodney, noticed something bulging out of her purse. His eyes widened with lust. She tucked her condoms back down into her purse and closed it. "Do you have a girlfriend?" She dug her manicured nails into the blunt. She tore down the middle of it, emptied out the contents, and rolled the blunt. She stood over the garbage can licking the blunt sealed. Rodney, opened another beer and took a few sips.

The girl sat down beside him on the couch. She talked about Canada, She told him the difference between Canadian men and American men. Rodney, finished his beer and looked at it, took a long glance at his bottle, and then smacked it across the girl's head. The sound of glass breaking along with her short yell. Savage, grabbed her throat and squeezed it. He held the broken glass with its rough edges tightly against her face.

"Make a sound bitch and it's over."

"I won't." Tears stung her eyes, but didn't come right away.

"Open that purse and give me that money." She sobbed as her blood dripped into her ear.

"Yo, its mighty quiet out here. What yall doing?" Main, came out the room in his boxers. He laughed until he saw Rodney, standing over the couch and the girl smushed into the cushion of the couch with a hand around her neck. Rodney, held the neck of the bottle and pressed the broken half into her face. "Yo, Savage, man chill." Main, grabbed him and tried to pull him off the girl. "What the fuck happened?" A look of confusion attended his face.

"Main, help me he took my money and now he wants to kill me." She screeched while looking helpless. Her life dangled in Rodney's, hands while he considered his next move.

"Let her go Savage," Main, pleaded in a soft tone.

"Get the fuck out of here." Rodney, tossed the girl to the floor. He backed up out of the living room and left the apartment building.

He walked through the park half way walking and partially running. He moved quickly holding onto the fistful of cash inside his pocket. He ran until he was at home, up in his bedroom, and counting the money. He put the money in the soles of each one of his sneakers, changed clothes, and went back outside.

Chapter 14
They bullshitted the bullshitter and found out he's a trigga happy nigga

Chairs smashed against the wall as Rodney, half turned and stopped, then backed up. His hands were locked behind his mother's head applying pressure to her neck. He had her in the full nelson shoving her chin closer to her chest. The more he twirled her around her arms flung loosely about.

"Help! Somebody heelllppp me!!!! He's crazy!" Her words fell dramatically out of her mouth. Janet, pushed her body backward using her little bit of body weight attempting to lessen the pressure her son had on her neck.

A man, her newest lover, walked into the house carrying a brown paper bag. His hand wrapped around the top of the bottle. His lips puckered up and pressed together as he whistled a tune. The sight of his part time lover being thrown around, but remaining in place in front of her son did something to him. Feeling heroic he sat his bottle down on the table and raced forward.

He waited for Rodney, to turn half way around then leapt on his back. He slipped off his body and fell to the floor. He tried to grab Rodney, from behind. Savage, thrust his leg backward powerfully and with acute accuracy. The sole of his sneaker crushed into his face. His eyes winced in pain. Another kick bumped into his face then another mule kick sped toward his head.

Rodney, shoved his mother to the ground and turned toward her lover. He approached her latest lover. He reached out and grabbed the man by the collar. He punched him in the face and fell in love with the feeling associated with violence and hit him a few more times. The man lay flat drooping in Rodney's, arms. He didn't move his unconsciousness wouldn't allow him to, but that didn't make Rodney, finalize the beating. Savage, was furious. Rage surged out of his pores and fell from his body with his sweat. Rodney, never allowed the man to fall to the ground. He held him, beat into his face, and swung him around until his back landed against the wall.

Rodney, rushed forward following close behind his knuckles. The punch banged into the man's nose. Blood appeared and smeared under the force of another punch. Janet, lay on the floor watching in horror. She screamed out at the top of her lungs. She sobbed loudly and cried for someone to help her. She yelled for Terry,

Terry, appeared in the doorway. His shirt was half way open. The knotted hairs on his chest twisted around in the center of his chest.

"Rodney!" He yelled loud as he could. His voice traveled around the living room, but only affected his and Janet's, ears. Rodney's, mind was gone and the guy was beat into a quiet sleep. He couldn't reason long enough to feel the pain being administered to his body let alone hear a voice crying out.

Terry, rushed forward and jumped on Rodney's, back and held onto him tight as he could.

"Rodney!!!" Terry, yelled attempting to calm Rodney's, anger. Savage, moved effortlessly carrying the older man's weight as if it was meaningless. Something the man said caused Savage, to stop swinging and allow the man's body to lay still on the floor. He turned toward Janet, "Rodney, that's your mother!" Terry, yelled while he rested on the boy's back. He yelled it again capitalizing on the word mother.

"She stole my money Terry." He expressed his hurt over being betrayed by his mother.

"No I did-N!" Janet, sobbed. She yelled out a few sounds that were supposedly meant to be a part of the pain that she felt, but it came out sounding phony, forced, and something that was suppose to help her lie sound more believable. Savage, looked at her in disgust. He turned to leave when he saw his mother's latest lover still on the ground. The man struggled to get to his feet.

Savage, stomped on his head three times. It bounced up and down until the front of his face landed on the floor.

"Rodney!" Terry, yelled again. He stood back and watched as the boy left the house.

"He's crazy Terry! That fucking boy is crazy!" Janet yelled at her neighbor.

Rodney, walked the street aggressively. Fury ran through his body. He felt stupid and wondered how the hell could have got caught slipping. He was only gone for one hour. He went and brought some clothes and a few pair of sneakers. He came right back home. When he walked into the house he saw Janet, she was drunk and sitting in front of the t.v. When she saw Rodney, she waved a friendly wave and said "What up nigga?"

Her words were slurred, but had a playfulness to them Rodney, looked at her. His eyes followed his mother as alertness swept over his body. Her easy going demeanor was a dead give-away. His suspicion led him into his bedroom. He fumbled through his clothes where he hid his money. His eyes shut in disbelief. He found the sock that he usually kept his money rolled up in. This time it was unrolled and empty. He threw the sock hard as he could. It floated, ran out of steam, and sunk to the floor. He raced down the stairs.

"Where the fuck is my money?" He stood before his mother questioningly.

"What, who, nigga what?" Surprise and shock filled her eyes. Downplaying her thievery. The smug look on her face encouraged his anger. That's what created his need to do something. He reached out and snatched her up. She fought back and swung wildly, but her open palm slaps did little to stop him. He spun her around and put her in the wrestling move.

Outside on the street while walking along the sidewalk. He moved and fumbled though his pocket. He felt the six twenty dollar bills that he had left over from his trip to the mall.

Disappointment swept through him. He thought about his next move. He thought about Pookie, then shoved his image out of his mind. He walked until he saw a kid about his age. He was dressed in stylish clothes and he stood alongside a building. A few scragglers surrounded him. They stood in front of him waiting for instructions.

He reached into his pocket, pulled something out, and gave something to each person. He took money from them then watched them walk away from him. Rodney, saw the people walking down the street with their hands in their pocket as they moved faster into the night.

Gotta be ready to take risks, jump out at destruction, and take the guerilla by the face. Dooski's, words echoed in his mind. Rodney, looked around, stooped down, and picked up an object and slid it inside the sleeve of his shirt.

"Yo." Rodney, called out while he approached the boy.

"What's good my nigs?" He spoke flatly hoping to give off an air of being cool. Rodney, looked at him and wondered where the hell he was from talking like that.

"I need to buy some weight. I need an eight ball." Rodney, pulled out his money. He counted the six twenty dollar bills like they were much more than their value. The boy stuck out his hand. Rodney, withdrew his hand.

"Can I see what I'm getting?" Rodney, asked looking at the boy. The guy nodded his head up and down, pulled out a sandwich bag filled with several eight balls, and handed one to Rodney, He looked at it, flipped it over, and examined it a little longer. "Do you have a lot of these, the same quality?" he put the bag up to his nose and smelled the substance through the plastic. The boy nodded his head up and down. Rodney, handed him the money and put the tiny package in his pocket.

The boy counted the money, pulled out a wad of cash, and added the money that Rodney, have given him to the knot. His eyes darted toward his pocket where he inserted the money into. The sound of an object swinging through the air whooshed until it exploded into a crackling sound. Wood rustled against his face. The stick that Rodney, carried hit him in the center of his forehead, the second blow struck his jaw, the third one bust open the skin around his right eye.

The boy fell to the ground. Rodney, beat the rest of his body with the stick. Money fell from his hand littering the sidewalk. Rodney, scooped the money up and filled his pockets with it. He quickly reached over to the boy's other pocket and pulled out the sandwich bag and added it to his own pocket. The boy let out a short moan. The sound of his agony created a stir inside of Rodney, one that encouraged him to plant three more blows across the boy's face.

Rodney, tapped around the rest of boy's pockets. He patted alongside his waist. He felt something. It was metal. He went under the boy's shirt and felt around. His hands ran across the handle of a snub nosed thirty eight revolver.

He pulled it from the boy's waist and stuffed it in his own waist line. The boy lay on the ground groaning out for help. Rodney, beat him in the head a few more times with the stick and kept swinging it until it broke in half. He backed up, looked around, noticed that no one was watching him, and took off running into the night.

Rodney, ran until he was a few blocks away. He slowed down and walked at a moderate pace. Once he felt safe he slowed down and walked regular, but kept checking over his shoulder to see if he was being followed. He walked up the street until he saw a yard that connected to his mother's backyard. The only thing that separated the yards was a small fence. He cut through the yard, hopped the fence, and walked along the side of the house.

"I'm telling you Rodney, aint nothing to fuck with. He beat the shit out of his mother's new nigga friend." Terry, spoke informing the people who sat on his porch of Rodney's, notoriety. People sat around drinking, playing dominoes, and talking shit to one another. "He beat the shit out of that nigga literally. Today he beat that boy until he shitted on himself. He busted a blood vessel in his eye and broke his lower leg." Pride slid across his face as excitement filled his voice.

"Fuck that shit Terry, cut the music back on." A man's voice yelled at him from somewhere on the porch.

"Fuck you Wally, this is my house." He swallowed some more of his liquor. He looked over at his brother in law, then laughed his signature laugh. The one that started off slow, skipped into a stutter, grew increasingly annoying, and ended up sounding like the crypt keeper. A minute later the music roared out of the speakers.

Rodney, sat on his bed counting his money. He had nine hundred and twenty dollars in cash, twenty two eight balls, and a brand new pistol.

I had an Accura Legend at fifteen kid .It's nothing something light. Dooski's, words rung out in his mind.

Pookie, sat on the bench with his legs spread apart. His arms hung over the edge of the bench. Music played, people talked, and women gathered around crowding the area where Pookie, and his workers posted up at.

Savage, sat beside Pookie, His baseball cap hung down over his eyes. He sat still watching the activity absorbing everything around him. The smell of hamburgers cooking on the grill filled the air. Clouds of smoke rose from the grill when Loop, opened it up to check on the meat.

Some people ran around in the grass chasing after a volley ball. Savage, watched Tiffany, biting into a hot dog. Her husband a brown colored stocky man with average features stood beside her. He held her by the waist. He kissed her on the cheek. He watched the other women move around the park, but maintained his embrace on Tiffany,

Little kids ran around the park chasing each other, some stood around holding onto paper plates waiting for the meat to be served, and others dribbled a basketball up and down the court.

"What's been up with you?" Pookie, spoke to Rodney, without looking at him.

"I've been out here putting a few things together and trying to get my feet wet. I got to get my weight up." His eyes lingered around, but followed Tiffany, He watched her shorts run out of material just below her crotch area. He followed her as she walked off with her husband.

"I heard about your work with the Canadian broad." Pookie, looked left and right then straight forward.

"I had to have it. I can't take this being broke shit." Rodney, looked at Tiffany, smile, pout, and playfully punch at her husband. He grabbed her and pulled her closed to him. She lifted up her hand revealing a hot dog. He bit it and chewed it up. Tiffany, smiled at him and walked off to get him his own hot dog. He smacked her on the butt while she walked away.

Rodney, looked at her and her husband. Pookie, adjusted his position on the bench and placed his arm around Rodney's, shoulder.

"Yo, I like your style. I'm about to put you down, but you can't hustle in the park. You got to get your own area." Pookie, stared straight ahead. His words created a tingling sensation inside Rodney's, chest.

"That's what I have been looking forward to doing. Getting my own shit started I'm not a little boy anymore I can't be hero." He caught himself and held onto to his point of view, careful not to say too much too fast and kill his chances of getting a chance to come up.

"You can't be what?" Pookie, leaned in closer to him to hear more clearly.

"I can't be no hero type nigga like you. If all I do is sit up under you." Rodney, smiled hoping his flattery would lessen Pookie's, inquiry.

"I tell all of my niggas that if they want it. Its out here to be got and all they have to do is go for it." He focused his attention on a few females walking across the park. "I told all of my niggas that if they show some initiative and buy a car. I'd hook it up for them."

"You said that?" Rodney, looked for Tiffany, but didn't see her. His eyes scanned the park looking for her.

"The only one who took me up on the offer was Loop, He came out strong, made his money, and situated his own thing." He looked at Rodney, "He helped step up the way we do shit out here in the park." Rodney, looked over at Loop, and watched him move with finesse, He entertained people, passed out food, kept a careful eye on the workers who hung out further in the park handling business as usual. Loop, watched everything while appearing to be solely interested in everybody's well being and making sure that they were having a good time.

"Who is that?" Rodney, pointed at Tiffany's, husband.

"Tezo," Pookie, frowned. "Corny ass nigga. He aint about shit, be sniffing up Peru." Pookie, shook his head.

"That's her husband?" Rodney, asked already knowing the answer.

"Yeah they got a daughter together. It's not really his baby, but he's been with the bitch since her daughter was a baby." Pookie, looked at Tiffany, then over at Rodney, "You like her?"

"I was just asking." Rodney, lied shaking his head side to side. He looked away attempting to avert his attention from her, but couldn't. His eyes rolled around the park looking at other objects, but frequently rotated around to where Tiffany, was.

"She's jive corny. My brother use to fuck her before he got locked up." Pookie, smiled at something that happened inside of his mind.

"Her daughter is your niece?" Rodney, looked puzzled.

"My brother was hitting that before she met her baby father."

"Who is your brother?"

"Turtle," Pookie, looked around the park, then at the street, absorbing each car that drove by, but slowed down only to pick up speed and drive off. "He was official all about his business, kept his paper right, and the nigga's gun game was sick." Listening to Pookie, talk about his brother. Rodney, listened to the tales and wanted his name to fall out of peoples mouth with the same level of respect.

"Yo, are you going to give it to me tonight?" Rodney, asked referring to the drugs.

"I'm going to see that you get it before you leave the park. Pookie, looked at him and sucked on his bottom lip and looked up. "Out here everything goes, it aint no love in this shit. It don't have too many happy endings. "

"I'm not looking for happiness, I'm l looking for money, cash money my dude."

" I hear You." Pookie, looked straight ahead. Rodney, looked straight ahead and everywhere else that Tiffany, moved to.

Upon leaving the park Rodney, received the four and one half ounces of already cooked cocaine. He stuffed it deep into his pocket and walked away. He took the drugs home. He sat in his room looking at the drugs wondering where he was going to sale them. He thought about what he was going to do with the money once he got it.

Its about stacking that paper B, stack that grip, hold your head son, don't let those bitches play you B, One honey who I was loving did me filthy. She screwed my man Boog, son. The hurtful thing about it was Boog, is a corny ass fronting ass nigga B, that just goes to show tha game don't stop, hoes think that they are players and it's important not to get played, but if it happens its cool it happens to the best of us.

Rodney, thought about Dooski's, words and then thought about a girl who he could be with on a serious level. He didn't know any, but he didn't' want to waste his money giving a girl reasons to love him only to find out that she was loving him only to use him as a come up.

Soon as the sun looked like it was somewhere in the midst of the cloud. Savage, walked out of his front door carrying all twenty two eight balls that he had stolen. He walked around all the areas that he knew where the people who used drugs hung out at. He walked around the area looking for one of the users. He saw one, then another, and a few more, but neither of them had more than ten dollars. He sold it to them and kept walking around. He walked up on a skinny woman who looked like a man with a woman's voice.

"Yo," She clapped her hands together seeking to get Rodney's, attention.

"What's up?" He looked around at her. She walked up on him.

"Do you got something?" She spoke to him quietly like she was relating top secret information.

"What you need?" He looked at her.

"Hold on." She ran into the house and returned one minute later with a fat lady. "She need something. She got some money and she wants to get looked out for and."

"Bernie, I know how to talk." The fat woman pulled away from her friend.

"Talk then." The skinny woman wiped her mouth eager to get her hands on something to smoke. She looked at her friend and ushered her forward.

"What's up?" Rodney, looked at them and watched them intently.

"I have one hundred dollars, but I want to make sure it's good. Some young boys came through here earlier and sold me some shit that fucked my pipe up."

"I don't do business like that." Rodney, looked at her. She pulled out her money, held onto it, pulled it closer to her chest, and asked him to give her something for twenty dollars first so she could test it.

One minute later she was opening her mouth, licking around her teeth, and rubbing her hands across her knees. She pulled out the rest of her money and handed it to Rodney,

"What's up?" He asked looking at her. She nodded her head, pointed at him, and nodded her head some more. He counted her money and pulled out some pieces and handed them to her.

"If you want to you can sit over here and make some money." Bernie, looked around. "Sissy, don't care. You can do whatever you want as long as you look out for us. I mean her." Bernie, looked at Rodney, and hoped that he would take her up on her offer and keep his good and powerful drugs nearby.

"I'll think about it." He looked nonchalantly for a few seconds. "You know what I'm going to take you up on that offer." Bernie, looked at him and smiled. Within seconds she disappeared inside the house and appeared just as fast side by side with Sissy,

"Here she is ask her." Bernie, looked at Rodney, her eyes beamed with happiness and a deep concentrated want. She looked at her friend. Rodney, looked at Bernie, wondering what she was up to. "He wants to sit in here and make some money."

"You know Darius, and his friends be over here." The fat woman looked at the skinner one.

"But they aint here now and this boy got some good dope." The smaller woman rubbed her hands across her face. Her friend thought about it for a second.

"He could come in until they decide to come over here." She looked at Rodney, he looked at her and walked into the house. He looked at the house. It resembled his own. It was nasty, disgusting, full of people, funky scented, and a little boy walked around late at night in a pair of cut off shorts, eating a bowl of cereal with water.

"You can sit down." Bernie, offered him a seat. He took a look at the furniture and thought about it. He shook his head side to side to decline. He stood up and leaned against the arm of the couch.

The house turned out to be one that was flooded with activity. People came in spurts, quick lucrative spurts. They knocked on the door, the windows, and called out for Bernie, Once they got a taste of the cocaine that Rodney, had they came more rapidly, they kept coming, and came back with more people some of which brought merchandise with them.

He stood inside the house and sold every last piece of crack that was inside the sandwich bag. The same one that he took from the person he robbed. Once he sold out he left the house quick as he could. The money in his pocket felt good pressing against his thigh.

"Are you coming back?" Bernie, looked at him curiously.

"Later." He turned and walked off.

Chapter 15
Game recognize Game

Rodney, sat in his house looking at the money that was stacked into a few neat piles on his bed. He looked at it and felt proud. He picked up the money, put it into a sock, rolled it up tight as it could go, and stuffed it in the front of his underwear. He lay down and went to sleep.

Later when he woke up, he washed, got dressed, put on some clothes, and went over to the park. When he got there Loop, was sitting there by himself.

"Savage!" Loop, yelled out to Rodney, soon as he saw the boy enter the park.

"Loop!" Rodney, yelled back and smiled to himself. He walked over to the bench and sat down. Rodney, pulled out his money and showed it to Loop,

"Put that shit away. You can get locked up for having money on you. If not they can take your money and either way you end up fucked."

"How can they take my money?" Rodney, asked truly naïve to the game and what was expected and allowed from the players. He didn't know any of the rules associated with the treachery that came with getting money.

"This shit is illegal. Niggas go to prison over this shit. Niggas get killed over this shit, bitches get pregnant, and weak niggas get strung out over this. It's not too many happy endings." He looked at Rodney, and searched his eyes for the truth and found it in the boy's innocence, inexperience, and ignorance. "Let me holler at you." Loop, stood up and walked away. Rodney, walked behind him.

Once they walked two blocks away from the park. Loop, pulled out a set of car keys form his pocket and opened the door to a silver Range Rover. He got in the driver's seat and opened the door for Rodney,

"This aint no career shit. You get in, get what you got to get, and get low." Loop, spoke to him while starting up his truck.

"But you have been out here for a long time and your still out here." Rodney, reasoned.

"That's beside the point. I'm in too deep. It's no other way for me. I'm thirty five years old, been out her since I was a shorty." Loop, steered through traffic.

"Your that old Loop?" Rodney, asked not believing him. Loop, didn't look a day over twenty one.

"Hell yeah. I've been lucky not to be all cased up and caught up in bullshit."

"How old is Pookie?" Rodney, questioned.

"About twenty eight or twenty nine." Loop, looked at the road. "Why are you selling this shit Rodney?"

"I want some money." He looked at him like that was obvious.

"There is money in a job. Why this, why the streets?"

"It's this boy who I was locked up with and he knows everything about cocaine and he use to tell me."

"Did he tell you how it tastes?" he looked over at Rodney, briefly then back at the street.

"He didn't use it. He just sold it." Rodney, spoke in Dooski's, defense.

"So he doesn't know everything about it. He's just a young kid running off at the mouth."

"He said that he had a whole kilo of cocaine before."

"Did you see it?"

"No."

"So it was strictly hearsay." Loop, looked at the street then turned his steering wheel and swerved around a car that was moving too slow. "Listen to me Rodney, niggas will tell you all type of shit, claim to love you then come to your house when you least expect it, and fucking kill you."

"Why?"

"That's what it is out here. Everybody is going crazy and looking out for themselves."

"Yeah, but only crack head niggas do shit like that."

"Really?" He looked at the boy. "Look at me. Do I look like a crack head?"

"Because your not."

"Not anymore, but I use to be." He looked over at Rodney, "I use to sell weed in high school, then coke came out. Everybody was doing it. It was considered fun at that point, just the latest fad, but then it caught me by the ass and drug me around for a few years.

"Pookie, too?"

"Just Turtle, but he was about his business. He had a hold on his habit, but its not too many niggas out here who can do that." He sighed then slowed down until his truck was completely stopped at a red light. "What are your goals, what are you trying to do out here, and what do you want?"

"I don't really know."

"Get a fixed number in your mind, get an exact date on when you plan to have it, take no shorts, get it, save every fucking penny. Once you get the money that's only the beginning what are you going to do with it when you get it?"

"I'm going to buy me a car and some more clothes."

"Its only so much shopping you can do, it's only one car that you can drive at a time, and pussy comes free." He pulled up in front of a sneaker store and got out of the truck. Rodney, got out with him.

They walked around the store buying sneakers and finishing their conversation. By the time they had left the store Rodney, was informed on some more pointers about street life that he never heard of before, even considered, nor did he remember Dooski, talking about them.

When they parked, got out the car, and walked to the park a few of the normal faces were spread out in their usual places. Rodney, walked along the street side by side with Loop,

"Why do you park your truck way over there and walk to the park?"

"For one I don't want the cops knowing my shit like that, for two I don't want people guessing how much money I'm playing with, and for three that's how Turtle, put it down before he left."

"Who was Turtle? Everybody talks about him like he was.."

"A king?" Loop, finished his words for him. "The boy had money, still has money, and they use to call him King Turt," He looked at Rodney, "Pookie, is getting money, but his brother is that dude."

"I thought you said that he was getting high?"

"He was, but he had a grip on it, and he had a connection that he kept paid."

"What about Tiffany, and her husband?" Rodney, asked only because he was curious.

"That sucka ass nigga Tezo, He's a full of shit ass nigga, still sniffing, and fucking all of the young girls." He scouted out the park as he moved closer to it. "Tiffany, is your typical cute face. A fat ass and no direction. She's depending on a nigga to take her to the promise land."

"Did Turtle, take her to the promise land?"

"Damn near, but he had mad bitches. It would be two and three hoes standing right next to each other claiming this nigga. That man had money."

"What did he look like?"

"A turtle, that's how he got his name, the nigga looked like a ninja turtle with glasses, but the boy had a heart of gold. That's who started the park jams, the cook outs, and this whole situation out here." He looked at the people sitting on the bench and shook his head. "You sort of got a style like Turtle, quiet, you keep to yourself, and you're about your business. You're quick to act without second guessing yourself."

Rodney, smiled at Loop, and shook his hand. They parted ways as Loop, headed to work and Rodney, went home. Rodney, walked up the street thinking about his life and what it was that he was going to do with it. He walked in the house and saw Terry, sitting in the living room.

"Your momma went to jail today, she had a warrant all this time and didn't tell nobody."

"What is her bail?"

"She got one. She has to do six months."

Six months?" Rodney repeated his words just because.

"Yeah fucking with that no good ass nigga, up there stealing steaks and taking shit out of those people's store." Terry, looked disappointed at his friend and neighbor. "If you need anything, I will be next door. I don't know how you are going to pay rent." The older man shook his head. "I got a little money saved up we can use that."

"I'll be alright Terry," Rodney, smiled at the man and closed the door.

Over the next couple of weeks Rodney, used the hell out of Bernie, and her fat friend Sissy, He met Darius, a light skin chunky kid. He was the fat lady's nephew. He had a friend named Freddie, He was mulatto with a bush hair style. Rodney, sold them double ups, he sold his own pieces, and had fun hanging out with the boys.

Darius, was funny all he did was tell jokes. He picked on his aunt and played tricks on her and her friends. He would see that they had smoked up all of their money, tell them that he lost some pieces, and if they found them they could keep it. They would be down on their knees looking for stuff that wasn't there in the first place. One time he filled a Vodka bottle with water and left it on the table with a note.

Freddie, was a guy who thought he was a player. He wanted money so he could buy a real pretty girlfriend. He spent his money on magazines about models and what they wanted from a man, what characteristics they thought to be sexy, and other shit that was solely designed to sell a few more copies of the magazines.

Living alone was like living in the boy's home except Rodney, had to get his own food. He couldn't cook therefore he brought boxes of cereal, cold cuts, and microwave pizzas, and apple juice. The dishes in the cabinets were corroded with filth. Rodney, tossed them in the garbage and brought different plates, bowls, and silverware.

Rodney, walked out of his house and prepared to meet up with Pookie, and give him his money. When he got to the park he noticed the drug task force standing in the park. They had a few people on the ground searching through their pockets. Two black detectives had Chris a dark skin heavy set brother hemmed up against a tree.

"Spit it out you fucking monkey," The baldheaded cop yelled as he choked the boy. His thick neck rattled around inside the angry cop's hands.

"You're going to get yourself killed you drug dealing piece of shit." His partner another black cop stood beside him looking like beating up on black teenagers was an everyday occurrence.

"Come on man. You're choking the shit out of my man." Courtney, a guy who hung around the park just to smoke weed said from the ground.

"You want to get fucking choked too! You black pastard!" A white cop yelled at him angrily mispronouncing the word bastard. He walked over to Courtney, stooped down over him and wrapped his pale hands around the back of his neck and squeezed. He shook the boy's neck around in his hands. Rodney, walked away he never looked over his shoulder. He walked a few feet until he escaped the area where the confusion was taking place.

The sound of a car engine crept up behind Rodney, he felt his heart increasing in weight and slinking down into his stomach. He walked concealing his nervousness by walking coolly along the sidewalk. The driver of the car beeped the horn. Rodney, ignored it and kept walking.

The second beep accompanied by a familiar voice caught his attention. Rodney, turned to see Loop, creeping along the street moving slowly. He pulled over to the curb. Rodney, jumped in the car and they sped off.

"What's up? It's hot over here." Rodney, was disappointed. He was on the verge of getting his money correct, but now the police were fucking everything up.

"This is what it is out here, they got a job to do. We got a job to do. The trick is to not get caught up in their business, cause if you do then you're getting arrested for possession or a sale of a narcotic." He drove the gray Dodge Spectrum through traffic with ease. "Now if they get in your business. Its conspiracy, CCE that kingpin shit, and with that come long ass prison sentences."

"My mother went to jail yesterday." Rodney, expected Loop, to offer him some guidance on how to handle being on his own.

"For what?"

"Crack head shit." Rodney, looked out the window.

"How old are you?"

"Fifteen next week."

"A fucking baby forced to be a man." Loop, spoke out expressing compassion and a seasoned understanding of what direction the boy's life was headed in. "What's you next move?"

"I'm going to keep getting money."

"I mean about your living situation."

"I'm going to keep the house until my mother get out." Rodney, spoke with confidence. His attitude and willingness to make a bad situation better caused Loop, to smile.

"I know you will it's all in your eyes."

"What's in my eyes?" He questioned the man who made the comment.

"Determination and devotion." Loop, drove up to a factory warehouse and parked the car.

"What's this?" Rodney looked at the building.

"You need some shit for the house don't you?" Loop, walked into the front door, Rodney, brought up the rear moving close behind him.

Thirty minutes later Rodney, sat in the passenger seat feeling good. He brought some furniture for his mother's house. Two bedroom sets for his and her room, a living room seat, and a kitchen table. He also brought a safe. His happiness came mixed with nervousness due to spending five thousand dollars out of his money. He wondered when he was going to make the money back. He spent majority of his profit.

"What are you thinking about?" Loop, asked form the driver seat.

"Nothing really." He lied not wanting to seem cheap.

"Money comes and it goes only to be made all over again." He stopped at a light. "Its called a wise investment. You brought furniture to have a place to rest your head. You brought a safe, somewhere to keep your money for the time being. You brought blankets, chairs, and a table. It's all shit that you need."

"But I damn near spent up my profits."

"You'll make it back and it teaches you how to separate your needs from your wants."

"When will they bring the furniture to the house?"

"A couple of days." Loop, looked at his watch, then picked up a handful of change out of the ashtray, and pulled over at a corner store. He got out the car and went into the store. He came out within seconds talking on his cell phone. He got back into the car and drove away.

"You got that paper with you?" Loop, looked at Rodney,

"I just spent it, but I got it at home. Run me by there so I can get it."

Outside Rodney's, house Loop, sat in the car waiting for him to come back to the car. Rodney, returned and handed Loop, the money. Loop, counted the money, slipped it in his pocket, went under the arm rest, and handed him a huge sandwich bag.

"That's two hundred and fifty."

"Dollars?" Rodney, asked in disbelief.

"Grams, that's two thousand more than what you just paid." He stuck his hand out and shook Rodney's, the boy eased the drugs in his pocket and got out of the car. He went upstairs into his bedroom and hid his drugs.

One hour later he was at Sissy's, house. Bernie, sat around waiting for something to happen that would end up with her having something to smoke. Sissy, sat around looking at t.v.

"Hey Rodney," Bernie, said happy to see him or serve as a taste tester and give her honest opinion about the product. He handed her a twenty dollar rock, then gave one to her friend.

He walked off to where Darius, kept the scale. He weighed up the pieces that he brought out the house with him. He sat a t the kitchen table looking at the numbers on the digital scale flicker until they stopped at sixty two grams. He broke down the drugs and placed them in a few baggies and set it aside for Darius, and Freddie,

"That's better than the last stuff you had." Bernie, came out the room walking slow and talking like it hurt her throat to speak.

"That's what they saying." He lied to her. "Yo, call Darius, and tell him I need to see him." Rodney, got up from the table and went and sat down on the couch.

Hours went by and people came by the house in droves. Rodney, sold pieces and kept selling them until the empty space in his pocket was crowded with dollar bills. He was in the process of selling someone something for seventy dollars when Darius, came walking through the front door.

"What's up nigga!" Darius, yelled at Rodney, he ran up on him, wrapped his arms around him, and hugged him tightly. He rested his forehead against Rodney's, chest. " I missed you." He sounded like his girlfriend instead of his homeboy.

"Get the hell off me." Rodney pushed the boy away from him. "I got something for you." He walked away and came back with three eight balls and handed them to him. "I got three for Freddie, too."

"We about to get paid." Darius, put the three packages in his pocket. He smiled and walked over to Bernie, who was turning the dial on the radio. She looked for good reception slowly moving the knob. The sound of Kirk Franklin, yelling GP are you with me, caused her to throw her hands up in the air and dance. She moved her body around rocking her leg as she moved.

Her fat friend came out from somewhere in the back. She danced her way up into the dining room and moved her body while singing along with the song. Darius, danced around then walked up behind Bernie, and started grinding on her while he danced against the spot where her butt used to be, before the cocaine ate it off her body.

Rodney, sat on the couch laughing at what he was seeing. Enjoying being the reason why everyone was laughing Darius, made a silly face and danced harder on Bernie, She was dancing like her life depended on it.

"Agghhh." Darius, leaned all the way back until he was on the ground in a crab position thrusting his hips up. Bernie, going along with the joke squat her narrow ass over him and danced around.

A knock on the door brought everything back to normal. Bernie, straightened up and went over to the front window and peeked out of it. She looked at her friend who turned down the radio. Darius, got up from the floor and walked over to the window.

"Oh shit that's my man. He be spending like two or three hundred." He looked at Rodney, Darius, opened the door and invited the man inside the house. He broke off some pieces and pushed them into the man's hand.

"Um is Bernie, around?" The guy asked nervously.

"Bill I'm right here. How come can't see me and I'm right in front of you?" Bernie, got out of the chair that she sat in. She looked at Sissy, asking for permission to take the guy in one of her backrooms. The two women conversed with their eyes.

"Are you going to look out for her?"

"Don't I always?" The man walked toward the back of the house. A few rapid knocks came at the front door. Darius, answered it.

"The police got somebody stopped over there." Rodney, Darius, and his aunt all bunched up together looking out the front window. They watched as the police had a few guys leaned up against the car. "That's Arthur, that boy is making some money. He threw something over there before he stopped." The lady who related the information stood there looking over Rodney's, shoulder as she peeked out the window.

A second later the police were arresting the two boys and placing them into the back of the squad car. Once the police pulled off. Rodney, grabbed the lady by the arm and took her into the back of the house.

"Yo, where did you say he threw his shit at?" She looked at Rodney, wondering did he know who he was fucking with. He pulled out a couple of twenty pieces and handed them to her.

"He threw it in the garbage can, but you didn't hear that from me." She took her earnings and walked into the back of the house. Soon as she disappeared with her friend. Rodney, stepped out of the house and walked down the street, looked around, saw that no one was watching him, and began searching the garbage can at the corner. He moved around a few trash items before coming across the cocaine. He picked it up and walked off in the direction toward the house.

He used the scale to weigh up his findings. He watched as the numbers jiggled around and stopped at one hundred and eighty three grams. He put it back in the bag and went home.

In his house he hid the stuff, got his gun, and went back over to where he had just left. He walked into the house and saw Darius, lying on the couch face down.

"Get up man." He slapped his hand against his foot.

"I thought you were gone for the day." Darius, sat up on the couch and looked at his friend.

Twenty minutes later Arthur, and two other people were knocking on the door. Bernie, answered it.

"Bernie, who is that nigga that took my shit out the garbage can?" His voice was calm and steady.

"I don't know I just got here." She lied. He looked at her and shook his head to her. He walked up in the house uninvited and barged up into the living room. "What's up Darius?" He looked at Darius, while standing side by side with his two friends.

"What's up Art?" Darius, was obviously afraid of him.

"We never had problems before. I mean we alright aint we?" He asked like his words were enough to demand his product back.

"No, we cool."

"So that mean I can get my shit back?" He spoke intending to intimidate Darius,

"That means fuck you nigga." Rodney, stood up. He walked up over to where the boys were standing.

"Who is this?" Arthur, pointed at Rodney, assuming he wasn't from around there because no one in his hood would dare speak to him like that.

"Unimportant." Rodney, looked at him challenging him to say or do something.

The first punch came from Arthur, it flew over Rodney's head as he ducked under it. The second one came from Rodney, it came from the floor and banged into the boy's chin. Arthur, stumbled back in time to get hit three more times. One of his boys jumped in punching Rodney, in the head. Darius, jumped up and ran at him and began fighting with him. The third boy jumped in to get Rodney, off of Arthur.

The first shot came from the ground. The second caused a voice to cry out in pain. Rodney, stood up swinging his pistol around. He aimed it at the boy who was on his back and squeezed. The bullet tore through his thigh. Afraid of being killed the boy struggled to his feet and hobbled to the front door. He forced his way through it.

Arthur, busted out the window and leapt through it. The third boy ran out the house. Rodney, ran behind him aiming at his ass cheeks and shot. Rodney, ran up the street after the boys. He shot as he ran behind them. Bullets skipped up from the ground and scraped into garbage cans, hit the side of buildings, and caused people to run for their lives.

Voices yelled out in fear as people moved out of the way. Rodney, ran behind the boys firing an empty gun. The barrel spun around only to click on an empty chamber. He ran after the boys although he had nothing to hurt them with.

Fear pushed them into a car that waited for them at the corner. The driver took a look at Rodney, and put the car in drive and sped off. Rodney, ran up the street and disappeared before the cops came.

Rodney, dropped the gun in a sewer drain and ran to Terry's, house. He walked in the front door calmly.

"What's up Rodney?" The older man sat up and looked at his neighbor.

"Somebody got shot and they probably think that I had something to do with it."

"Somebody got shot?" Terry, walked around his living room with his arm crossed over his chest. "Where at?"

"Over on Highland and Fairfield." Rodney, looked at Terry,

"Go and chill in the back room." Terry, went and got his girlfriend and their daughter, got in his car, and drove over to the crime scene to see what was happening.

Rodney, snuck in his backdoor and went into his bedroom and hid his drugs and came down and went back into Terry's, house and waited for him to return.

Thirty minutes later Terry, came walking through the front door. He looked at Rodney,

"What happened?"

"Nothing when I got there the police was asking questions, but nobody said nothing." He looked at Rodney, "I don't think Arthur, will tell he's from the street. Randy, and Carl, is street niggas too. If anything they will come back on you."

"I aint tripping." Rodney's, look scared Terry, who walked up on him.

"Be careful Rodney, take it easy you just came home. Remember where you just came from and where your not trying to go back." His eyes contained love and compassion. Rodney, nodded his head up and down.

After changing clothes Rodney, called Loop, Ten minutes later he walked down the street looking over his shoulder prepared to run if need be. He stood at the corner near 15th and Michigan where Loop, told him to meet him. Two minutes later Loop's, car pulled up.

"What the fuck?" Loop, stepped out of the car with both hands raised high in the air. "You keep shooting mutha fuckas." He walked across the street, grabbed Rodney, and pulled him by the shirt until they were in the car. He pulled off.

"Loop, it wasn't my fault. The shit happened so fast." Rodney, tried to explain.

"What the fuck Savage, cut this shit out. Who the fuck did you shoot now?" His eyes swelled up with anger.

"Some nigga named Arthur,"

"Light skin?"

"Not really, but he aint all that dark either." Rodney, sat in the passenger seat looking at Loop,

"Fuck it just fuck it." Loop, threw his hands up in defeat. "For what, how did it happen?"

"The nigga tried to play me." Rodney, maintained a straight face as he lied concealing the real reason for the shooting.

"How?" Loop, was on the verge of exploding behind the steering wheel.

"I found some coke in a garbage can and he tried to say I stole it from him. He acted like he wanted something and I did what I had to do."

"You just found it?" He looked at Rodney, in disbelief. "Did you find it the same way you found that Canadian girl's shit?"

"Something like that."

"Rodney, man!"

"Loop, fuck that nigga. I just need a gun in case they come back for me." Rodney, cut him off.

"You don't need a fucking gun you need to cool the fuck out." Loop, looked at him.

"Loop, I need a gun that's why I called you, for you to give me a gun, not for you to baby me."

"Oh your grown up now?" A gesture of pure mockery covered his face. Loop, had both hands on the steering wheel. He rode around, looked over at Rodney, and back at the street. "Crazy world that we living in, it's a fucked up and crazy world that we living in."

Before long the two men were sitting outside a green house. Loop, rubbed both of his hands over the top of his head, and down the back of his neck.

"Rodney, you're getting money it takes time, and you can't keep robbing every damn body."

"I didn't rob him I found it." Sincerity filled his eyes displaying his way of seeing the situation. He looked at Loop, expecting him to believe him and help him out by placing a gun in his hand.

"Here you have your mind made up." He put his hands down in his lap and pulled out a gun. "That's a glock ever see one of those?" He handed Rodney, an extra clip. He stared straight ahead and breathed heavily through his nose. He took Rodney, home and dropped him off.

Rodney, walked around the house with the gun tucked inside his jeans ready to pull it out and use it if he had to. He sat on the edge of his bed. He counted his money, looked at his cocaine which was scattered across his bed packaged up in sandwich bags, and plastic baggies. He imagined how the stack of money would look when he sold everything.

Chapter 16
Déjà vu

The sound of someone knocking on the front door woke Rodney, up. He sat up, stared around the room until the contents of the room came into focus. He looked around at the bed. His money was spread across the bed looking like someone had run a hand over it and stretched it out. Packages of drugs were stuck to his stomach. He peeled the bags off of him and wondered when; did he fall asleep.

He put all of his money and product away. He walked down the stairs and up to the front door.

"Who is it?" He yelled through the door.

"Delivery guy, we are here with your furniture." A cheerful sounding voice stated its purpose.

Rodney, looked out the window then opened the door. He stepped out the way and let the man in. He signed a few papers and told them where to put the furniture.

After everything was in place Rodney, sat around feeling the texture of the new furniture. He looked at his screen t.v. and realized that he needed some cable. He went next door to Terry's, house.

"What's up Rodney?" Terry, answered the door half sleep

"I need your help." Rodney, looked at him.

"Hold on." He pulled his raggedy burgundy house coat tighter to his body. He walked outside following Rodney, He hand on a pair of red and white boxers and a pair of fake, but beat down leather house shoes. They were busted and cracked on the sides. He walked down his steps and up on his neighbor's. He walked into the house. "Holy shit Rodney." His eyes widened as he looked around. He walked over to the t.v. and stood in front of the blank screen admiring the size of the television.

"I need your help. I got to get some cable for this t.v." Rodney, looked at him then at the t.v.

"Alright." The older man looked at the table and chairs in the kitchen. He looked at the newness that filled the house in amazement. "Rodney, remember where you came from and be careful."

Fear didn't control Rodney, respect was a word in the dictionary as far as he was concerned. Long as he had a gun and some bullets. He would forever refuse to back down and shrink in the face of danger. A few days after shooting Arthur, and his two boys. Rodney, was back over at Sissy's, house worry free. Although he had started some shit, didn't know how it was going to play out, or how long life was going to occupy his body, but judging by how fast money came to him just sitting in Sissy's, house. He wasn't willing to be chased out of paradise.

Two months later Rodney, accumulated more money, brought a jet black Accura Legend. He put rims on it, redid the interior of the car with leather, a t.v., and a banging stereo system. He ran into Arthur, on several occasions, he reached for his gun, waited for something to happen, and when it didn't he would pull off.

One day Rodney, rode around listening to Mary J. Blige, you remind me. He pulled up at a stop light and stopped. A group of girls were walking by when one of them stopped and waved at him. He looked at her, but couldn't remember her. He tapped his horn out of routine. He was in the process of pulling off when his memory kicked in.

"Oh shit." He pulled to the side of the street. He backed up and stopped a few feet from the girls. "Dena?" He asked stepping out of his car.

"Yeah." She smiled at him. Her hair hung down to her shoulders. She stared at him.

"What's up?" He walked up on her and opened his arms preparing to hug her. She walked into his arms.

"How long have you been home?"

"A few months."

"Why didn't you call me or try to get in touch with me?" Dena, held onto his body. She squealed out in delight. They rocked back and forth in each other's arms.

"You look good." Rodney, backed away from her in order to take in a better view of what she had to offer.

"You do too." She looked at him with as much attention that he paid her.

"Who is that Dena?" A dark skin girl with a short hair style asked looking up and down at Rodney,

"You don't remember him?" She looked at her friend giving her enough time to figure it out. "Rodney," She looked at her friend like he was equally important to them as he was to her.

"Do you need a ride?" He looked at her.

"Well I'm with my friends and we were about to."

"Yeah we want a ride." The dark skin girl smiled, then pushed her hands into Dena's, back. She shoved her toward the car.

Rodney, jumped in his car. The dark skin girl attempted to climb in the front seat. Dena, grabbed her by the arm. She looked at Dena, who was staring at her intensely.

"Oops my bad." She giggled before getting into the backseat. Rodney, waited for them all to get in the car, then he pulled off. His phone rang.

"What's up?" He spoke into the phone.

"Where are you at?" Freddie, asked.

"I'm with some girls. I'm about to drop them off."

"Drop them off where?" Excitement rushed through the phone. "Bring them over here."

"Man these girls don't want to sit up in that nasty ass house."

"Let's take them out and then to a motel or something. I'm about to go get Darius, come and get us." He hung up.

"Where are yall going?" He looked over at Dena,

"Just over to my house, but aint nothing going on over there." The dark skin girl spoke from the backseat.

"What's your name?" Rodney, looked at her through the rearview mirror.

"I'm Ebony," She smiled a bright and fun filled smile.

"Yo, I'm about to pick up a couple of my mans and we can go and hang out."

"I don't know." Dena, said unsure of what to do or say.

"Why we not doing nothing." Ebony, spoke up again.

"It's better than sitting at Ebony's, house talking all day." Dena's, head snapped around as she gave the girl beside Ebony, a murderous look. The girl went silent mid sentence.

Rodney, pulled up in front of the spot. Darius, and Freddie, got into backseat.

"Oh brother Freddie," The light skin girl said in a tone that could of suggested that Freddie, was corny or didn't want anything to do with him.

"Melody, I should of known you were somewhere around here. I've been smelling rotten cheese."

"Keep eating it." Her words caused everyone in the car to laugh. Rodney, pulled up in front of the place where Ebony, suggested they go. They all got out the car, went inside, and paid for their gear. Once everyone was dressed and secured from possible injuries. They paired up into teams. The boys against the girls.

Ebony, fired the first shot. Her paint ball exploded close to Rodney's, private parts. He looked at her with surprise. He aimed his own paintball gun and fired. She jumped out of the way, rolled across the floor, got up, and took off running.

Before long everyone had forgot about being on teams. It was every man and woman for themselves. Rodney, shot Darius, in the back, who turned around and shot him in the stomach. Freddie, ran after Dena, while Melody, ran behind him shooting and hitting him directly in the back.

When it was all over with they all sat in Rodney's, car talking and laughing. Rodney, drove around the city for a little while. He stopped at a red light across the street from a fast food eatery.

"Oh I am hungry." Ebony, said out loud.

"Me too." Darius, looked at her. She rolled her eyes and looked away. Rodney, cut his blinker on and turned left and drove through the drive thru where he waited behind two cars. When his turn arrived he pulled up to the intercom.

"I want a double burger, some fries, a vanilla milk shake and." Ebony, looked at Rodney, "What do you want?" She pointed at him.

"Order what you think I will like."

"Can I have a double burger with cheese, a large fry, and a large soda." She looked at Rodney, he smiled at her. She gave him one back and sat back in her seat.

"I want three double cheese burger, two medium fries, and two medium sodas." Everybody looked at Freddie, "What? I'm hungry." He shrugged his shoulders.

Everybody order and Rodney, paid for the food and drove until he reached Ebony's, house. He let the girls out.

"Do you want my number?" He asked Dena,

"I don't got my phone with me." She stared at him.

"What's the number I can remember it." Ebony, stuck her straw in her mouth and sucked on it. Rodney, gave them the number. Ebony, repeated it out loud three times then assured him that she had it stored in her mind. Rodney, waited for the girls to get in the house then he blew the horn and pulled off.

"Yo, that bitch was all up on Rodney," Freddie, spoke his mind freely as he referred to Ebony,

"I know, but what about Melody?" Darius, asked.

"I already be fucking her. She lives next door to my grandmother."

"That's why you made that cheese comment?" Rodney, asked focusing on the street.

"Yeah that bitch keeps a yeast infection."

"ILL!" Darius, yelled out.

"That is some nasty shit." Rodney, laughed as he drove toward the spot.

A couple nights later Rodney, sat on the edge of his bed counting his money. He lined each stack of money neatly beside other stacks of money. He picked the money up and placed it in the safe.

Once he locked the safe and secured his money. He walked down stairs and into the kitchen. His cell phone rang. He answered it.

"Hello is Marcy, there?" A white girl asked.

"You have the wrong number." Rodney, looked at the front door anticipating leaving out of it.

"Are you sure because I just called her last weekend."

"I just got this number not to long ago." Rodney, cleared up the miscommunication immediately.

"Alright well." Rodney, cut her off by hanging up on her. He turned to leave the kitchen when his phone rang again. He looked at his phone and didn't recognize the number. He secretly wished it was Dena, He let the call go to his voice mail and called the number back.

"Hello." The caller answered the phone on the first ring.

"Did somebody call me?"

"Who is this?"

"It's Rodney,"

"Oh hey how are you this Ebony, I didn't even know that this was your number." She gasped letting out an exaggerated sigh. " I don't know why, but this number kept floating through my head and I just called it."

"Is Dena, with you?" Rodney, asked hoping that she was.

"No she's probably with her boyfriend." There was a brief silence for a minute or two. "Oh you didn't know that she got a boyfriend?"

"She never mentioned it." Rodney, responded with a flat tone and pitch.

"That doesn't mean nothing people always have somebody, but still mess around with other people. All guys do it, some girls do it too." Friendliness crept out of her voice and slipped through the phone and pulled Rodney, into a conversation.

"Everybody does it?" He asked her looking for a reason to keep her on the phone.

"Um-hmmm."

"You do it?"

"Do what? It's not like I'm a hoe. No it's not like that." She laughed a chuckle that went against her words. "I mean if I like a person and we have been talking and we are good friends. I might hook him up, but as far as just running around doing stuff just to be doing stuff is nasty."

"I." Rodney, attempted to say something.

"You what?" Ebony, spoke, stalled for a second, and waited for his response.

"Its..like..well..we have similar ways of looking at things. I think that girls should be able to benefit from knowing what they want out of life." He tossed out a quick and random line of bullshit. He looked up toward the ceiling.

"What do you mean?"

"Yo, Ebony, I have to go and I will get in touch with you sooner or later, but I really have to go."

"Wait." There was a slow pause between them. "What time are you going to come back home."

"Why?"

"I can..if..you..were just sitting around and doing nothing....I could come over to your house and we could talk about." She ran out of words that would cover up her real intentions.

"Where are you I will come to you?" Rodney, nodded his head up and down pretending to memorize the address as she gave it to him. He walked out of his house and got into his car.

Two hours later he was in front of Ebony's, house blowing the car horn. A curtain moved to the side, a head flashed across the window, and one second later Ebony, came walking out the front door. She walked up to the car slowly. Her hips rocked side to side filling up her tight blue jeans. She looked better than Rodney, had remembered. He sat behind the steering wheel looking ahead pretending not to notice her. She grabbed the door handle, but it was locked.

"Can you open the door?" Her smile lit up across her face. Her disposition was charming, unpolished, and straight off the block. Rodney, felt something tingle inside his stomach. He felt a churning sensation burning in his lap. He unlocked the door for her. She climbed into the car, sat back, and put her seat back.

Rodney, moved through the streets. His music blasted and rattled against the glass. Ebony's, head rocked on beat to almost every song that came out the speakers. He drove over to Sissy's, house, reached under the arm rest, and pulled out the packages that he had for Freddie, and Darius,

He adjusted his shirt by straightening it out. He acted like he wanted to conceal his gun better, but his true purpose was to impress Ebony, Her eyes lit up and came alive with desire. She looked away pretending not to have noticed it .

"I'll be right back." Rodney, got out the car. He stopped and leaned his head back into the car. "What did you say?"

"I said I'll be right here." She smiled at him.

"Alright." Rodney, walked up on the porch, knocked on the door, and disappeared through it once it opened.

He entered the living room. He walked up on Darius, and shook his hand.

"Here this is an ounce and give this one to Freddie,"

"Where are you going?" Darius, looked at his friend who was dressed to impress and smelling good.

"I'm about to get up with this girl." Rodney, spoke coolly.

"Ebony?" Darius, knew, but needed confirmation.

"You already know."

"I'm not going to hold you up." The two boys shook hands.

Back in his car Rodney, navigated his car until he was in front of his house. He stepped out the car. Ebony, stepped out in sync with him. He led the way up to the porch.

"Rodney," Terry, poked his head out of his front window and hung over the ledge. He took a look at Ebony, over at Rodney, his eyes brightened with happiness. "Your mother called me tonight. She asked about you and told me that she got saved." Terry, laughed out loud. His voice shrilled out and rippled through the air. He pulled his head back into the window and shut it.

"Who is that?" Ebony, laughed at his silliness.

"That's my neighbor he's a good dude." Rodney, used his house key to open the door. He walked in and cut the lights on. Ebony, looked around the house and hid her smile.

"Just you and your mother live here?"

"Yeah, but she's in jail right now." He closed the door and locked it.

"For what?" She looked at him faking concern for a complete stranger.

"Crack head shit." He walked toward the stairs.

"Where are you going?" Ebony, walked behind him. He stepped up on the bottom step. She walked closer to him and stood a few feet away from his face.

"I want you to give me a kiss." He ignored her question.

What?" She smiled and looked away. She turned to face him. "You mean a little friendly kiss, a small peck on the cheek that's my friend kind of kiss?" She asked seeing if she could succeed at pulling wool over Rodney's, eyes like he was willing to fall for the I'm not that kind of girl line.

He looked at her without speaking. His eyes maintained focus while he stared directly at her. She walked up on him. Her feet reached the edge of the steps where he stood. He was able to look at the top of her head because he was on the step and she wasn't.

"Come down here." She prepared to kiss him.

Come up here." He stepped up another step giving her room to step up herself. She climbed up on the step and stood face to face with him. She closed her eyes and curved her lips into position while leaning forward. "Not here." He backed up and broke her concentration. She opened her eyes, looked at him, and blinked. "In my bedroom silly." Rodney, smiled at her then turned and began jogging up the stairs two at a time.

He heard her feet moving along the stairs behind his. He walked in his bedroom and kicked off his sneakers. He dove in his bed, rolled over on his back, and spread his arms wide as he could.

Ebony, looked at him. Her shoes clanked against the wooden floor. She walked up to the bed and climbed into it. Her hands touched the bed softly, her arms went forward with her knees as she crawled over to Rodney,

She crawled on top of his chest. He touched her hip and pushed her over until she was laying on top of him. Her legs dangled on each side of his body. The center of her mid-section rested against the stiffness that bulged up from the center of his mid-section.

Their kiss was wet, tongues twisted, tangled around, and flickered against the tips of each other's. The movements of their mid-sections pushed and pulled. Her body pushed down, ground around careful to keep the hardness in his lap center with the heat behind her jeans.

Hands touched then met the others palm, unfastened buttons, untangled belts out of belt loops, and pulled them out with one smooth stroke.

Nakedness danced around on top of his comforter. Sweat rolled down their bodies, pleasure hurt filling up her hairy opening. Sweetness enticed the sensitiveness that ached to be fed from the juices that came out of heated walls.

Lower backs arched, dented, swiveled, rotated, and stayed in place pushing to the limit, reaching for something slightly beyond its reach, yet determined to touch it.

Her lips pursed as she moaned. Her head swayed side to side. Sweat flattened her hair, made it look like it was spilling off her head. Passion took over her reasoning, love came natural, and kept digging inside of her as Rodney, held her legs against his shoulder. Her legs were inches away from her chin, he pushed harder into her pussy, his balls banged up on her butt cheeks and slipped around the entry of her asshole. She clenched it shut by pulling it tighter together.

He panted, groaned, felt the goodness of her wetness. He crawled higher on her body bringing her legs with him. He pressed her toes into the mattress and dug into her body. It felt good. He dug his toes in the bed, but slipped and lost his footing, but the power of the P.U.S.S.Y. picked him right back up, stood him up, and got him hotter and hornier. He took her by storm, did it to her like she needed to be did it to that way. He tore it up, gave that pussy a new identity, and finished the act by bouncing up and down.

"Oh Rodney, please Rodney, oh god!!" She dug her nails into his back.

"Um..mmm..mmm." He moaned as he banged and pounded. "Umm..mmm.mmm." His pleasure increased as he dug deeper in search of it.

"Rodney, I feel it. Oh god…I…feel it…it's in my stomach ooh." The last word rolled out of her mouth like a terrifying scream that wounded the soul when it sounded.

She came first, second, third, and fourth. He came last. He came the hardest it poured out of him. The pressure of his pleasure created a need to empty it out. He bounced around and downward until it was out of him and squirting into her.

He lifted up off her and sat back. She lifted up breathing hard. She grabbed him by the waist and hugged him, squeezed him tight, and kissed his stomach. She brushed her face across his stomach, touched his abdomen with the edge of her lips. She kissed him, hung her head low and planted a soft kiss against the massiveness in between his legs that was decreasing, losing blood, and shrinking down to its original size.

"I love you Rodney, whenever you need me come and get me. You don't have to buy me nothing, take me anywhere, or nothing." She breathed harder allowing her air to blow against his body. "You don't have to give me shit. I swear to god." She hugged him and pulled him closer to her. He leaned backward until he was laying flat on his back. He looked up at her, didn't say a word, just kept her in view. Her eyes looked into his and recognized his need. She brought her face to his penis and took him in her mouth.

Twenty minutes later Rodney, lay flat on his back cool as a fan. He looked up at the ceiling and reminisced.

Don't go home and let those bitches fuck your head up. Have you spending up your money. You have to take care of yourself. It's rough and it seems unfair, but life aint fair. You got to start form where you're at and come the fuck up and go to where you want to be. I love you B, you're my man. It would hurt me, fuck me up in the chest to hear about you falling off letting some bitch lead you around by your dick. Pussy don't mean love and dick sucks aren't enough to keep you feeling obligated. Don't let no hoes get you feeling obligated. The sense of duty is a strong urge. You gotta overcome that B.

Dooski's, words played out in Rodney's, mind. He lay in bed feeling the caress of smooth female hands coiling around his sex. He felt the power of her strength when she ran her hands up and down his thigh. He felt the urge to stiffen and grow harder in her hand.

"Rodney," Ebony, whispered his name soft and delicate forming the syllables that pronounced his name. He looked over at her. The top of her head appeared darker, sweat added color to her mane. She stuck her tongue out and pressed it against his skin.

"What up?" He placed his hand on her back and reached down and palmed her ass cheeks like a soft ball. He squeezed it and felt the softness crushing in his grip.

"Do you want a relationship or do you want to just be fucking partners?" Her bluntness meant nothing to Rodney, Her fascination with his dick size didn't enlarge his ego and the touch that she pressed up and down against his skin did little to break his focus on what was important to him.

He stared ahead leaving her to contemplate his silence and wonder did she go too far and scare him off. One second went by with no response, no words came forth. The only sound that filled the bedroom was the sound of cars driving down the street.

"I can handle it if you just want to be fuck buddies. I'm not all that pressed for company, but I think we look cute together." She held her head close to his body and snuggled up on him like a kitten. She buried her face into his side. She sniffed his body and thought about the force he used to invade her pussy and take her insides hostage. She wanted some more of it, if not tonight then at least some other night. "I need to know so if a dude, come to me on some yo shorty was up type of shit. I can know how to address the situation." She waited for him to give her an answer, but it never came . "Rodney," She called out to him again.

"What's up?"

"Did you hear me?" She squeezed him tighter and spread her leg over his.

"I heard you."

"So what's your answer?"

"I don't know how to answer."

"I was saying because if I don't have a man or someone to cuddle up with and a dude approaches me." Her voice trailed off and came back more audible. "Then I would be like let me get your number. I don't have anybody so." Her voice was polite and considerate as if she was really turning someone on.

"I see."

"Then if I have a man. I could be like don't come at me like that. I don't appreciate it and I'm sure my man won't either." Her voice became stern and chilling. "So what do you want to do?" She pulled him closer to her.

"I want to get paid."

"Besides that I mean boyfriend and girlfriend wise."

"We don't really know each other and we should get to know what's going on with us."

"That's cool, but I'm going to think and act like you're my man." There was a silence that came from wondering what was going to happen next.

"Act like what?" He questioned.

"I mean I'm going to be here when you need me. Put it down every time it pops up." She giggled.

"Fuck buddies."

"Deal." She kissed his stomach and ran her hand down it until she felt his balls rolling around in her hand.

Chapter 17
If that girl starts acting up, then take her best friend

When the morning came Rodney, was in the shower and washing away the night before. He got dressed and took Ebony, home. When he pulled up in front of her house she looked at him.

"I'll be in touch with you sweet little fuck buddy." Rodney, smiled at her.

"I'll be waiting my even sweeter boyfriend." She leaned forward and buried her lips into his and stuck her tongue in his mouth. She took his breath kissing him like it was the last time that they would ever see each other again. Within an instant she was opening the car door and getting out. She waved by to him and turned around switching all the way to her front door knowing damn well that he was watching her. He looked at her ass swerve side to side and thought about how her ass was much bigger, softer, and rounder than it appeared in her jeans. Rodney, smiled and pulled off headed to the park.

Pookie, sat on the bench. He had a look of discontent on his face. He was mad. Somebody had pissed him off. His eyes glared around looking at everyone. He turned his head side to side then spit on the ground.

Rodney, walked up moving smoother as he bopped hard across the cement. He was happy. It was a happiness that came from the center of a woman's body, dead smack in the middle of her legs; something to smile about.

Rodney, moved along the park. He shook a few hands, called out a few names, and hugged a couple cats who he didn't don't know. He hugged Loop, and the two girls who were sitting beside him. Christopher, looked at Rodney, in disgust. He knew about his car, about the things that he overheard Loop, talking about, and about the amount of money he was making. He thought about himself and realized that he was older than Rodney, had been in the streets longer and was down with the right people, but he still was stuck in the same low position. He didn't own a car. He used girls for their cars and he thought about Rodney, and how he robbed the Canadian girl, busted her in the head with a bottle and took her money.

"Pookie, what's up with you?" Rodney, sat down beside him and wrapped his arm around his shoulder.

"Aint shit these sorry ass niggas can't get shit right." He looked over at Loop, who sat with his head down and looked away. Rodney, looked at Pookie, and wondered what was happening.

"Pookie!" A girl yelled for across the street in between the buildings that were in front of the house where Pookie had his people stationed at to answer the phone whenever the connect called. He stood up and walked away.

"Yo, Loop, what's going on with Pookie?" Rodney, looked at Pookie's, back as he walked away.

"Some money came up short and it's been happening." Loop, looked away.

"How?" Rodney, looked at him like it as if he was the one who had been shorted on his money.

"One of these niggas is fucking up and slipping their own product in the bunch. Out here selling their own shit in our park."

"Who?"

"If I knew his ass would be stretched out there right fucking now getting stomped to the tenth power." Loop, looked frustrated and ready to settle the problem.

"I'm almost ready for some more shit." Rodney, looked at Loop, whose face lit up. On the verge of smiling he looked at Rodney,

"You might be the one to turn this shit around." He shook his hand and walked toward his car. "Call me tonight."

Rodney, walked away feeling good as he enjoyed the memory that dazzled his mind, left him weak in the knees, and his penis aching to be inserted into something similar to what he got last night.

Later that night when Rodney, met up with Loop, he was sitting in his car. He was parked on a dark street by himself. Rodney, looked around, peered over his shoulder, looked upward as if he could hear cameras snapping his picture while he walked toward the car. He got in.

"What's up?" He stuck his hand out and shook Loop's,

"Aint shit." Loop, handed him the package of drugs. "That's one thousand grams of coke. You got to cook it yourself." Loop, looked at the money. "How much is this?"

"Ten thousand dollars." Rodney, said putting the coke into a black plastic bag that he pulled out of the front of his pants. Loop, told him the difference that he had to pay. They shook hands and Rodney, got out of the car.

Two days later Rodney, Freddie, Darius, Melody, Ebony, and Dena, each drove individual go cars speeding around the track. Rodney, rolled by and yelled at Dena, who didn't hear anything that he said. The force of the wind blowing in her ears drowned out everything except the whistling in her ears.

Freddie, rolled up on Ebony, flicking his tongue out at her. He moved it up and down even slid it side to side. She looked at him and rolled her eyes. She stepped on the gas attempting to leave him in her dust. Melody, rode alongside Darius, they flirted with each other as they raced to the finish line.

After riding around in the toy cars they all piled up in Rodney's, car. They laughed and cracked jokes on each other. They ended up at a movie theater that they didn't understand it was in French, therefore they read the subtitles and laughed at the punch lines and corny jokes.

When the night wound down Rodney, was standing on Dena's, porch kissing her. They held hands and looked into each other's eyes. She looked at him and waved bye then went into her house. Rodney, got back into the car.

"Man that girl aint trying to give you no pussy." Darius, said smiling at him.

"I don't know why you wasting your time." Freddie, watched her front door close. "I think that bitch fuck around with Cedric, some pretty ass nigga."

"Fuck that I do what I want to do." Rodney, silenced their talk by pulling off. He dropped everybody off except for Ebony, He made sure his boys had crack to sell and everyone else was dropped off and away from his business. He drove to his house. He got out the car and walked into the house. Ebony, was right behind him.

Rodney, lay flat on his back exhausted. His body was tangled around Ebony's, She lightly scratched on his chest while fondling his private parts.

"I got to pee." Ebony, got up out of the bed. She walked downstairs and into the bathroom. When she came out of the bathroom she walked into a woman carrying a brown paper bag filled with clothes. "Oohh." Ebony, jumped back startled. She looked at Janet, who stared back at her.

"Is Rodney, here?" Janet, asked looking away doing her best not to make the girl feel embarrassed.

"He's upstairs."

"Tell him Janet, is here." Janet, sat her bag down and went into the living room.

"Rodney, there is a lady named Janet, downstairs." Ebony, stood over him looking down into his face examining his reaction to her information.

"She's down there now?" He calculated the time up in his mind. He wondered how she could be home when she had to do six months and only four months had passed., He got out of the bed, slipped on his pants, and waked to the edge of the stairs. "Ma!" Ebony, stood directly behind him feeling relieved that the pretty woman was his mother instead of her rival.

"Yeah it's me." Cheerfulness accompanied her voice as it rose up the stairs.

"How did you get out of jail so soon?"

So soon?" She came walking up the stairs and stood before him. "What do you mean so soon. Being in jail for a day feels like a lifetime to me." Janet, smiled. Rodney, looked over his mother looking for any changes.

Catching on to his intentions. She walked into his bedroom and cut on the light, lifted her hands up, and turned around slowly showing off her new body weight.

"How do I look?" Her smile radiated across the room while she twirled around in front of her son. Ebony, sat on the bed under the covers smiling at Janet,

"You look fatter."

"Fat?" Her eyes slanted into a look of disagreement. "I look good boy. I don't drink and smoke. Don't even want to be around it." She lowered her head and lifted it back up. "I got saved." She peered at her son waiting for his reaction.

"If it will keep you from that other stuff I guess It's good." He shrugged his shoulders and looked back at her.

"Whose car is that parked in front of the house?" Janet, looked at her son.

"Mine." He looked at her. "Did you see the furniture?"

"Yes and its nice."

"Alright I will see you in the morning." He spoke to her like her husband instead of her son. He backed up into his bedroom. He looked at his mother and nodded his head to her and closed his door. Janet, walked downstairs mumbling the words got damn to herself.

Rodney, was in the passenger seat of his car checking his glove compartment. He reached around until he felt what he was looking for. He pulled out the money and went back into the house.

When he walked into his bedroom Ebony, lay on the bed looking like she had been rummaging through his drawers looking for something, but then she heard him come back into the house, and jumped on the bed pretending to be lost in a deep thought.

"Did you find it?" He walked over toward his bed. He pulled his shirt over his head, dropped it on the floor, and unsnapped his pants. He got into his bed.

"Find what?" Ebony, sat up in the bed. "I would not do nothing like that because if I can't trust a nigga then." Her mouth opened wide with each word she looked at him. "I don't have to be watching what you are doing."

"Shut up." He grabbed her and pulled her into his arms. She pulled away from him and slapped him on the shoulder. He pushed her down on the bed, rolled her over, and slapped her on the ass. She rolled over onto her back so she could face him.

"Nigga aint nobody scared of you." She stood up and swung a few weak slaps. He caught her hands and held them while she struggled to get him off of her. She tussled until she became weak and her arms trembled. He pushed her down on the bed and climbed on top of her. She crossed her legs at the ankle. He placed his hand in between her legs and slid it further between her legs, and with one sweeping motion he wiggled her legs apart. She giggled and tried to hold them tight as she could. "Wait your hurting me."

"Stop playing then." He rolled over and lay on his back staring up in air. One second later a pillow banged into his face. Ebony, leapt on his lap. She grabbed his arms by the wrist and attempted to hold him down.

"Now." She glared down at him. He looked at her and easily overpowered her. His muscular body covered her girlish figure.

"I will give it up freely." She opened her legs welcoming him in between her legs.

"I don't want it." He stood up and got off the bed.

"Oh you're going to get this." She scooted down the bed and stood up. She reached out to grab his arm. His hand caught her wrist and spun her around. He pulled her into him and held her tightly against his body. "Let me go." She backed her body up into his pressing her booty into his genitals. The heat from her body being close to his burned him up with desire.

He shoved her down on the bed. She looked up at him and turned over. Her legs spread opened revealing an enormous patch of pubic hair. His eyes followed her legs as they opened and closed like she was using a thigh master. He grabbed his dick, held it, leaned down toward his bed, and aimed at the slit in between her pubic hairs.

Downstairs Janet, and Terry, sat in the living room talking.

"Terry, how did Rodney, get all of this stuff?" Janet, asked trying hard to conceal her pride in her son's self reliance.

"The boy been though so damn much. He didn't really have a choice, but to survive." Terry, sat on the couch beside his neighbor and good friend,.

"Terry, how does he have a car. He's not sixteen yet?"

"He can afford it and he's been bringing a cute little girl over here too." Laughter followed his words. His smiled remained long after his giggling stopped.

"I saw her." Janet, looked away remembering last night. "I saw her real good." She said softly.

"Come on bitch let get us a drink."

"I'm done with that shit."- Her face scrunched up in sadness. "I don't ever want to see a jail again Terry,"

Rodney, came walking down the stairs Ebony, trailed close behind him. She playfully attempted to trip him from behind. He spun around quickly. She put her hands up, a startled reaction, the first thing to do in order to block the blows coming at her. She giggled a girlish laughed and bawled her leg up into her upper body.

"You better stop playing Rodney," She stood still waiting to be sure that he wasn't still expecting to get her back.

"What did I tell you about playing too much?"

"Shut up." She came walking toward him. He flinched at her and she stumbled backward before swinging wildly at him. He spun her around and pressed her against the wall and held her there. He stole a feel on her left titty. "Pervert." He squeezed her nipple harder. "Ouch." She laughed out.

When they were down stairs Janet, looked at Rodney, and Ebony,

"You two look cute together." Janet, smiled at her son and the girl who stood beside him.

"I told you." Ebony, leaned over toward him putting her mouth close to his ear.

"Shut up." He elbowed her softly in the side.

"What's up Rodney,?" Terry, waved at him.

"Terry," He acknowledged his neighbor.

"He is so ignorant." Ebony, said walking up on Janet, "I'm Ebony," She stuck her hand out and shook Janet's,

"Rodney, your girlfriend is pretty." Janet, spoke truthfully.

"I'm not his girlfriend he just wants to be my."

"Shut up." Rodney, said playfully cutting her off. Terry, laughed out and Janet, let out a little chuckle.

Chapter 18
Sleepwalkers get rudely awakened

Ebony, got out the car and kissed the palm of her hand, held it open, and blew on it. Rodney, laid down in his seat pretending to let the imaginary kiss fly over his head. She ran back over to the car and opened the driver's door. She stuck her head in the car and stopped in front of his and planted a kiss on his lips.

Rodney, left after dropping Ebony, off and rode around for a little bit. He saw a few people crowded around a guy on a motorcycle. He pulled over a few cars down the street, giving him enough room to see what they were doing, but not close enough to let them see him watching them. His eyes focused on the bag that the man reached into and pulled something out. One second later he pulled his helmet down over his face and pulled off fast as he could go. Rodney, started his car and drove up to the corner of the street.

The guy came back up the street going the other way doing a wheelie up the street. Rodney, watched him zoom pass his car. He let a car, a bike, and another car get in between him and the motorcycle. He rode behind the cars, but concentrated on the sound of the motorcycle he watched it turn the corner. He turned the corner after it and slowed down allowing some distance to creep in between them.

A few blocks later the guy pulled up in the drive way. He cut his motorcycle off and got off it. He took off his helmet and carried it in the house with him. Rodney, watched the house. The boy who rode the bike came out the side door of the house. He walked behind the house and came creeping down the driveway in a deep brown caddilac.

Rodney's, eyes memorized the facial features on the boy. He sized up his body and the type of build he had. After the car turned the corner Rodney, started up his car and drove off. He followed the car for a few blocks until it stopped at a house where three more cars were parked.

The boy stepped out of his car and walked over to the porch where the other three boys were standing. Rodney, parked his car and sat there watching the interaction between the four guys.

"Got your punk ass. Cold busted." Rodney, spoke to himself. He saw Christopher, walk up the street and go up on the porch. He shook everyone's hand. He walked around and grabbed a blunt and inhaled a few tokes of the marijuana filled cigar. Rodney, watched him reach in his pocket and pull out a wad of money. He counted it and handed it to a light skin boy with braids that swirled around his head in different angles and patterns.

Christopher, walked down the stairs, looked both ways, and started walking down the street. Rodney, waited ten minutes before starting his car.

He waited until none of the men were on the porch then he pulled off. He looked at the house, marked down the address in his mind and drove off. He pulled up at the corner and wondered which way did Christopher, go. He rode slowly up the street. He decided to go to the park. Once he arrived at the park he saw Christopher, hiding his bags across the street from the park. He came out the backyard walking carefully looking around. He looked both ways then walked into the park and sat down. One second later Loop, came out and walked around checking out the area. He searched for undercover narcotics detectives. When he didn't see any he gave the signal for the boys to bring out the product.

Rodney, watched them. He saw Christopher, get his pack and run and hide it somewhere other than the backyard. He watched what was going on around him. He started his car, put it in reverse, and backed up. He made a u-turn and drove up and parked a few streets over from the park. He walked around observing the scenery. He looked at a few people going about their business barely noticing him.

He looked up on a porch were an old lady sat. He walked passed her noticing that her yard was the one that he had to go through. He kept moving until he got to the house next door. He cut in between the house, walked a few feet, hopped over the fence that led into the old lady's yard. He ran across her backyard. He climbed over her fence, landed in another backyard and ran a few more feet, until he was climbing a fence that led into the backyard where Christopher, was in.

Rodney, crept along the yard moving quickly and smoothly. He leaned over and looked in the same spot where Christopher, had hid something. He moved the garbage around, picked up a bag, and opened it. The smell of cooked crack came screaming out of the bag. He closed the bag and put it in his underwear. He backtracked the same way he came, scaling as many fences as it took until he was walking out the yard next door to the old lady's house. He looked at her and smiled a friendly one at her then walked around the corner.

Once he got back in his car he pulled off. He drove home and weighed up the drugs. He found two hundred and fifty grams. He walked over to his safe and hid the drugs. He went outside and got back in his car and drove over to the park. He got out of his car and walked down the street until he was sitting in the park beside Pookie,

"What's up Pookie?" Rodney, stuck out his hand and embraced the older boy's.

"Out here getting this money right." Pookie, looked around.

"Oh I'm going to need to come and see you shortly." Rodney's, head nodded up and down.

"Whoop-whoop!" A boy wearing red and blue yelled and turned around to walk away like he had nothing to do with what was going on in the park. Two people who had drugs on them ran. Pookie, sat still Rodney, slid off the bench and walked casually. His feet moved toward the end of the park, a few feet away from the commotion. A hand grabbed his shoulder. He felt the force gripping him then turning him around. A white cop flung him to the ground.

"What do you have in your pocket scum!" The cop reached around in his pocket feeling around, but came up with nothing. He dug his hands in his back pocket. "Where's the gun and drugs?" He asked feeling in between his leg squeezing his ball bag. His hand opened and ground down tightly on his nuts. "Say something." He placed his big head next to Rodney's, ear. "I didn't hear you. You say something!" The cop yelled in his ear.

"I didn't say anything."

"What are you doing out here selling drugs for Pookie? Or is it Loop? Which one?"

"I was going to the store and you stopped me."

"How old are you?"

"Fifteen."

"Got any identification?"

"I said fifteen not fifty."

"What did you say?" The cop bawled the back of Rodney's, shirt into his hand.

"I'm too young for Id." The cop attempted to pull him up by his pants, but couldn't so he stepped on his butt. "Get the fuck out of here." Rodney, got up and walked away. Pookie, was still sitting on the bench.

"If I can catch you your going to jail, now run!" The cop yelled at Loop,

"Come on man I don't feel like running." Loop, looked at the cops pleading with his eyes.

"Run you mother fucker!" The cop's face turned bright red as he yelled. Loop, turned and jogged a little bit. He ran behind him. "I can catch you-you better run you black drug dealing son of a bitch!" Loop, picked up speed and ran.

Rodney, turned the corner and walked up the street. He got into his car and pulled off. His phone rang, he looked at, and didn't recognize so he didn't answer it. He dialed the number back.

"Did somebody call me from this number?"
"Rodney?"
"Dena?" A broad smile slid across his face.

Chapter 19
Your ass got took

Rodney, rode around holding onto his steering wheel he looked at Dena, while he drove. The cool look on his face camouflaged the desire that burned in his lap, and how bad he wanted her butt to press down on it.

Rodney, and Dena, pulled up at the mall, got out the car, and walked along the sidewalk. He reached out and grabbed her hand. She smiled feeling his hand swallow hers up in his.

The short stroll ended in front of a glass door which Rodney, held open for her. She giggled girlishly and walked through the door. Rodney, caught up with her and grabbed her hand. They walked around until they ended up in a souvenir store where she brought Rodney, a shirt. He walked around the store until he found a friendship bracelet and brought it for her.

Three hours later Rodney, had dropped her off at home and went over to Sissy's, house. Darius, wasn't there, but Freddie, was. He lay on the couch talking on a phone.

"When did this get here?" Rodney, asked pointing at the telephone.

"Today." Freddie told him.

"Did you finish?"

"Yeah." He nodded his head up and down. He reached into his pants pocket and pulled out some money. He counted it, took some of the bills out of the wad, put them back in his pocket, and tossed the rest to Rodney,

"Where is Darius?" Rodney, counted the money while he talked. He made sure that it was all there before putting it in his pocket.

"I don't know, but yo lets get up with Melody and her girls tonight."

"Who are you talking to?"

"Melody," Freddie, smiled. Rodney, laughed at him then sat down on the couch.

The next time Rodney, saw Christopher, he was sitting in the park by himself. He had a black eye and his nose looked crooked.

"What the fuck happened to you?" Rodney, looked at him feeling sorry for his anguish.

"I was up in Rochester, over my people's house on Goodman and Short." He looked away then back at Rodney, "Some niggas hopped me." He said referring to being double teamed by a group of people.

"Some niggas beat your ass for nothing?" Rodney, questioned him.

"Well it was some bullshit I was with my people out in Rochester, and one thing led to another and I wound up in the middle of some shit." Christopher, looked at Rodney, making facial expressions that could re-enforce his lie.

"Alright I'm about to get up out of here." Rodney, stuck his hand out and shook Christopher's, Rodney, walked off and got into his car. He pulled off only to park around the corner and creep back around to the park. He stood crouched down behind a house looking at Christopher, he watched as the boy sat on the bench squirming around. A look of desperation filled his face. He got up, sat back down, and stood up and walked away. He threw a few punches in the air. He looked around making sure no one was watching him. When everything appeared to be cool he walked in between the building toward the houses where Pookie, kept telephones that the connect called when he needed to talk to Pookie,

Rodney, waited for a few seconds then emerged out from his hiding place. He moved briskly barely touching the ground when he walked. His eyes peered through the night air searching for nothing in particular just immune to watching his back. He moved in between the buildings carefully alert he could be seen by Loop, Pookie, or somebody else who would have want to know what the hell he was doing back there.

Christopher, looked around checking over his shoulder. Concern shook around his pupils when he opened up the door to the apartment that contained the backup stash. He went inside the apartment and moved around until he found what he was looking for. He picked up the drugs, weighed it up, when two hundred and fifty grams appeared on the scale. He quickly pocketed the drugs. He looked over his shoulder, when he saw no one he turned, and walked out of the apartment.

In the hallway he searched for someone. When he saw no one he put the house key back where he had gotten it from. He walked until he went through the door that had an exit sign above it. One minute later Rodney's, head peeked out into the hallway from where he hid. He moved down the hallway until he reached the apartment door that Christopher, had left moments earlier. Rodney, looked briefly over his shoulder, stooped down, grabbed the key, and walked into the apartment.

Inside the apartment Rodney, moved around and bumped into a few things. He cursed to himself realizing that the noise could possibly alert someone. He walked around looking through the drawers, closets, and under the cushions on the couch. He reached his hand under a heater and gently felt along the bottom of the heater feeling for what he was looking for. He turned and moved quickly and went over to the kitchen. His mind raced quickly as he processed information.

Where would I hide this shit if I was Pookie, I would be in charge therefore I wouldn't hide it. I would have someone else hide it. Who would I trust? His mind churned out names rapidly. *Loop, no Christopher? Maybe.* He thought for a second and smiled. *Yeah Christopher, were would I put it? I would be in a rush. I'm stealing. I'm looking for a way to pay back my other people. The ones who I fucked out of nine ounces and the ones who beat me down. I would be afraid, scared for my life. I would steal from Pookie, then cover my tracks by leaving it in a place where someone else would have access to it. That way it could be stumbled over and greed would make someone take it, I could pretend like I had been in a rush and got caught slipping.*

Rodney, smiled and walked over to refrigerator where a chair rested a few feet away and got up on the edge of his toes.

He felt around on top of the refrigerator. His hand moved around until he felt something. He recognized the shape of it to be a scale. He pulled it down. He reached around some more until he felt a huge plastic bag. He pulled the bag down.

A blue zip lock bag fell into his hands. He sat the bag down on the table, opened it, and pulled out the drugs. He took out a handful of chunky blocks of cocaine and put the rest back. He walked out of the apartment, locked the door, and put the key back in place before leaving. He moved casually looking around then he emerged out from in between the buildings and went around the corner and got back into his car.

Rodney, pulled up at his house and got out the car. His phone rang. He pulled it from his pocket and read the number it was Ebony, he pressed the button and shoved it in his pocket. He walked into the house and saw Janet, with a man. One of her past lovers, he sat on the couch smiling and leaning over next to Janet, Rodney, gave her a look, held her in his focus. He turned his glare on her friend.

"Hey buddy." The old flame stood up and extended his hand out toward Rodney, The boy's face grew stone. It was void of any emotion or human compassion. The happiness that once settled on the man's face sunk away and transformed into a look of spine tingling fear. The guy, the old lover and old fling that was now flung to the side looked over at Janet, He smirked weakly at her then looked at Rodney, who ignored him altogether and went upstairs to his bedroom.

"Ok, Janet, it was nice catching up with you." The man said as he looked at the boy's back moving up the stairs.

"Bye." Janet, said signaling for her old flame to give her a call by pressing her thumb against her ear and her index finger against the corner of her mouth. She walked behind the man, shut the door behind him, and walked into her bedroom.

Upstairs Rodney, was at his dresser weighing the drugs up. He kept putting pieces on the scale until it read three hundred grams. He thought for a second then decided to forgive himself for not talking all the drugs. He tied the drugs up in a plastic bag and took them to his safe. His eyes viewed the contents. He saw the stacks of money, the nine ounces that he stole from Christopher, the five ounces that he had left over from his own package, and the ten and one half ounces that he just stole from Pookie's, stash house.

Rodney, calculated the estimated amount of money he would have when he finished selling all of the drugs. The number that rolled around his head was close to fifty thousand dollars. His phone rung again. He pulled it out of his pocket and checked the number. It was Ebony, again. He pressed the button on the phone and put it back in his pocket. He closed his safe and made sure that it was locked. He went outside and got into his car and pulled off.

"Did someone just call me from this number?" Rodney, asked into the phone. He sat in his car watching the street and paying attention to the activity that was going on around him.

"You know who called you." Ebony's, voice sounded seductive flowing into his ear.

"What's up?"

"I wanted to hang out with you tonight."

"That's cool because Freddie, wanted to see Melody, anyway." He looked at a black Caprice Classic, cruise pass the corner. "Yo, call your girls and see where they are and if they feel up to it."

"I wasn't talking about with everybody else. I meant more like you and me." The seriousness of her statement came forth in her request.

"Me and you?" Rodney, thought about it, scrunched up his lips, and put the phone closer to his mouth. "Why don't you want to be around everyone else?"

"I just want to be around you by myself. I wanted you to treat me like you treat." Her voice trailed off.

"Like I treat who Dena?"

"And everybody else." She let out sigh.

"Yo, call your girls and I promise we will hook up by ourselves." He spoke then hung up. He got into his car and drove over to Sissy's, house.

Darius, was on the porch with a beautiful girl. Rodney, looked at her. His eyes went up to her face studied the flawless features sketched into her brownish yellow complexion. He looked at the hair style that fit around her head perfectly. He looked at her body and watched it fill out until it formed a slender athletic build. When he walked pass her he stole a glance at her ass. It was nicely proportioned and connected to her body just right.

"Darius, " Rodney, called his name and waved him toward him. The two boys walked into the house. "Who is that?" Astonishment filled his eyes and voice. Rodney, looked at Darius, as he waited for his response.

"Tasha,"

"You fucked her?" Youthful admiration filled his voice.

"Hell yeah."

"That's your girl?"

"Dude that's a crack head."

"Get the fuck out of here." Rodney's, eyes blackened with shock. Surprise filled his face. His eyes searched Darius, for a lie. "How do you know?"

"I told you I fucked her."

"I don't believe you." Rodney, shook his head side to side.

"Watch this." Darius, went out on the porch and returned with the girl. "Tasha, my man Savage, want to hit that." She looked over at Rodney, and studied his face. "So what's up?" Darius, looked at her. She shrugged her shoulders.

"Do you want me to go back in the room that we were in?" She questioned Darius, He nodded his head up and down. The girl turned and walked down the hallway.

"Yo, she's a crack head?" Rodney, whispered to Darius,

"I told you."

"You are so fucking nasty fucking crack heads." Rodney, punched at him in a playful manner.

"Its good." Darius, ground around and pumped hard into the air. Rodney, walked into the room to find the girl already naked and sprawled across the bed. His eyes stretched outward growing with appreciation. He turned around and quickly left the room. He walked into the living room and stopped in front of Darius,

"I don't got nothing on me."

"Here." Darius, handed him a twenty dollar rock. Rodney, took the drugs and looked disgusted.

"What you want me to give her more?" Darius, looked misreading his friends disgust.

"Yo, I aint never fucked no crack head before. Those bitches probably got AIDS." His eyes looked sad at possibly passing up fucking the very beautiful girl. "How old is she?"

"About twenty six or seven. That broad don't got AIDS."

"How do you know?" Rodney, didn't wait for a response. "When I was locked up I learned a little about that shit."

"Nigga Ebony, can give you AIDS. That bitch not no virgin."

"But she's not a crack head."

"Use this." Darius, handed him a condom.

Chapter 20
Hey Mr. Dope Man, you think you slick?

Rodney, walked in the bedroom. His heart pounded into his chest as he approached the bed. He walked to the edge of the bed and stood there. The girl turned over. Her breast sat up nice and even on her chest.

"Do you want me to suck your dick first?" She moved her tongue around in her mouth loosening it up and working up some saliva. He looked at her and thought for a second. Common sense told him to abandon the idea, but lust made him greedy. He wasn't satisfied with just seeing it, he wanted to touch it, but he didn't want to pay the high price of gambling with his life.

"I don't know." Rodney, answered truthfully.

"Is this your first time?" She scooted closer to the edge of the bed. Her lips were within inches of touching the tip of his dick through his jeans. His lust grew straight in his pants. She slid her hands up and down caressing it through his jeans. Confusion swirled around his mind and chest as pleasure and fear competed for his brain.

She opened his pants and pulled his dick out. She jerked it slowly and opened her mouth wide, prepared to insert Rodney's, member into her mouth. The heat from the back of her throat came streaming forward out of her mouth and warmed the tip of Rodney's, penis. He grabbed the side of her face before she could close her mouth around him.

"Hold up." He turned her around. "Put your ass up in the air." He grabbed her waist and helped her get into the position. She backed her ass up in the air and arched her back. She lay her head flat on the bed.

"Like that?"

"Push it up some more so I can see your pussy."

"Can you see it?" She asked scooting back and arching her back some more.

"I can't see it." He pulled her up by the waist and lifted her ass cheeks up. He split her legs.

"Turn the light on. You may be able to see it better." She spoke without turning her head around. Rodney, walked over to the light and clicked it on. He walked back to the bed and stood behind the girl. The smell from her ass and pussy crept out and consumed the room. Rodney, moved closer to the bed, pulled his pants down, and got up right behind the girl. He pushed her further down on the bed.

"Can you see it?"

"A little bit."

"How about now?" The girl leaned over some more and gave him the best view in the house, as majority of her pussy hairs were visible along with her clit, and the slit surrounding the opening of her pussy, plus the snug wrinkles that spiraled around into a deep brown colored asshole.

Rodney, stood behind the girl sliding his hand up and down his penis. He stroked it smooth and ferociously. He pulled it, yanked on it, shook it around, and tussled with it. Tasha, reached in between her legs and gently flickered her fingers against his balls. He bent over and got closer to her body. The heat from her ass snuck out and touched the tip of his penis. Unconsciously he moved closer to her asshole all the while she was backing it up and pushing her ass out to him.

Lust overpowered his senses and drowned out his common sense as he was at the edge of her asshole. He let go of his dick and pushed her further into the bed.

"Hold your ass open." Rodney, said expecting to get his way.

"Umm." The girl lay flat on her stomach, reached around, and grabbed each one of her plump ass cheeks in her hands then spread them apart. She pulled them far as they could go. Rodney, climbed over her and rested over her butt aiming his dick down at it. He leaned down close enough to feel the heat surging out of her ass without actually touching it.

"I'm about to cum in your ass." Rodney, pumped harder and faster. His eyes revealed a perverted freak as he jammed his dick in and out of his hand.

"Do you want me to make some noise?" the girl moaned. He ignored her and kept pulling on himself. "Ooh cum in my ass. Put some cum in that ass ooh baby cum in it." She squealed out in delight. Rodney, grew harder in his own hand and pulled fast as he could. The first drop of semen came grouped together in thick spurts of white fluid. The first squirt hit her ass cheeks and dripped down into her ass. She squealed out louder. He pulled on it faster as she opened her asshole wider.

"Get your ass up here. Get that ass up here." Rodney, climbed closer to her. She inched backward moving closer to him bringing a wide open asshole with her. The rest of his fluid poured out of him and shot directly into her butthole. He rested over her butt draining his penis until it was depleted and relieved.

"Are you done?"

"Stay there for a minute." Rodney, stood up and looked down at her butt hole. His cum filled her asshole and overran smearing her butt cheeks with creamy semen that looked like powdered milk spilling from a bowl of cheap cereal. She held her ass cheeks in her hands and squeezed them. He shook his dick and let all of the left over cum land on her back.

"Do you got something I can use to get this out of my ass?" the girl never looked back at Rodney, he looked around, saw a shirt, picked it up. He didn't care if it was clean or not. He tossed it to her. She caught it and wiped herself clean with it. She turned around and sat up with her hand out. Rodney, gave her the small piece of drug, and looked at her. "Is that all you want?"

"I'm good." He pulled his clothes up. The girl got up and got dressed. She looked at Rodney, like she wanted to say something, but decided against it. "What?" He looked at her.

"Do you look at movies and jerk off?"

"Why did you ask me that?" Anger flashed across his pupils. He felt offended by her words.

"Not like that. Most dude would have been trying to fuck me with or without a condom. You paid to look at me and jerk off."

"I don't watch movies." Rodney, turned and walked out of the room. She got up and walked out behind him.

"That shit was good wasn't it?" Darius, looked excitedly at Rodney, then at the girl. "Tasha!" He said her name like she was a celebrity. He laughed and she shook her head and walked away. She took a long look at Rodney, and walked out the house.

Rodney, pulled out his cell phone and called the number that he missed messing around with Tasha, He dialed the number.

"Hello." He spoke first.

"I can't find Dena, she's probably with her man." She became quiet and waited for his reaction.

"Where's Melody?" He asked not missing a beat.

"She's here, but."

"Here we come." Rodney, hung up the phone and tapped Darius, on the shoulder. "Come on let's go get these hoes."

"Man I'm satisfied." A lazy look crept over his face.

"I thought you wanted to fuck Melody?"

"I do, but I already fucked Tasha, She's been over here all morning." Darius, smiled as an indication that he spent most of the day sleeping with the girl. Rodney, picked up the phone and called Ebony, back.

"Hello."

"What's up?" She sounded upbeat and cheerful.

"Yo, aint nobody here with me. We may have to get up later."

"Melody, and whoever can get up later, but me and you can get up now." Ebony, sat on the phone waiting for his answer. Rodney, thought for a second. He didn't really want to fuck, he also didn't want to sit around Darius, and listen to him brag about a crack head's pussy, but he didn't want to waste the rest of his night either.

"Alright here I come."

"I can come to you."

"I'll be there." He assured her. They hung up and Rodney, went outside and got into his car.

"Yo, Darius, called out before stepping onto the porch. He extended his arms in the air and mouthed the words I need you. Rodney, nodded his head up and down. He drove home, got the drugs, and drove back to the house.

"That's six, three for you and three for Freddie," He looked at Darius, I'm trying to do something right quick. We will see what happens after this package."

"What's up?"

"I'm in the process of doing something just trust me." Rodney, looked at his friend truly being honest with him. He was putting together something, but the reward was solely for him, but if his friends stacked their money, they would at least get some money out of the deal. He wasn't sure what they were going to do, but his mind was on getting some cash money.

Chapter 21
Reunited and shittin on fly bum ass niggas

Rodney and Ebony, sat together in his car. She reached out and took his hand in hers and held onto it. He looked at her, but didn't move his hand away.

"Why do you look at me like that?" Ebony's, eyes batted making her appear prettier.

"I look at you because you're beautiful." He lifted her hand up to his mouth and kissed on her knuckles. She smiled and allowed herself to be wrapped up and scooped like ice cream. Rodney, leaned over and whispered in her ear. He talked to her and threatened to beat her down with his dick.

"I'm going to bust your booty open."

"Why my booty, why not my pussy?" She turned to face him. She slid her knee into his seat and placed it against the back of the seat.

"That too, I'm going to rock them draws."

"I don't wear draws I'm not a boy." She looked at him enjoying his filthy talk. He reached over and grabbed her breast. She smiled at him and made herself available for his pleasure. Rodney, looked at her, but something caught his attention. He looked at the boy who rode the motorcycle, hung out on the porch, and secretly supplied Christopher, with the drugs that he sold in the park and undercut Pookie's, money.

The boy rode his bike up the street and rode right pass Rodney,

"Who is that?" He pointed at the motorcyclist.

"I don't know." Confusion took over her face left her wondering what the hell Rodney, was trying to prove. "Do you think that I sleep around?"

"I don't care if you did anyway." He was serious.

"Well I don't anyway." She was more serious than he was.

"Dang." He stretched the word out. "Look at you all up in my face with your feisty self." He laughed at her.

"Don't play with me." Her facial expression became more intense.

"Girl I will whoop your ass up in here." He was being funny and trying to defuse the situation. "Matter of fact get out and walk your ass home."

"I live right there remember?" She pointed at her house. Rodney, smiled. He had forgotten that he was parked outside of her house. He started the car and pulled off.

"I'm about to fix that right now."

"Whatever." She laughed. Rodney, looked at her and smiled. He drove over to his house and prepared to park when something urged him to drive over to the park. He rode through and saw Christopher, out here in the park all by himself doing whatever it took to get those people their money. Rodney, looked at him and thought about a way to make some more money. He would handle that later, but for now he was going to handle Ebony,

Rodney, lay in his bed looking at Ebony, She danced around in her bra and panties. She shook her ass to dance hall tunes. When Ghetto red hot by Super Cat came on she went crazy. She got even wilder listening to Mr. Lover man. The look in her eyes represented sexuality and desire. She moved around attempting to seduce Rodney, It was working until one song came on. It broke her trance and changed her mood.

"Listen to this song." The beat came on and sounded funny to Rodney,

"What is this shit?" He looked at her.

"Just listen." She started rocking back and forth moving her body like she was a dancehall queen. *"All that you can say, years gone by and still, words won't come easily."* She stood in front of him and told him that he could say baby, my baby can I hold you tonight.

Rodney, looked at her and smiled. He kept his eyes glued to the front of her panties. He watched the area through the lace.

He smiled at it. Ebony, knew what brought him pleasure and gave him more of it to look at as she wound her body around.

"Rodney, are you hungry?" Janet's, voice came through the door.

"I' am." Ebony, slipped on one of Rodney's, shirts, and opened the door.

"Ma what time is it?"

"About three o'clock."

"In the morning?" He asked.

"People eat breakfast this time of day." She asked Ebony, what she wanted to eat.

"What do you got?" Rodney, watched as Ebony, and Janet, walked down the stairs. Rodney, sat up in his bedroom thinking about money. He felt his phone vibrating around inside his pocket. He picked it up and looked at the number. He smiled and got up to call Dena, but decided against it, he decided to do it anyway. He got up and went downstairs.

"We are not really together, but I like him." Ebony, sat down at the kitchen table talking to Janet,

"He likes your friend and you sleep with him hoping he will like you?" Janet, looked at her wondering if she was hearing her right.

"Not really, but it seems like that, Dena, doesn't like him." She looked around then over at Janet, "She think she's a player and prides herself on having dudes all over her without actually doing nothing with them."

"So she's a virgin?"

"A what?" Ebony, looked at Janet, and rolled her eyes. Janet, fell out laughing.

"Well why won't she give it up to Rodney?"

"I won't let her. Whenever she tries to get close to him. I be all up in the way." She smiled. "Dudes be dumb sometimes, but Rodney, isn't dumb, but he is capable of thinking from the waist down."

"Ebony, you are a mess." Janet, laughed. "How old are you?"

"Seventeen."

"What about school?"

"I graduated."

"Already?"

"Yeah." She smiled at Janet,

"What's up, what are you two doing in here?" Rodney, walked into the kitchen.

"Rodney, I like her." Janet, rubbed her hand over Ebony's,

"Oh me too." He mimicked his mother's voice. He grabbed Ebony, and put his arms around her.

"But you'd like me more if I was Dena," She looked upward looking into his eyes.

"I don't like Dena, she wrote me when I was locked up."

"That's what Dena, does she write people on lock down, gas them up, get them open, and she be sending all types of booty shots up in the jails."

"Why are you hating on your on your friend?" He looked at her.

"I'm not hating on my friend. I'm looking out for my friend." Ebony's, eyes sparkled with truth.

"I hear you." Rodney, gave her a smug look that represented arrogance and discredited her claim.

"See what I mean Janet, Dudes see a cute face and start thinking with their dick and get stuck on trick." Her eye lids fluttered. "Oops my bad excuse me Janet," Janet, erupted into a ball of amusement as she laughed loud as she could. "I'm saying though." Ebony, shrugged her shoulders, tilted her head to the left, and looked at Rodney, like he should pay attention to her wisdom.

"Ha ha ha ha. Look at this?" Rodney, held out his phone in front of her face. She leaned over and read the numbers. She looked up at him and rolled her eyes.

"Call her and see what she has to say." Ebony, chewed on the food that was already in her mouth, then used her fork to cut into her pancake, and swirled it around in her eggs until she had a forkful of food.

Rodney, walked over to the stove and dialed the numbers and waited for someone to answer. Janet, sat back looking at her son and Ebony,

"Watch this." Ebony, leaned closer to Janet,

"Hello." Rodney, spoke first.

"Hey Rodney," Ebony, spoke in a cheerful voice indicating what Dena, had to say before she got a chance to say it. Rodney, looked at her with a little frown moving across his lips. "I was just laying down and you crossed my mind so I called you." Ebony, used a voice of a person longing for something. She leaned over and rested her head on Janet's, shoulder. She batted her eyes as she looked up at Janet, Rodney's, mother covered her mouth with her hand to conceal her laugh.

"I was thinking about you too." Rodney, said into the phone all the while he stared at Ebony,

"I would like for you to come over and keep me company so bad." Ebony, leaned closer to Janet, and used an exaggerated voice. "But the timing isn't right. It's too soon and I don't want to have you thinking I'm a hoe." She tooted her lips upward.

"I wouldn't think that." Rodney, started to feel like a fool. "Yo, let me call you right back. I have to handle something." He hung up the phone.

"Don't be mad she pulls that shit on everybody. She think she's a player."

"I'm still going to hit that." He lied. He no longer had the desire for Dena, due to her playing too many games. He only spoke to maintain his status in Ebony's, eyes.

"No." She pushed her chair back and stood up. The t-shirt that she wore rose above her waist revealing her panties. She smoothed it out and pulled it down. "You're not." She walked closer to Rodney, staring at him with stern conviction.

"Watch me." He turned to walk away from her.

"Oh that's exactly what I'm going to be doing." She grabbed his arm and attempted to turn him back around, but he was stronger than her. He turned and looked at her.

"What exactly will you be doing?"

"Watching." She halfway yelled her response, but caught herself halfway through her statement. For a moment they stared at each other looking, watching, and waiting for some more words to come from either person. Rodney, looked at Ebony, who stood in his face with her arms crossed over her breast.

"Yall two are crazy." Janet, broke out into a huge and laborious laugh that sounded like it was long overdue.

"No he's crazy if he thinks that he's just about to be running around here chasing all of these other girls."

"Yo, we don't go."

"I will punch you in your face." She raised her arm and held it in a closed fist. Rodney, looked at her and assessed the weakness in her arms and laughed. Janet, laughed too.

"Go upstairs." He pointed at the stairs.

"Come with me." She pointed her own hand at the stairs. Ebony, looked at him with the same intensity that he glared at her with. There was a short silence that made the sound of Rodney's, phone vibrating inside his pocket grind out louder than usual. He pulled it out and looked at the number.

"Who is that?" Ebony, wanted to know.

"My business." He smiled. He slipped the phone in his pocket and walked away. He did that to keep her acting jealous. The number on his phone was Sissy's, house phone. The call alone meant that Freddie, and Darius, needed some more drugs. He walked up into his room, got dressed, grabbed a few more ounces, and came downstairs. Ebony, sat in the living room already dressed and waiting for him.

"Where are you going?" He teased her.

"The same place you are."

"You can't come." He hid his smile behind a fake frown.

"Well if I can't go you can't either. My friend shouldn't be anywhere I'm not allowed at." Her face contained a dedicated form of seriousness.

"Whatever." He turned to walk out the front door.

"We'll be back Janet," Ebony, got up and walked out the door behind him.

In the car he sat in the driver's seat giving Ebony, more reasons to worry about.

"Are you ready to see the truth?" He smiled.

"I don't know why dudes be cold fronting acting like they don't know when they got it good." Her eyes peered into his then over at the street. She nodded her head to the beat.

"I got it good?" He looked over at her pretending not to care as much as he did, but the strange thing is that he wasn't aware how he felt about her. He understood that he was comfortable around her, but still felt like he could get a better girl to be his real girlfriend.

He started up his car and pulled off. He turned the radio up and cruised off in the direction of Sissy's, house. He pressed the gas pedal then hit the break moving the car along with the baseline of the music that played.

"Alright if you get pulled over for playing." Her words drifted off and faded into silence. She did make sense and Rodney, listened. He drove correctly until he was outside of Sissy's, house.

"Yo, I will be right back." He looked over his shoulder.

"Boy I'm not about to be sitting out here all by myself." Concern crowded the edges of her face.

"You scared of black people?" He smiled at her.

"That's not what I'm saying. What I'm saying is that I don't feel comfortable out here at this time of night, in this neighborhood, all by myself."

"You should of stayed at the house." He got out the car and closed the door.

"You're not there." Her head stuttered side to side and back and forth.

"My mother is there."

"I'm not her company." She reached out and grabbed his hand and walked with him.

Rodney, knocked on the door and waited for it to open up for him.

"Rodney, what's up my dude?" Freddie, stuck his hand out and took his and shook it.

"Skinny girl." He gave Bernie, a fake hug of appreciation and a forty dollar slab.

"I aint thinking about you." She slapped on his shoulder. "Who is this? She is cute." She looked at Ebony, and moved aside allowing them to come into the house.

"Yo, it's crazy paper, mad dough, and mad customers." Darius, pulled out some money, counted it, and handed it to Rodney, He pocketed the money and handed him what was in his pocket.

"Half of those are Freddie's," He looked around the house. Crack heads moved freely looking lost and spaced out.

"Freddie!" Darius, called out. He walked around then stopped at the kitchen table. He sat down and put some of the drugs on the table and cut it up.

"What's up?" Freddie, came walking out of the backroom wearing a pair of blue basketball shorts. He walked out into the living room.

"Where are your clothes?" Rodney, looked at him like he was slipping. He had drugs on him, in a crack house, and he running around damn near naked.

"In the room." He smiled with pride.

"Whose back there?" Rodney, put his arm around Freddie, and walked off with him.

"Eb-bo-knee!" Melody, came walking out the back room. She was happy and glowing all over. "What are you doing here?" She looked around searching for someone else. "Where is Dena?"

"I don't know she may be at home." Ebony, answered.

"You and Rodney?" Melody's, eyes lit up with surprise and happiness for her friend.

"Not really, but we …he…well I don't know what to say, but I."

"Did you sleep with him?"

"Like four times so far." Ebony's, face appeared to rise upward a few inches elevated by her smile.

"How was it?" Melody, asked anxious to know.

"It was." She smiled and pulled her arm up in the air. "Real hard and wild, it's big too." She smiled and nodded her head up and down looking happy to be so lucky.

"What did Dena, say?"

"She doesn't know." Ebony, looked at her friend no longer smiling. "Are you going to tell her?"

"You didn't tell her and it's not my place to tell her because it's not my business."

"She shouldn't be mad because she doesn't even like him at all."

"Yeah I know, but you know Dena," Melody, smiled at her and looked around.

"Melody, bring your ass back in this room!"

"Shut the hell up Freddie!" She yelled out loud enough to be heard by him and everyone else in the house.

"Are you ready or do you want to stay here and hang out with Melody?"

"Rodney, it smells in here."

"What does it smell like in here?" He smirked at her while they walked toward the door.

"Like I don't know, I never smelled these scents before."

"That's crack burning and ass being sold for cheap." He looked at her seeing what type of affect his words had on her.

"Oh." Her words fell flatly out of her mouth and they walked out the door. They got into the car and Rodney, pulled off and drove home.

Rodney, woke up underneath Ebony's, touch. Her fingers gently strummed against his shoulders. His eyes opened as he looked around in disarray. He looked at Ebony,

"What's up?" Grogginess came out of his mouth quickly followed by the funk of morning breath.

"Your mother is knocking on the door." She rolled over and got under the covers. Rodney, sat up collecting his senses.

"Yo!" He yelled through the door not wanting to get up.

"Somebody named Dooski, is at the door."

"Who?" His senses quickly came rushing back to him. He climbed out of bed and got dressed. He put on the same clothes from the night before. He walked out of his bedroom and went downstairs. He walked up to the door and looked out the window and saw a silhouette that resembled his friend form not so long ago. He opened the door and stepped on the porch.

Rodney, reached out and grabbed Dooski, and embraced him.

"What's up B!" Dooski, yelled in Rodney's, face.

"Chilling kid, cold chilling." Rodney, smirked happy to see his friend. He looked at his friend felling happy that he would be able to show him that he was able of accomplishing what he set out to do. He looked over at Dooski, "That's what it's about, all of that heavy jewelry?" Rodney, grabbed his friend's chain. He dangled the bottom of the medallion against the palm of his hand.

"You already know, where is yours B?" He felt around Rodney's, chest then pulled the collar of his shirt back and looked for a necklace.

"I'm not into that shit. I respect that paper, cash money."

"That's what I'm here for B," He extended his arms apart and smiled.

"Well come in here then." Rodney, stepped aside allowing him to come into the house. They walked into the house and moved along the living room.

"Oh shit B, is that wifey?" Dooski, looked at Ebony, She stood at the bottom of the stairs staring at Rodney, and Dooski,

"Oh shit B, wifey is official." He looked at Ebony, with lust and desire spewing out of his pupils. His eyes fell to her feet, rose up her legs, parked at her thighs, and lingered around the pussy print in her jeans. He shook his head side to side slowly.

"My face is up here." Ebony, scolded him with a cold glare.

"Yo, she's mad feisty B," He let out a short laugh and ended it with a devious smile.

"I don't like him." Ebony's, face frowned up in disgust, hatred appeared on her face, but relaxed for a second and settled into distrust.

"Whoa…whoa….whoa." He lifted his hands in the air and patted them like he was patting something. "Easy ma-ma." He grinned at her and maintained his stare.

"It's Ebony," She corrected him before turning her back and going upstairs.

Rodney, and Dooski, sat down at the kitchen table. Rodney, listened as Dooski, told him that he was in town to knock off three bricks before he took off to North Carolina, He told Rodney, that he kept him in mind. He gave him one ounce of cocaine and told him to have his people check that out and get at him if they liked it. He told him to move quickly because he only had three left and he had to be out in a short.

Before long Rodney, and Dooski ,were shaking hands and parting ways. Rodney, walked Dooski, out to his car and watched his friend drive away in a rental car. Rodney, looked at the piece of paper with Dooski's, number on it and pushed it deep into his pocket.

Rodney, walked up upstairs and went into his bedroom. Ebony, stood at the door waiting for him. Her face contained discomfort and anger.

"What's up with your attitude?" He pulled his shirt over his head.

"I don't like him." She made her position known early.

"You don't know him well enough to not like him." He spoke on Dooski's, behalf.

"He's going t o be trouble. You just watch and see." She crossed her arms over her chest. Her eyes shifted toward the wall. She looked away understanding that nothing that she said could alter the way things were going. Rodney, had his mind made up and agreed to go into business with the devil's little cousin.

"What's that got to do with you?" He stared at her trying to cool the heat that jealousy caused to brew in his stomach. He misread the circumstances of the situation. Insecurity had him believe that Ebony's, reaction and disapproval toward Dooski, was really a secret desire to have him as a lover.

"Everything." She was mad and her anger ran out of room to run inside of her so she let it out, frustration stained her eyes.

"How?" Confusion interlaced with anger became the foundation to Rodney's, thinking.

"If something were to happen to your Rodney," Tears welled up in her eyes. "I would be so hurt." Anguish came out of her throat like vapors rising above cough drops.

"Nothing is going to happen to me." He frowned assuming that she underestimated him and prejudged his ability to take care of himself.

"If you mess with that boy it will." Sadness enveloped her and numbed her senses, but she held onto her tears. She wanted to be tough. "Rodney, that boy doesn't care about you." She ached internally for not having the proper vocabulary to express the negative vibes she experienced upon seeing Dooski, someone who she felt was sneaky and would use Rodney, up until there wasn't anything else to use.

"That was my man when I was locked up."

"When you were locked up people called you Savage, referred to your musty armpits as dew-dew strings, and made fun of you." She looked at him. "He's your friend, but your not his friend." She spoke with confidence like she was there to witness their relationship.

"What?" Anger cornered him, pushed into his chest like two powerful hands shoving him backward and challenged him to use her resource of violence. He contemplated slapping Ebony, but thought against it. He decided to let her finish speaking her mind so that he could hear her out.

"People made fun of you before you went away."

"They don't do it now." He wished a mutha fucka would say that to him. He would stomp his foot so far up their ass that he would leave sneaker prints along the lining of their small intestines.

"He does." She spoke quickly fully aware of the emotions that surged through him as he looked at her. "He wasn't talking to Rodney, he was talking to Savage, " She let out a short sigh. "He doesn't see you as no one, but what he remembers about you. A musty ass country bumpkin who he plans on using for his benefit."

"How do you know? You act like he told you all of this."

"He doesn't have too, I can see it when I look at him."

"What do you see when you look at him?" His eyes focused on her waiting for her reply.

"He's so phony, just look at him. He's trying too hard to be something he's not."

"How do you know?"

"He looks out of place. He doesn't look real he look like he's acting." She let out another sigh. "Rodney, you have a demeanor that says fuck you and stay out of my way. Even when your pretending to be nice people can still see it."

"That's what you think?"

"I think that you don't need that boy for anything."

"Yo, he has a couple of bricks that he's letting go for cheap."

"He probably stole them, can't go back to his city, and plans on hiding out here." She looked at him like she wasn't capable of being wrong.

"You act like that nigga soft." He extended his arms and gave her a funny look.

"He just might be, you never know." She walked closer to Rodney, "I have never heard you sit back and talk about what nobody won't do for you. I don't know what you do, but I know that you will make it happen for yourself and you don't look for or expect any body to help you."

"What's wrong with you?" Rodney, looked at her. He stretched out and laid down on his bed. "I have a headache. You're stressing me out." He rubbed his hands over his temples. He looked at Ebony, "I need to fuck to lessen some of this tension."

"Call Dena," She was serious.

"What?" He sat up and looked at her. "What did you say?" He laughed outrageously and loud. He got up off the bed and walked up on her and stood in her face. He grabbed her, lifted her up in the air, and rested her belly on top of his shoulder. He held her in place.

"Put me down." She giggled .

"Gangsters don't talk like that." He moved her around on his shoulder pretending that he was going to slam her on the bed.

"Quit!" She sung out. "Rodney, stop I'm not playing with you!" She laughed some more. She reached for any body part that she could get her hands on, in order to prevent being slammed. She grabbed at his knee, but touched his stomach, somehow she managed to grab his legs, however he spread them apart and she lost her grip. He slammed her "No!" Her voice screeched until it was drowned out by being slammed down on the bed.

He stood up and looked down at her.

"That's for talking shit." He pulled her leg until he drug her toward him. She kicked and wiggled her legs. He scooped her up in his arms and held her high in the air and placed her back on his stomach. "This is for agh!" He crumbled beneath her. She fell down on top of him. She held his balls in her hand.

"That's for slamming me." She got up and tried to run out of his bedroom, but he clipped her at the ankle. Rodney, grabbed the bottom of her jeans. She fell down on the floor. She kicked her feet backward until she was being drug back into the bedroom.

She grabbed the door frame and hung on. Rodney, tugged at her while she gripped tighter to it.

"Janet, help me!" She yelled out laughing. Rodney, held onto her ankles. He climbed on her butt and started humping away against the back of her jeans. "Janet, ha..ha..ha..ha..he is humping me." She couldn't breath due to laughing hysterically. Laughter took over her as she lay flat on her stomach. Janet, watched her body disappear out of the doorway with one quick tug. She got off her bed and walked over to Rodney's, room.

"Rodney, get off that girl with your nasty self." She swatted on his back and pulled his arms. Once she got his arms she pulled at them hard as she could. "Ebony, run girl. Hurry up and run."

"Janet, I'm not leaving you." She laughed until her and Janet, both were wrapped up in Rodney's, arm's being pent down.

"Ebony, girl you got us both jacked up." Janet, said laying on the floor unable to move.

"Rodney, my side hurt, you're hurting me, stop!" Ebony, pretended to be angry.

"Good." He rubbed his chin on her back. She laughed some more.

"Rodney, get off of me!"

One hour later Rodney, had showered, changed clothes, and dropped Ebony, off at home and went to get up with Freddie, and Darius, He walked in the house and pushed Bernice, down on the couch and hemmed her up.

"Rodney, what is wrong with you?" She asked laughing at his youthfulness.

"He's in love." Sissy, said walking out of the kitchen. She held a stem in her hand.

"Where is everybody?" He looked around.

"By everybody you mean Darius?" Sissy, asked him.

"That would be so true." He laughed.

"He went to the mall."

"Tell him to call me." Rodney, turned to leave the house, but stopped and handed Sissy, and Bernice, both one gram of cocaine a piece. He went outside and got into his car and pulled off. He drove around until he was cruising down the street near the park. He drove by at a normal speed, but his eyes searched the crowd looking for Christopher, He saw him, but kept driving because Loop, and everyone else was in the park too.

Rodney, drove home, went upstairs into his bedroom and checked his safe. He looked at the money and counted out eighteen thousand dollars and took it over to his bed. He put it in a bag. He put his gun in his waist and went out to his car on his way to meet up with Dooski,

When he pulled up at te hotel he parked and got out the car. He left his money in the trunk of his car. He walked up to room 314 and knocked on the door.

"Who is it?" Dooski, called out.

"Its your boy." Rodney, stood outside listening to the lock unfasten, once the door opened he walked inside. He sat down and noticed a girl sitting in a chair near the bathroom.

"Who is that?"

"Oh this is my shorty." Rodney, looked at her and studied her features. She looked Spanish, but he wasn't sure. He just stared at her. She stared back, but didn't say a word. "Wanda, say what up."

"What up?" She said never taking her eyes off Rodney,

"I came to see what's up with the business." Rodney, turned away from the girl and looked at Dooski, he walked over to his friend and sat down on a chair.

"What's up, what do you need?"

"I need what we talked about." Rodney, looked at him.

"The whole thing?" Dooski, wanted to be sure he understood where Rodney, was coming from.

"I'm nine thousand dollars short, but I can have that by tomorrow no problem at all."

"That's your word B? This is different than group home shit B, this is real money." Dooski, looked at Rodney, questioningly.

"We are too old to be hero worshipping. I came home and made it happen for myself. Nobody helped me, but they all respect me." Rodney, looked at his friend. Wanda, slowly nodded her head up and down behind Rodney's, back. Dooski, looked at her and recognized her movements and went into the bathroom and got the drugs. He came back with what Rodney, wanted and handed it to him. Rodney, went out to his car, popped the trunk, and pulled out his money.

He entered the hotel room and handed Dooski, the money. They shook hands and left each other's presence. Rodney, looked back at Wanda, and smiled his irresistible smile. She held hers back, but smirked with her eyes.

Rodney, drove home and put the drugs up. He wanted to kill some time until the day shifted over and made way for the night. He didn't have anything to do. He didn't want to sit around the house. He decided to go over Ebony's, house. He rode over to her house without calling or checking to see if she was home.

When he pulled over in front of her house his eyes fixed into a gruesome stare. He looked at Ebony, standing in front of her house talking to someone. The man stood in front of her looking at her. He had his arms crossed at the chest nodding his head up and down.

Rodney, got out of his car and walked over to them. Ebony, saw him approaching and a sly smiled slid across her face. She watched Rodney, walk over to where she was standing.

"Yo, what's up?" The man stuck out his hand to shake Rodney's,

"What up?" Rodney, just looked at it. Ebony, smiled and it grew wider as she smirked.

"Jeff, this is my boyfriend Rodney, and Rodney, this is my older brother Jeff,"

"I thought some other shit." That was Rodney's, way of apologizing for his rudeness.

"What's up boo, I mean boy?" Ebony, smiled and let out a little girl laugh.

"I came to see you and spend some time with you."

"Didn't you just get done spending time with me?" She looked at him seductively.

"That's my cue to leave." Her brother stepped backward and walked toward the house. "When Cheryl, pull up, come, and get me." He walked away.

"I might not be here." She walked down the street toward Rodney's, car. "I saw you-you were about to act up out there when you thought that my brother was some dude that I was seeing." She smiled from ear to ear pleased to have proof that Rodney, cared.

"No I wasn't I was just about to say that I knew that she wasn't no good."

"That's not what I saw. What I saw was a look that said. I wish this nigga is over here fucking with my bitch." She laughed at him and leaned over toward him. "I forgive you for calling me a bitch in your mind." She rested her head on his shoulder.

"That's not what I was thinking." He lied.

"Yes it was. If that wasn't it, why didn't you shake his hand?"

"I don't know that nigga." He said serious enough to mistaken for being honest.

"But you knew that he was up in my face and you wasn't 'trying to hear that." She leaned back in the passenger seat feeling loved. "Where are we going boo?" She smiled at Rodney,

"Stop calling me that it sounds corny."

"Well Rodney, where are we going?"

"I need some new clothes."

"You don't have to buy me Rodney, I'm with you for you."

"That's good because I wasn't buying you nothing anyway."

"Now that we are on the same page and you realize that I can't be brought." Ebony, looked out the window and daydreamed about a future with Rodney,

When they pulled up in the mall Rodney, spent three thousand dollars. Two on him and one on Ebony, She wouldn't accept his gifts until he threatened to give them to Dena,

After dropping Ebony, off and making a promise to come and get her before the night was over, he pulled off and drove over to the park to find Christopher,

He parked his car and walked over to the park. He sat around watching Christopher, sell a few pieces and walk away.

"Yo, Christopher, come here for a minute."

"I'm sort of busy." He said not really wanting to be bothered with Rodney,

"It will only take a moment." He walked over to meet him half way. The two boys met up in the middle of the park.

"What's up Rodney?" He stuck his hand out not really wanting to shake his hand.

"I got some serious business for you."

"What's that?" He rolled his eyes and looked away.

"Oh you playing me out of pocket?" Rodney, looked at him, and slapped him to the ground. He grabbed up his neck and put his gun in his mouth. "Do you want your face shot off?" Rodney, looked around to see if anyone saw him or if the police were coming. "Bring your ass over here."

"Come on Rodney, man all I got is three gees kid, don't do it." He whined out in pain.

"That's what I'm trying to do, put some money in your fucking pocket." He walked over to his car and opened it. "Get in nigga." Christopher, sat down in the passenger seat.

"What's up Savage?"

"Yo, I need you to sell some of my shit in the park on the down low."

"I can't do no shit like that Pookie, will fucking kill me." He stared at Rodney, hoping he brought into his lie.

Rodney, pulled off, rode around the corner, and pulled over. He pulled out his gun and stuck in his face.

"Is that why you broke in his house and stole nine ounces after you fucked up them Rochester, niggas money, then you pumped that shit in the park until you paid them!" Christopher, looked down at the ground.

"Why are you doing this Rodney?"

"Shut the fuck up nigga were not friends." Rodney, handed him five ounces of cocaine. "That's some good shit and it's better than that shit Pookie, has out there. It will move quick." He looked at him. "Try some funny shit and I will tell Pookie, what I know. If you fuck with my money I will get rid of you." Rodney, didn't smile. He punched Christopher, in the mouth three times. "Get the fuck out of my car nigga." Rodney, pulled off before Christopher, was completely out of the vehicle. He backed up, rolled down the window, and gave Christopher, his cell phone number.

"How much for this?"

"Five thousand dollars, a thousand dollars each. You still will make a fortune you bitch ass nigga." Rodney, pulled off thinking of a way to get rid of Christopher, when he had no further use for him.

Chapter 22
So I relate to, choke your ass out, until ya face blue

Rodney, drove over to the spot to check on Freddie, and Darius, when he pulled up and got out the car. He saw them outside standing on the porch talking to a few girls.

"Yo we got to step it up a few notches." He handed them each two more ounces. He got back into his car and drove home. He went in the house and got dressed in all black. He tucked his gun in his pocket and left the house. He rode around until he was three houses down from the house that he saw Christopher, buy his drugs from. He had been watching the house for the last three weeks and learned that every night around this time the boy who rode the motorcycle was at some fat girl named Conswayla's, house.

Rodney, got out of his car and walked down the street. He moved along the sidewalk smoothly and calm. He was careful not to draw attention to himself. He walked up in the driveway. He knocked on the door. He waited for someone to answer the door. No one came so he knocked again. He used his foot to kick into the bottom of the door as he knocked again. He kicked until the door came open.

He disappeared in the house and shut the door behind him. He pulled his gun out of his pocket and cocked it. He walked through the house. He went through the whole house and found nothing until he went upstairs into a bedroom. He saw a huge safe. He checked it, but it was locked. He looked around the room something to take, but found nothing. He became frustrated and walked out of the house. He walked down to his car, got in, and pulled off. He parked around the corner, got out of his car, hopped over a few fences until he was in the boy with the motorcycle backyard lying in the grass.

Hours later the boy returned home. He pulled up in his driveway, shut off his car, and got out of it. He walked up to his house, he looked at his door and looked around only to see a light flash off of Rodney's, gun as it smacked into his head. Rodney, pulled his mask down over his face while the boy fell to the ground. Rodney, drugged him into the house, beat him with the gun, forced him upstairs, and threw him on the floor.

"Open that mutha fucking safe nigga." Rodney, ordered.

"Yo, it aint no money in." The first bullet hit him in the stomach.

"I'm not here to play or get arrested. Open that safe." The boy struggled to his feet and moved slowly to the safe. The second shot tore a huge piece of his ass muscle off. He stumbled forward crashing into the safe. "Open it." Rodney, raised the gun.

"Please-please I'm opening it." He twisted the knob around until the safe came open. Rodney, grabbed his pillow, dumped it out of the pillow case, and loaded it up with his money and jewelry. Rodney, aimed his gun at the boy. "Please man come on I gave you the money please." The boy begged for his life Rodney, aimed at him and shot him in the shoulder and hurried out the house.

"Hey." A lady said witnessing a man dressed in all black including a black mask creep out of her boyfriend's house. Rodney, shot her in the abdomen and ran through the backyard and didn't stop running until he was a few blocks away. He pulled off his mask, put it in his pocket, and walked calmly to his car. He got it, started it up, and pulled off.

He got to his house and opened his safe. He pulled the contents out of the pillow case and counted the money. He ran out of paper after saying eighty two thousand and three hundred and fifty dollars. He took nine thousand dollars out the pile of money and set it aside. He put the rest of the money in his safe and shut it up tightly. He walked downstairs, pulled out his phone, ordered something to eat, and called Ebony,

When she arrived at the house she and Janet, were getting out of two separate cabs at the same time.

"Hey Janet,"

"Ebony, is that you girl?" Janet, smiled at the younger girl.

"It better be me and not nobody else."

Rodney, was upstairs in the shower when Ebony, came walking into the bathroom.

"I paid for the food." She said standing in the bathroom holding the shower curtains open.

"Get out of here." Rodney, grabbed the curtain and pulled it closed.

"I can look at you." Ebony, snatched the curtain back open.

Rodney, got out of the shower, dried off, got dressed, and stood in front of the mirror admiring himself. He stared in the mirror looking at his face. He made a few expressions and smiled at himself.

"You are not all that." Ebony, stood in the doorway. She walked into the room smiling. She walked up behind him, looked over his shoulder looking into the glass peering into his eyes. She slapped her hand on his ass and walked over to the bed and plopped down.

"Yo, would you fuck me if you just met me?" He asked staring down at her."

"I'm not the right person to ask that question, being that I've always thought that you were sexy." She looked at him and waved her hand around. "To me anyway, you may have to ask another girl her opinion." She looked up at him.

"So you think I'm cute?" He glared downward looking at her eyes which looked upward.

"Sexy."

"What's the difference?"

"Cute is adorable, while sexy makes you want to find out more about the person."

"That means you would fuck me if you just met me?" He told her while making it sound like a question.

"Why are you asking me this?" Her eyes lit up.

"Just asking." He reached out and grabbed her arms and pulled her up into his arms. "Let's go somewhere."

"Where?"

"Anywhere." He shrugged his shoulders.

"I want to stay here and be with you." She pulled away from him and walked back over to the bed. "We could watch a movie. Let's go to the video store and pick up some movies." She suggested.

"Like what?"

"Well we can go and see what they have to offer."

Inside Rodney's, car Ebony, sat beside him fastening her seat belt. When the car rolled away from the curb the music roared out loudly as he moved along the street.

When they pulled up in front of the video store they got out the car. Hand and hand they walked across the parking lot and into the store. Rodney, and Ebony, walked around the isles looking at the movies lined up against the wall.

"Ooh look at this." Ebony, held up Love and Basket ball. Rodney, looked at the movie and shook his head. "Boy we are getting this." She moved down the isle holding onto the movie. "Where are you going?" Ebony, looked at Rodney, as he moved into another isle.

"Everything over here is love shit. I'm looking for some gangster shit." He walked over to another section of the store where the independent movies were located. He checked the selection before picking out two movies and walking away. His feet carried him over to the isle where Ebony, was a few moments ago. His eyes shifted around in every direction looking for her, but he didn't see her or anyone who resembled her.

Rodney, walked down the isle until he was standing in the horror section. He looked around.

"Boo." Ebony, grabbed him from behind attempting to scare him. "Were you scared?" She walked around to face him.

"Not the least bit." He smiled at her confidently then leaned in closer to her earlobe. "I got a gun on me." He smirked at her and held it in place while she stared at him.

"Ebony," Dena, walked down the isle approaching her friend.

"Hey Dena," Ebony, said doing her best to hide the uncomfortable feeling that peeled away at her insides.

"Dena," Rodney, smiled at her, nodded his head, and turned to look at the movies on the wall.

"What are you doing here?" Dena, pried for information.

"Hey Ebony," A light skin boy with wavy hair, green eyes, and a six foot three frame said. He walked up behind Dena, and placed his hand around her. He held her gently and swayed with her in his arms. Dena, looked at Rodney, then at the floor. "Are you going to introduce me to your friend?" He reached out to shake Rodney's, hand.

"I'm Rodney," He shook the boy's hand and turned back to the movies.

"Is that your boyfriend Ebony?" He asked smiling.

"Cedric, mind your business." Ebony, looked at him smiling. "Is Dena, your girlfriend?"

"You better believe it." He smiled proudly as he hugged her.

"Well Ebony, call me in the morning." Dena, gave her a weak smile, made a little eye contact with her, then at Rodney, and walked away.

In the car Rodney, rode around blasting his music and rocking his head back and forth. He pulled up at a street light. A car pulled up behind him, flashed the headlights, backed up a few feet, and turned out from behind his car, and stopped beside him.

The driver looked at the passenger who rolled down the window and leaned back. Rodney, pressed on his gas pedal. He sped through the red light and reached for his pistol. He pulled it out, smashed on the gas until he had a sizable lean on the car that was behind him, and slammed on the breaks. He made a sharp u-turn, rolled down his window, stuck his gun out the window, and sped toward the car firing shots.

The car veered to the left and slammed on breaks. One second later the driver jumped out of the car.

"Rodney!" His arms went up in the air. "What the fuck is wrong with you!" Dooski, yelled out loud as he could. Rodney, noticed who the car belonged to, but couldn't stop. He had a gun on him, he let off a few shots, and violated a few traffic regulations. He sped off until he made it home. He hid his car and went into the house with Ebony, and called Dooski,

"Yo, my fault I overreacted." He sighed. "I'm saying its real out here and you pulling alongside a nigga like it's all good." Rodney, let out a short laugh.

"B, you could of killed me and shorty son." There was a short silence. "I thought maybe you didn't want to see a nigga with that short."

"Ahh I been had that."

"It's like that out here?" Excitement filled his voice.

"I told you already."

"Can I come and get that?"

"I'll do you one better I'll come to you." Rodney, smiled at himself.

"That's good B," One second later they hung up. Ebony, walked into the bedroom pretending that she didn't hear the conversation.

"Was that- that boy?" She asked disgustingly

"Yeah why?" Rodney, looked at her.

"What's his real name?" She pulled out a pen a piece of paper out of her pocket and prepared to write.

"Why?" He looked at her confused.

"In case something happens to you. I can tell the police that he was the last person that you were with." She was serious and it showed in her face.

"Nothing will happen to me." He walked away from her.

"Do you need me to come?"

"No." He shook his head side to side and walked out the house. "Don't start the movies without me."

"Hurry up." Ebony, walked downstairs and looked out the window. Rodney, drove directly to the hotel and parked in front of the room. He got out the car and walked into the room.

"What's up?" Rodney, said shaking his friends hand.

"Yo, B, your crazy, B. You could of fucking killed us, not to mention you scared shorty." He looked over at the girl and back at Rodney,

"It was ..that's my bad I be ready for niggas." He laughed.

"Yo," Dooski, clapped his hands together. Rodney, handed him the money, looked at the girl, focused his gaze on her, and stared until his pupils sparkled with interest. She recognized it. Curiosity spread throughout her body, a smile didn't appear on her face, but it was present in her mind.

"Easy." Rodney, smiled at Dooski, and shook his hand then walked through the door.

"Yo, B, we got to get up so you can show me how yall do it over this way."

"I have been waiting for you to come out and play, bring the misses, and we can do it up real big." Rodney, extended his arms and held them open.

"We'll see what we can do." Dooski, looked at his girl. Her eyes maintained a distant aura. "We definitely are going to see what's up."

"Alright." Rodney, walked away, got in his car, and pulled off. He didn't stop driving until he pulled up in front of his house. He got out the car and went upstairs into his bedroom.

The next day after dropping Ebony, off at home Rodney, went and rented a garage. He went to the car lot and brought two new cars, a black Tahoe and a cream Audi. He drove the cars individually to the garage and stored them.

Rodney, spent most of the day insuring his car and truck, getting a for sale sign, and putting it in his back window. When he finished taking care of his business he drove over to the park looking for Christopher,

Pookie, sat on the bench with his legs spread apart looking menacing. His eyes watched all the movements that took place in the park. He looked over at Loop, who stood in the park with his arm crossed over his shoulder looking around. He saw other people standing around or either sitting around pretending to play card, chess, or checkers.

Rodney, blew his horn at Pookie, who nodded his head. He drove until he saw Christopher, he gazed at him then broke his stare after allowing his eyes to convey his message.

Rodney, pulled up in front of the address that he found in the phone book. He looked up to make sure that the address on the building matched the one on the piece of paper that he held in his hand.

He stepped out of his car and went inside the building. He walked into the building. Soon as the employees saw him two of them approached him.

"Can we help you?" They both smiled long stretching smiles. Rodney, smiled at the people and shook his head no.

"I'm just looking right now." He smiled and kept walking until he saw a younger employee with pimples scattered across his face. "Do you work here?"

"Yeah." The white teenager responded looking tired as his sleepy eyes hung low.

"I'm looking for some home security. Some shit that will let me know when a nigga is trying to creep up on me." Rodney, spoke to the kid like he understood him.

"Some down low spy tech government shit?" The boy waited for Rodney's, response.

"Will it help me stay on point?"

"Let you know everything going on inside, outside, and anywhere near the house." The white boy stared at him.

"How much is all of this shit?" Rodney, looked at him.

"Not much." The boy took him to the isle where he found all types of hi-tech equipment. Rodney, paid for all of the items and walked out of the store. He moved casually until he reached his car.

He jumped in his car and drove over to the house where he was suppose to meet the landlord and get a set of house keys to his new house.

Rodney, got out the car and walked over to the porch. He walked up to the man who stood on the porch checking his watch.

"Your right on time." The man said rolling his wristwatch around his wrist.

"That's good business." Rodney, pulled out the money and handed the man enough to secure the house for one year. The man gave him the keys and shook his hand. Rodney, walked around the house and checked it out. He walked out the house and got into his car.

Inside his car he rode over to the furniture store that Loop, took him to and purchased furniture sets for two houses. One he kept in storage and the other he scheduled to have delivered to his new house.

When he returned home night fall had fallen over the street and cloaked the city with darkness. He stepped out of his car and moved toward the house. `

"Rodney!" Terry, yelled out his name a little too loud. Rodney, reached for his gun.

"Everything alright Terry?" He asked looking at his neighbor.

"Everything is good is your mother home?"

"I don't know." Rodney, wondered why Terry, was speaking loud, was he trying to warn him about some unseen danger, was there someone in his backyard, or what? He looked around anticipating the worst. He walked toward the house. He stuck his key in the door, hesitated before walking completely into the house.

He walked around the house looking paranoid. No none was there. He was all alone.

"Ma!" Rodney, yelled out. He listened to the silence in the house. He moved along the house. He walked into the kitchen where his mother and Ebony, sat at the table seated around a birthday cake. The cake was blue and white with sixteen candles glowing on top of it.

"Happy birthday!" They cheered together.

"What?" He looked at them intensely. He calmed down long enough to remember that today was his birthday. He thought about it again and laughed at himself.

One second later a knock came at the door.

"Come in!" Janet, yelled out to the person behind the door. The door pushed open and Terry, walked in hand and hand with his girlfriend.

"Happy birthday Rodney,"

"Thanks Terry," He took the present that the older man handed him.

"Are you happy?" Ebony, stood up and walked around the table. She stood in his face, wrapped her hands around his shoulders, and kissed him on the lips. "I wanted to invite Freddie, and Darius, but I never saw them over here before and I didn't know if you trusted them like that." She looked at him looking to see if he approved or disapproved her choices.

"Thank you." He kissed her back and sat down at the table.

"Happy birthday to you." Everybody sung out in union. When they got to the end of the song Terry, the only voice yelled out loud and drunkenly.

"What's your girlfriend's first name?" His girlfriend and Janet, looked at each other and laughed.

"Ebony!" The girl held onto his side yelling her own name out loud. When the night ended and the next day came Rodney, was at his other house.

He looked at the movers put the furniture in the house. He shook their hands, watched them leave, got back in his car, and pulled off. He drove over to his mother's house and picked up five more ounces and drove over to Christopher's , house.

He knocked on the door hard and forceful like he was the landlord coming to collect the rent money. Christopher, opened the door and wiped around the corners of his eyes.

Rodney, reached out and grabbed his throat. He yanked the boy forward.

"Where the fuck is my money?"

"I got it-I got it, chill Savage, I got it." Christopher, said between clenched lips. Rodney, shoved him backward and stuck his hand out. Christopher, handed him his money. The boy rubbed his neck and looked at Rodney,

"Here." Rodney, handed him the drugs.

"These mutha fuckas is loving this shit." Christopher's, eyes beamed with delight. "I'm making me a little paper on the side." He smiled and nodded his head.

"Move this shit faster." Rodney, turned and walked away without waiting for a response.

Rodney, rode over to Sissy's, house. He stopped in front of the house and got out the car. He ran up on the porch. He twisted the doorknob expecting it the door to be open. He knocked on it.

"Hey Rodney," Bernie, said after letting him in the house.

"Yo, I'm finished already." Darius, handed him two handfuls of money.

"Where is Freddie?"

"His money is in there too."

"Where is he at?" Rodney, looked his friend directly in the eyes.

"Shopping, tricking, and spending money on Melody, Trina, and Davida,"

"He's bugging like that?" Rodney, asked not caring at all as long as his money came correct.

"Like that." Darius, laughed.

"Yo, we going out tonight to have a little fun." Rodney, smiled. "We going to show my man Dooski, a good time."

"Dooski?" Darius, looked at him funny. He never heard that name before.

"It's a cat I know from way back." Rodney, shook his hand. "I got to go breath easy." He turned and walked out of the house. He walked down the steps and moved along the sidewalk until he was inside his car.

He pulled away from the curb and rode until he was at his house. He went inside the house and stopped in front of Janet,

"Ma, where are you going?"

"I'm getting ready to go to one of my meetings." She rushed around picking up her belongings. "Jackie, should be here in a minute." She walked over to the window and looked out the window.

"We got a new place to live." He handed her a set of keys. He gave her the address to the house and jogged up the stairs and went into his room. A short while later he had showered, got dressed, and stood in the mirror checking his appearance.

Rodney, walked out of his house and up to his car. He got in and drove out to the hotel to hook up with Dooski,

Rodney, knocked on the door and Dooski, opened it.

"What's up B, your looking real good." Dooski, laughed then grabbed his old friend. "Samantha, come on ma, we about to get our boogie on." Dooski, walked out the door with his friend.

"Follow me." Rodney, said before getting in his car. He pulled off moving quickly through the street. Dooski, moved at a fast pace keeping up with Rodney, he wheeled his car around traffic attempting to keep up with Rodney,

Rodney, pulled up in front of the spot and blew his horn. Darius, Freddie, Melody, and Tasha, all came out and got into Rodney's, car. He pulled off and headed for a night club.

Inside the club everybody, but Rodney, were drinking, smoking weed, and acting a fool. He was moving around entertaining his guests, but his focus never left the reality of who he was or what he did for a living. He looked around viewing all the people and watched to see who was watching him. All the while he partied, held up bottle after bottle of liquor he did not drink.

Samantha, looked at Rodney, her eyes followed him around. She looked around keeping her eyes jumping from person to person to disguise her true focal point. He walked around moving smoothly appearing to sneak around a room full of people unnoticed. He knew her eyes locked on him like a heat seeking missle. When the night was over Dooski, was all over Rodney, drunk and breathing hard and looking at his friend.

"Yo, I want to fuck shorty." Dooski, looked at him.

"Which one?" Rodney, asked already knowing who he was talking about.

"Tasha, Taysha, whatever the fuck her name is."

"Tasha," Rodney, looked at him. "I'm saying that's one of my broads." Rodney, lied. He looked over at Tasha, a beautiful crack head.

A crack head who was doing exactly what she as paid to do. Hug up on Rodney, look cute, flirt with Dooski,and go with the flow and end up wherever the night took her.

"I'm saying B, we go way back. I got you your first piece of ass."

"I appreciate that, but times have changed were not in a boy's home anymore." Rodney, smiled at him."A favor for a favor." He looked over at Samantha, and smiled.

"Oh that." He blew out a gust of air. "I don't give a fuck about shorty." He looked up at Rodney,

"Let her know what's going down."

"Cool." Dooski, walked over to Samantha, and looked back at Rodney, while whispering in her ear. He walked over to Rodney, leaned down toward him and got close to his ear. "Yo, its in place." He smiled at his friend and looked over at Tasha, "Your turn B," He rubbed his hands together in excitement.

"Hold up." Rodney got up and turned around and whispered into Tasha's, ear. She looked at Dooski, and frowned at Rodney, and stomped her foot.

She tossed her drink on the floor and walked away with an attitude. Dooski, looked at Rodney, and put his arms up in the air. Rodney, walked out of the club after Tasha, Dooski, and Samantha, walked out the club and stood out front and watched the interaction between Rodney ,and Tasha,

"Why do you want to come at me like that?" Tasha, said making a scene.

"I'm saying I asked you to do me a favor, you claim that you love me, and now its time to prove it, and you create confusion." He reached out and grabbed hold of her arms. "Are we together, are you my woman?" Her eyes lost luster and became one with his as she gazed into his eyes. His voice spoke forcefully and powerfully. "Tasha, Tasha!" He shook her. She came back to her senses and looked at him.

"I will do it, but this is for you, and you better not change the way you feel about me or how you treat me." Tasha, pointed her finger in his face, made an uncomfortable face, and turned away from him.

"She's good." Rodney, said to Dooski, he jumped in the car. Dooski, opened the passenger side door and held it open for Samantha, when she got into the car he closed the door.

"Yall two have fun." He tapped on the top of the car and walked away to his own car where Tasha, sat holding her hands against the side of her face. She looked sad. "It will be alright." Dooski, rubbed his knuckle across her cheek.

"Let's just do this and get it over with." Tasha, looked at him with an attitude.

Rodney, rode around for a short while until he pulled up in front of his mother's house. He got out the car and opened the door for Samantha, He grabbed her hand and held it. He walked her into the house and took her upstairs in his room.

Chapter 23
Promise you won't rob him?
I promised, but of course you know I had my fingers crossed

"Suck that dick, suck it you pretty mutha fucka suck that dick." Rodney's, voice was low and swanky. The tip of his dick budded out from in between the tip of her breast. Her tongue flipped back and forth touching the opening of the head of his dick. She closed much of her lips as she could around the tip of his penis. She sucked it hard and fast focusing on the tip. He slid it further into her mouth. He climbed up her body dragging his balls across her flesh as he moved them directly over her mouth and dipped them in and out of her mouth.

The heat from her mouth warmed his testicles as he moaned out in pleasure. Samantha, looked up at him and started speaking in a foreign language.

"Your Spanish?" He asked not expecting an answer.

Samantha, said more words in a lusty tone. Rodney, turned around rearranging his balls in her mouth. He reached down and pulled her legs toward him until she was half way balled up with her pussy sitting in his face.

His tongue touched the tip of her asshole, licked around, left behind saliva. He sucked on her clit with brute force, he licked up and down the walls of her pussy, and stuck his face and tongue all the way inside it. She murmured out in pleasure.

Thirty minutes later he was on top of her wiggling his dick around every square inch of her vagina. He dug deep into her and pushed hard as he could. He rode her from the back and banged his hips against her soft and juicy ass cheeks as they bounced around. He reached around and played with her titties. He squeezed them, twisted her nipples around in between his finger tips.

"Turn that ass over." He backed up away from her and watched her rotate her body. She moved quickly landing on her back. Her legs split open and welcomed him into the circumference of her body heat. He lowered down into it and drove his dick pass the entry part of her pussy and got inside of her center. He moved fast and rough causing her titties to jiggle around and flap against her skin where they made a smacking noise.

Rodney, moved along her body and didn't stop until the birds chirped. The sounds of a new day found Samantha, fast asleep beneath Rodney, as he pounded on her pussy. He kept going although she lay out cold. Her head lay to the side and bounced around as he pumped on her.

His cell phone vibrated in his pocket and shook against the floor. He wanted to answer it. It could have been some money. He got off of her and pulled on his dick fast until his movements became faster. Sperm squirted out and flew over the top of her head, some fell on her face, and the rest hung from the tip of his dick looking like a long string of yarn.

He backed up and reached down for his phone . He looked at the number. He called the number back while walking downstairs.

"Hello," Tasha's, voice came over the phone.
"Did you fuck him?"
"Yeah." She sounded disappointed.
"What happened?"
"He had a big mouth, talked all of that shit, and had the nerve to pull out a little boy's dick." Frustration flooded over the phone.
"How long did it last?"
"He's been done, went to bed, woke up, ate me out, and played in my ass for an additional three minutes."
"I got you." He paused for a second. "Tasha, don't get caught up, this shit is strictly business."
"Trust me."
"I do." He prepared to hang up.
"Hey." She yelled attempting to catch him before he hung up.

"What's up?"
"You got me right?"

"You know I do." There was a pause and another silence then they hung up.

Ten minutes later Rodney, called Dooski,
"What's up?" Rodney, spoke first.
"Shorty pussy was the truth. The pussy was all that."
"Yo, I already know." Rodney, lied.
"Yo, B, where's my shorty?"
"She's upstairs you need her?"
"Tell her to get ready I'm on my way to get her."
"Will do." They hung up the phone. Rodney, walked upstairs and woke up Samantha, she rolled over and groaned out of tiredness. "Dooski, is on the way over here for you." He looked at her. "Are you alright?"

"I'm ok." She looked at him assessing where he was going with his line of questioning.

"I hope you don't feel disrespected, but I couldn't resist you." He looked at her apologetically, yet her feelings meant nothing to him. "They your not from here so I wouldn't be able to see you again." He paused pretending to search for words to describe his feelings.

"I wouldn't have done anything that I didn't want to do." Her eyes contained traces of the truth and portions of uncertainty.

"If you ever need somebody to talk to while your hear. I mean like when Dooski, isn't around and you're all by yourself, you could come over here, and be with me." Rodney, squeezed her hand inside his. She smiled believing he enjoyed her love making, assumed that he wanted her, and was willing to be pampered by the boy who took her body through physical changes and gave her something to write home about.

"I don't talk much, but I understand where you're coming from."

"Do you think that you would need this?" He handed her a piece of paper with his cell phone number on.

"Probably." She reached out for the paper. Once it touched her hand Rodney, pulled her in closer to his body and stuck his tongue deep into her mouth and twirled it around. He wrapped his arms around her and held her in place while his mouth produced reasons to come back to him.

She moved her hands from her sides, down to his stomach, and into his pants. She pulled her hand along the length of his penis. She squeezed it, yanked on it, and fondled his balls.

"Rodney," Janet, stood in the doorway of the kitchen.

"Yo," He called back to his mother.

"Oh I was wondering who that was." She came closer into the living room. Her eyes peered around easily taking in the facial features of the white girl who stood in her living room kissing on her son. In her heart she felt bad for Ebony, but outwardly she knew to mine her business.

"Ma, go back in the kitchen for a minute." He backed away from the girl and buttoned his pants up. "Are you going to call me?"

"I don't know." She smiled at him.

"Well hurry up and decide because your ride is here." he opened the door. Dooski, hopped out of the rental car with Tasha, he squeezed her ass. Her face frowned up in disgust. Samantha, walked out of the front door.

"Yo, man I'm disappointed in you." Rodney, came out the door walking behind Samantha, he walked pass her and shook Dooski's, hand.

"What happened B?" Dooski, looked at his friend with concern.

"She didn't want to do nothing. She was on some Dooski, is my man type of shit." He looked at Samantha, who looked at Dooski, confirming the lie.

"It be like that sometimes you know how that thug love have them broads B," he laughed at his own joke. Samantha, laughed too, but turned to face Rodney,

"I'm on your side." He said low enough only to be heard by a woman or a person doing their best to hear a conversation that has nothing to do with them. Her lips pursed into a short smiled then went flat. She walked to the car and got in.

"She was the truth B," Dooski, bit on his lip and winked at Tasha, she looked away and came over and stood beside Rodney,

"How are you feeling boo?" Rodney, hated the way the word sounded coming out of his mouth.

"I'm good."

"That's still my pussy?" He asked Tasha, she wrapped her arms around him and hugged him tightly offering her affection as evidence. "Good girl." He held her in his arms.

When Dooski, pulled off he took Tasha, inside the house and questioned her thoroughly. She sat on the edge of his bed explaining her story.

"Now you saying he was feeling you right?" He looked directly in her face. He squatted down so that he was eye level with her.

"I guess so."

"No time for guess work either he is or he isn't." He looked at her seriously. "What was he saying, what was he doing?"

"He was eating me out."

"How long?" Curiosity filled his eyes.

"Most of the night."

"What was he saying to you?"'

"He kept saying oh I love this pussy and other stuff like that." Rodney, looked at her sternly. "Well he was asking me do I love you, how long have I been with you, and he asked me did I know about Ebony," She looked at him. "Oh yeah he said that he could take care of me."

"He said that?" He studied her face and searched for clarity.

"Yeah." She nodded her head up and down. 'Oh yeah he was screaming all sorts of stupid stuff."

"Like what?"

"Saying if I don't let him sleep with him again he would kill me and my shit is the best that he ever had and."

"Did he give you something?" Rodney, no longer smiled he got closer into her face then pulled her up from the bed.

"He gave me this." She pulled out a few hundred dollar bills. The look on his face let her know that he wasn't the one to be bull-shitted.

"Don't hold noting back from me, nothing." The look on his face increased her heart beat as fear seized her eyes.

"I won't." She shook her head side to side.

"That's yours he gave it to you." He pushed her hand away from his. "Don't lie to me. It's important that you don't." He walked away from her and picked up his cell phone off the dresser. He looked at the number and put his phone in his pocket. "Tasha, is your shit good like that?" He stared at her.

"I don't know people say it is." She raised her arms in the air signaling that she didn't know.

"I want to see." He placed his hand on the mirror and wiped away a few smudges that came from his finger prints when he touched it. "Go get in the shower and I'll be in that bed." He pointed at the bed that she once sat in. "Waiting for you."

"Where is the shower?"

"Downstairs." he pointed toward the floor.

"Alright." She walked away and headed downstairs. Soon as she walked into the bathroom. Rodney, closed his bedroom door and went in his safe and pulled out a half ounce. He put it in one of his dresser drawers and shut it.

"Ma!" He yelled out.

"What!" She responded from downstairs.

"Call Ebony, and tell her that I said I will call her back I'm in the middle of something."

"Alright!" She called back to him.

When Tasha, came out the bathroom and walked into his bedroom with a towel wrapped around her body. Rodney, looked at her and smiled. He lay in the bed underneath the comforter.

"Come on over here." He remained in the center of the bed.

"I'm coming." She switched over to the bed doing her best to please Rodney, she wanted to sleep with him since the day he turned her pussy down and chose to jerk his dick all over her instead of fucking her. Most men couldn't resist her although she was a crack head she was still a woman. A beautiful one at that. She smiled to herself while taking a shower, she was going to fuck the shit out of this little boy, and put it on him.

She climbed in the bed, slipped under the cover, and reached in between Rodney's, legs and grabbed onto a long surprise. Her eyes bulged around a little bit.

"I sort of forgot." She rubbed up and down on it amazed that he had already had on a condom. "I don't remember it being so big." She lowered her mouth to his penis.

When it was all said and down Tasha, lay sprawled across the bed fast asleep. Rodney, was up, fully dressed, and taking half of the cocaine out of her bag. He weighed it up and took more out of the bag until it was only an eight ball. He put it in a plastic bag and shook Tasha, until she woke up. She rolled over and looked at him. She sat up, put her clothes on, and got ready to leave.

"Tasha, I got a crib for you to stay in for the time being." He looked at her face. "You need to look the part, don't fuck with no drugs, and if you do make sure you get them from me." He walked over to her and gave her a hug, not because he cared, but because he wanted her familiar with responding cheerfully to him. He kissed her on the cheek and held her tight. She felt warm sensations crawl over her body. The feelings that come from falling in love.

"Alright."

"You have to get use to the house and everything." He walked over to his dresser and picked up the eight ball and handed it to her. Her eyes lit up as she put the package in her pocket. He handed her some money. "Buy some clothes, get some of that sexy shit the young girls be wearing."

Rodney, dropped her off at the house and gave her the keys.

"I'll see you later and stick to the plan."

"Will you see me later or see me later- later?" She asked wanting some more of his love.

"I'm going to call you." He pulled off and drove over to Sissy's, house. He got out the car and walked into the house.

"Yo, we have to move and set up shop somewhere else."

"Why what's up?"

"We've been here for a minute and shit starting to get hot."

"This is a good location money is coming off the hook."

"We are not leaving, but we are going to have to get another spot on this block to keep the shit at." Rodney, looked at Darius, and waited for him to understand what was happening.

"Alright I'm with it."

"Good." Rodney, walked away to see Sissy, before he left to put his plan in motion. He told her what he needed her to do.

Outside in his car he pulled off and drove around until he felt his cell phone vibrating inside his pocket. He pulled it out and looked at the number. He pushed his phone back into his pocket and drove over to the park.

When he pulled up at the park he saw Christopher, standing around interacting with the customers as they handed him money in exchange for the base that he held in his hand. He looked over at Rodney, and nodded his head letting him know that everything was going according to plan.

Rodney, rode around until he got tired of the person who kept calling him repeatedly. He answered the phone.

"Who is this?" He asked soon as the caller picked up the phone.

"Tasha,"

"What's up?" "Hold on for one minute please because someone is calling on the other end."

"Dooski, called me and he wants to come over." She waited for his response.

"Tell him no, your busy, and you got some shit to do."

"Alright." Rodney, sat on the phone for a few seconds then Tasha, clicked back over.

"I'm back."

"Who was that?"

"Him." She said referring to Dooski,

"What is he saying?"

"He asked were you here, when I told him no he asked could he come over." Rodney, smiled.

"Tell him that you're going to the mall and that's the only free time that you will have and if he wants to he could meet you there and yall could talk." He hung up the phone.

Rodney, rode around killing time waiting for Dooski, to go and hook up with Tasha, He rode over to the house that he got for Tasha, he used his key to get in the house. Tasha, was gone. Rodney, called Dooski,

"What's up?"

"Chilling B," Dooski, said sounding cool doing his best to show off for Tasha,

"I'm looking for my broad and I can't find her." Rodney, lied.

"Why would you be checking with me B? Shorty don't like me son." Arrogance accompanied his voice.

"Oh if you see her let me know." Rodney, hung up the phone and jumped in his car and drove out to the hotel.

He stepped out of his car and walked up to the room door. He knocked on the door. No one answered. He knocked again, but still no one answered. He looked around and walked along the walkway and around to the back of the hotel. He looked at the windows and became confused, all the windows looked the same and made it difficult to determine which window belonged to the room.

He came back around to the front and knocked on the door. He turned the knob, it was locked. He walked down counting the doors until he ended up behind the hotel. He began counting the windows until he got to the number of windows where the door should be.

He walked up to the window, pushed on it, and played with it until it cracked open. He pulled it all the way up and climbed through the window and landed on the bathroom floor. He walked out into the bedroom area of the room. He looked around moving quickly as he searched. He checked every square inch of the room. He searched the closet, searched the drawers, checked all the clothes. He moved along the room and back into the bathroom and looked under the lid on the back of the toilet. There it was two kilos taped to the top of the lid. He sat the lid back down and roamed looking for money.

He couldn't find any money he walked around looking frantically for it. He heard someone jiggling keys around inside the door. He looked over at the bathroom door. It would take him some time to get to the window and he would be seen going out the window. He started taking off all of his clothes until he was completely naked. He climbed under the blanket and lay in the bed with his arms resting behind his head.

The door opened and closed with Samantha, carrying a few bags of groceries. She noticed someone lying in the bed. She imagined it to be Dooski, until she got close and saw that it was Rodney,

"How did you get in here?"

"Front desk let me in. I told them I was your husband." He looked at her convincingly. He let out a short smile. She looked over at the floor and saw his clothes bawled up into a pile. She laughed.

"What if Dooski, was here?"

"That never crossed my mind. I was only thinking about you." His voice was even and calm.

"You are bugging out."

"I will leave." He stood up, got close to her, and pulled her into his body. "After I get what I came to get." They fell on the bed and attacked each other sexually. He gave it all to her and didn't stop until his phone vibrated. He looked at the number and assumed it was a number to a pay phone at the mall. He got up and got dressed. He sat down and rubbed on Samantha's, head while he picked her brain lovingly. He looked at her and kept talking while she gave him all the information that he wanted.

Chapter 24
Money bring bitches, bitches bring lies

Rodney rode around in his car replaying the information that he heard. He learned that Dooski, was really a runner who ran drugs state to state for a guy named George, and Samantha, wasn't really his girlfriend at all. Her real name was Destiny, she knew the guy who gave the drugs to Dooski, He sent her along with him to make sure that he didn't pull any funny shit with his money.

Rodney, rode around piecing together his plan inside his head. He rode around moving through traffic and navigating through his ideas at an even faster rate. He pulled out into traffic and kept driving until he was in front of his old house. He got out the car, went into the house, and got dressed.

One hour later he walked out the house and got into his car. He drove over to Ebony's, house. She wasn't there so he drove over to Tasha's, house. He stepped out of the car and waked into the house. Tasha's, eyes lit up.

"I did what you said."

"Did you follow everything to the letter?"

"Yep." Her head bopped up and down like a proud little kid happy to please her father.

"Good girl." He smiled. He handed her some drugs, but she declined them. He looked at her strangely.

"I want to be on my A game."

"Is that right?" He asked looking at her through slanted eyes.

"This is kind of fun." She let out a small chuckle. "It's like I'm part of this big scheme and everything depends on me. I feel good feeling important like this." She smiled at him. He walked up on her and hugged her. He held onto her allowing her to linger inside his embrace. He felt her hands rise over his shoulders and squeeze. He sucked on her neck, she tilted to the side and made it available for his pleasure, but he stopped. He pretended to use self control to prevent sleeping with her.

He sat down and talked to her for a few hours. He talked to her while slipping in a few compliments about her. He mentioned her intelligence, expressed appreciation for her love making ability, and other things. He talked to her until night fall crowded the city with more activity and a different breed of people. He kissed her on the cheek and left the house.

Freddie, was sitting on the porch when Rodney, arrived at Sissy's, house. Rodney, got out the car and talked to Freddie, he told him what he wanted him to do in regards to the stash house. He shook his hand and got back into his car and drove over to the garage, got into his Audi, and drove to the hotel.

He pulled up at the hotel when Dooski, was on his way out the door. He watched him climb into his rental car and pull off. Rodney, waited a few minutes then pulled off after him. He rode behind him, but kept a few cars between them. He watched him pull over and go into a few stores, then get back in the car, and drive over to a florist shop where he purchased some roses. He watched him ride away smiling as he thought about something or someone.

Rodney, watched him pull back up into the hotel parking lot and go into the room. Rodney, waited in his car for him to come back out. Five minutes later Dooski, and Samantha, both exited the room carrying bags. They got into the car and pulled off. Rodney, started up his car, waited a few minutes, and pulled off looking for Dooski, Rodney, followed behind at a safe distance. He was surprised when Dooski, stopped at an apartment building and switched cars, tossed two big bags in the trunk, got in the car, and pulled off. Rodney, watched him and followed him until six hours passed and Dooski, had pulled up in the hotel parking lot where the stake out first began. Rodney, didn't turn into the parking lot he drove home. He went home to the house next door to Terry, He walked in the house as his phone rang.

"Hey Rodney,"

"Where have you been all day?" He said in a playful tone.

"I went out to the college today. I'm about to enroll out there."

"What are you going to be taking up?"

"I'm going to become a registered nurse."

"They make a lot of money?"

"A little bit."

"Do they be giving it up?"

"What?" A laugh followed her words. "Don't be nasty."

"Do you want to come over and tell me about your day?"

"No I want you to come over here."

"Why?"

"So you can meet my mother."

"I don't want to meet your momma." He sung out the words shake it like a polaroid picture. The two of them laughed before he agreed to come over and meet her family. He hung up and went over to Ebony's, house.

After visiting Ebony, and her family Rodney, was back inside his Accura Legend, cruising around the street. His eyes were glued to the streets. People stood around looking at each other, some were hustling, and others yelled vulgar language at some females who walked by.

Rodney, pulled over and got out of his car. Something about the looseness of the scenery caught his attention. He leaned against the front of his car. He watched a few guys drive slowly up the street showing off their cars, he looked at the girls scantily dressed giving the fellas meaty flesh to lust over. Rodney, watched the environment and looked at all the girls moving up and down the street.

"Hey Rodney," He looked to his left following the direction of the voice that called his name.

"What's up?" he looked at the girl and tried to place her face to a name. He thought again, but she was too far off. The closer she came he instantly recognized her. "Tiffany?"

"Hey what's up, what are you doing over here. I thought that you were one of the park niggas. I didn't think that I'd see you on this side of town." Rodney, never considered looking at the city in terms of sections he saw it as wherever some money or pussy was, he was going to be there.

"Aint no telling where I'm going to pop up at, but what are you doing over here?"

"I live over here on the dime." She pointed toward a few buildings.

"The dime?"

"Yeah, that's just short for tenth street." She smiled and let out a short chuckle.

"Oh the dime." He laughed more out of formality and phoniness. He looked at her then around checking the scenery.

"You don't have to worry about nothing over here. This is where my people are from." She noticed his roaming eyes.

"I aint worried. I'm accepted worldwide." He meant every word of his sentence.

"Oh you're not?" She looked at him, then her watch, and across the street. "Do you want to smoke some weed?" He didn't smoke and didn't want to start now, but his feelings for Tiffany, resurfaced within moments of being around her.

"I don't smoke a lot, but I can drop you off wherever your going." He looked up and down the street. He saw the difference between the people on her side.

"Well I'm from right over there." She said. "But since your offering I will get a little short ride. Where is your car?"

"Right here." Rodney, walked over to his car and got into it. Once Tiffany, got into the car he pulled off. He followed her instructions until he pulled up in front of her house. A young boy stood on the porch with a couple more guys.

"Is this your new man?" He asked knowing that neither of the men on the porch was her husband. Sadness crept over her face and stayed there for a minute.

"We not talking right now."

"Yo, I don't know how to roll up blunts."

"I'll show you."

"What's up Tiffany?" A brown skin boy stood up to speak to the girl.

"Boonie," She walked pass him and sat down on the porch. "Boonie, this is Rodney, Rodney, this is my brother Boonie, this is Al, and James, these are his friends." Rodney, shook their hands.

"Yo you that nigga that shot Carl?" The boy named AL, said looking at Rodney,

"Yeah that's me." Rodney, reached around his waistline and grabbed the handle of his gun. "That's your man?" Preparation came across his voice.

"Hell no, I just remember seeing you before. I was up there when that shit went down."

"Oh." Rodney, calmed down, but took his gun off of safety. He walked over to one of the chairs and sat down. Tiffany, rolled up four blunts and lit two of them up. She hit one a few times then passed it to her left. She lit the other one, hit it, and passed it to her right.

When the blunts reached Rodney's, hand he inhaled the smoke, but kept it in his mouth retaining the smoke from entering his system. He blew it out in powerful white clouds that came from not fully inhaling the smoke. He passed the blunts quickly keeping them rotating around the small circle of people formed on the porch.

"Boonie, did Tezo, call while I was out?" Tiffany, looked hopeful.

"Fuck that faggot ass nigga, Tiffany. He's over there fucking with that bitch and being straight up disrespectful." He sucked in some of the purple clouds that rolled around in front of his lips. "He can't deny it, he's over there living with a bitch and telling you he can't fuck with you right now because your stressing him out. Fuck that nigga." Boonie, was angry and it showed all over his face.

"Yo, that nigga is wack. I saw him the other night he looked at me like was going to blow up his spot." Al, looked disgusted. "Like mutha fuckas get down like that."

"He's not all that bad." Tiffany, spoke on her husband's behalf. " When he was over here looking out for yall he wasn't that bad."

"That nigga was always wack." Boonie, smoked some more of the weed and blew out a short cloud.

"Boonie," A small and fragile looking woman in a brown coat that was too heavy for the weather called from the street.

"What's up?"

"Do you got something?" The lady called from the street. He walked out toward her and took her behind one of the buildings. One second later he came back counting some money. He stuffed it inside his pocket and walked up on the porch. "Yo, Tiffany, you need to plug us into Pookie, so we could get this money for real." He looked at his sister with sincerity in his eyes.

"Boy Pookie, don't be messing with little shit like that." She sounded annoyed to have to keep reminding him of this fact.

"How much money do you got?" Rodney, said putting himself in their business. Everybody's eyes looked at him, then away, then back at him.

"Rodney, people know how you give it up and people might be a little distrustful of you." AL, said hoping that he didn't offend the boy.

"And they should be. You should never trust nobody in this game." He looked at them. "But realistically I mean you aint got, but so much money. That makes you an underdog and that's my kind of nigga." He inhaled some of the weed smoke, held it in his mouth, then he blew out a full stream of smoke. "Now if you want some money you'll fuck with me. I'm no day to day survival ass nigga I do shit for a reason."

"I got like forty two hundred dollars." Boonie, looked directly at the man.

"I'll do something for that." He smiled at the boy. "And my shit is fire." He got in his car and pulled off.

Twenty minutes later he was pulling up in front of the house he had left moments earlier. He got out the car and walked toward the house. He knocked on the door.

"Who is it?" Tiffany's, voice came from behind the door.

"Its Rodney,"

"Hold on." She opened the door. "Come in my brother ran to get some more weed, but he left the money with me." Rodney, pulled out the drugs and handed them to her. "Damn." Her nose scrunched up. "You can smell it through the bag."

"That's fire." He took the money, counted it, and stuffed it in his pocket. "Yo, tell him if he's about his paper we can get some money, but if not I can handle his money as long as its consistent." He turned to leave.

"You can wait for him." Her voice contained a sense of urgency that made him want to see where this night would go.

"Alright." He walked over and sat down on the couch. He sat there pretending to smoke weed. He listened to Tiffany, talk about her husband and the problems that they were having.

"Rodney, if you had a girl like me would you cheat on me?" Her eyes began to dampen, but she held onto her tears. "I don't know what's wrong with him. He does what he wants to do, but be all over me." Rodney, listened to her and didn't have anything to say. She wasn't looking for answers she wanted someone to listen to her. She wanted a way to release her pain.

If no one else wanted to listen to her due to hearing the story too many times, Rodney, would listen. He didn't care he wanted something from Tiffany, since he was younger and he would listen to any story if it brought him closer to her pussy. She stood up and walked away only to return with a bottle of liquor.

"Do you want some of this?" She asked looking at him.

"No, I'm good." She walked in the living room and sat down and poured herself a drink. She drunk it like it was water and made another one.

"I haven't had sex in six months-six fucking months." Frustration filled her face. She looked over at him. "I've been trying to keep it real with this nigga waiting for him to come around so we could sort this shit out." She let out a heavy sigh. "But no he wants to run around on some childish shit and fuck this ugly ass black bitch, throwing it up in my face." Anger and sadness spilled out of her mouth. "When I find somebody to fuck I'm putting it on them. I'm giving them all of this watch and see." She was hurt and it needed to come out and it did. A few tears slid down her face.

"Yo, I have to go, but give this to your brother and tell him to call me." Rodney, walked away after giving her his phone number. He walked down the steps and got into his car. He pulled off. He wanted to stay and comfort her, but that would have lessened his chances of fucking her. He definitely wasn't trying to be friends.

Chapter 25
Get money niggas be living it up, all the sexy young bitches be giving it up AKA: A long ass Chapter

The next day Rodney, was buying two kilos of cocaine from Dooski, he had someone test it and make sure it was the same quality. Once he learned it was. He paid him and took it to his house and put it up.

He rode over to the spot and gave Darius, and Freddie, some drugs to sell. He got back in his car and took Christopher, some and went back home. He sat around counting money when his phone vibrated in his pocket. He didn't recognize the number, but answered it anyway.

"Hello." He said soon as the caller picked up the phone.

"What's going on, what are you doing?" Tiffany's, voice was unmistakable.

"Chilling why what's up?" He wondered what was going on.

"My brother wanted to see you again."

"Alright." Rodney, hung up the phone and got into his car and pulled off. He went home, picked up some more drugs, and stashed them in his car, and headed to Tiffany's, house. He felt his phone vibrating in his pocket. He pulled it out, saw Tiffany's, number, but didn't answer it.

He pulled up in front of the house and got out of his car. He walked up to the door and knocked on it. She opened it looking like she was getting ready to go on a date.

"Where is Boonie?"

"He didn't get here yet." She stepped back letting him in the house. "You can wait for him."

Rodney, walked in the house and sat down.

"Rodney, I had a dream about you last night." She walked by him and into the kitchen like her words were meaningless.

"What were you dreaming?" He asked looking at her back as she looked around inside of her freezer and pulled out a bag of chicken.

"Something nasty." Rodney, thought about her using him as a get even fuck and saw nothing wrong with it, but it wasn't going to happen right now being that he had some money to get. "Did you hear me?"

"I heard you and I was wondering if you are aware that dreams are a way of showing us what's to come."

"What?" She laughed.

"Where is your brother?" He asked looking at her.

"He will be here." She walked into the living room and bent down in front of him showing off her ass, but she didn't need to. He had her body etched into the deep areas of his mind.

Rodney, and Tiffany, talked for one full hour giggling and laughing, smoking, drinking, and getting familiar with each other.

A short while later Boonie, came walking in the front door. He walked up and took the blunt out of his sister's hand and inhaled it. He reached in his pocket and handed Rodney, the money. Rodney, took it and counted it in front of him.

"I didn't bring enough for all of this, but I'll be right back with the rest." Rodney, stuffed the money in his pocket and left the house. He got into his car and rode away. He returned with the rest of the coke and a few extra ounces. He got out the car and handed it all to Boonie,

"Yo, I put some extras in there so you don't have to call me so much, that should hold you over for a couple of days."

"I thought that you don't trust people?" Boonie, asked smiling.

"I'm not scared to pop that ratchet." He flashed the handle of his gun.

"I respect your handle no problems." He shook Rodney's, hand and walked out of his sister's house. "Yo, Tiffany, I will see you later!" He yelled to his sister.

"Alright." She moved quickly to catch up to him before he was in his car and out of her business. "I guess I will go to sleep and dream a little bit more." She looked at Rodney, he smiled and got into his car.

Rodney, rode around then headed back to his house. When he got in the house his phone rang. He answered it.

"What's up Dooski?"

"Samantha,"

"Hey girl."

"I'm alone by myself and Dooski, is gone."

"Where he at?"

"I don't know and don't care."

"Do you want to come over here?"

"You come over here." She said.

"Here I come." Rodney, hung up the phone and got in his bed. He had no intention of going anywhere.

Rodney, woke up to the sound of Ebony's, voice.

"What are you doing ignoring me?" She leaned over and kissed his ear.

"How did you get in here?" He said still half asleep. He rolled over on his back and looked up into her eyes. She sat beside him and wrapped her arms over his upper body. She lowered her head close to his face.

He wrapped his arms around her and pulled her into the bed and rolled around until he was on top of her.

"Get off of me boy." She smiled while pretending she didn't want to be touched.

"You don't mean that. If you did you wouldn't be here." He ground his hips around on top of her.

"Nasty." She let out a giggle. "Ooh Rodney, stop." She laughed and attempted to get from under him, but her efforts were useless. He overpowered her and sucked on her neck, moved along to her collar bone, and grabbed a mouthful of her breast through her shirt.

"Rodney," Janet, stood in the doorway of his bedroom. "I hope you don't mind, but I let her in. She said that she wanted to see you and it showed in her face." His mother waited for his response.

"She's good." He looked back at his mother.

"I better be."

"Yo, where have you been?" He rolled off of her and sat up. "I've been looking for you." She closed her eyes, smiled, and shook her head side to side.

"I'm not answering that." She let out a short laugh.

"I see how you are." He got up out the bed and looked at his phone and checked the time. He pressed the button and searched all of his missed calls. He overlooked all of them except Christopher's, He called him back.

"What's up?"

"Where are you?" Christopher, asked.

"I'll be there." Rodney, hung up on him and got dressed. He prepared to leave the house.

"What about me? I didn't come over here to be alone." Ebony, crossed her arms over her chest and pouted at him.

"I'm sad too." He pouted back at her. "I'll be right back." He grabbed his gun and left the house.

Rodney, pulled up in front of Christopher's, house. He banged on the door until it opened.

"Yo, my kids are sleeping." Christopher, said looking worried that Rodney, wouldn't care.

"Give me my fucking money." He snatched the money out of his hand and tossed the drugs to him. He turned and walked away. He rode over to Sissy's, house and gave Darius, and Freddie, some more drugs. Once his body was secure in the driver's seat of his car, he pulled off and headed home.

Rodney, got out of his car and walked into the house Ebony, and Janet, was sitting around the television watching a movie. He sat down beside them.

"What are yall watching?" He asked.

"Shhh, be quiet." Janet, swatted at his leg.

"Rodney, I'm trying to hear." Ebony, said leaning her head closer to the television.

"Oh shit." Both women said together.

"I knew he did it!" Ebony, pointed at the tube. "It's always like that a person be acting like he want the people to succeed, but in reality his is really working to destroy them."

"That bastard, he did that girl like that." Janet, said shaking her head at the television like the characters were real people who she interacted with everyday.

"That's messed up." Rodney, added his own brand of disappointment.

"Rodney, shut up you wouldn't care anyway."

"He wouldn't he's a man." Janet's, words followed closely behind Ebony's,

Rodney, grabbed his phone and looked at the number vibrating across his screen. He walked into the kitchen and dialed the number back.

"Hello." Tiffany, sounded sweet and seductive.

"What's up?"

"My brother wants you."

"Here I come." He hung up the phone. One second later the same number came shaking across his phone again. He dialed the number back. "What's up?"

"Could you bring me something?" She asked. "I will pay you when you get here."

"Alright." He hung up the phone and left the house. His mother and Ebony, watched more of their girly programs. "I'll be back."

"I'll be here." Ebony, stared directly at the screen.

Rodney, went upstairs to his bedroom, came back down, and climbed into his car and headed over to Tiffany's, house.

Thirty minutes later he was getting out of his car, walked up on the porch, and knocked on the door.

She opened the door looking astonishing. Her hair was pulled back in a tightly wrapped pony tail which hung down to edge of the crease in the center of her back.

Her shirt fit snuggly around her body and pushed her breast outward. They stood up in his face like two melons being held up on a silver platter. He looked down at her legs which were flowing out of her shorts that looked like a pair of basket ball trunks.

"Come in." She turned around switched into the house. Her booty moved like it was linked to a speaker blasting dancehall tunes. He walked in the house doing his best not to focus on her behind.

He walked into the living room where the t.v. showed some movie that he wasn't interested in. He walked over to the couch and sat down. He reached inside his pocket and pulled out an ounce of weed and handed it to her.

"I didn't want this much." She smiled nervously.

"Don't worry about it." He waved his hand in the air like spending five hundred dollars for an ounce of weed was nothing. He could have brought some regular weed, but he wanted to make a good impression on her. He went out of his way and brought some purple haze.

"This is a lot of weed." She smelled the weed through the bag. Her lips curved into a smile. "You're trying to get me fucked up?" She bent over in front of him allowing his eyes to roam over her booty as it poked out in his direction. He smiled, but cleared it off his face when she turned around unexpectedly to see if he was looking. His eyes remained fixated on the t.v. screen pretending to be interested in the show.

"What is this you're watching?" He asked not caring. "This is crazy. Why are these people killing these kids and women like this?" He recalled the last scene.

"I don't know, but Don, something is playing the lead character." He walked around her house then looked out the window. Here it comes."

The music from his car speakers blared throughout the neighborhood.

"I told him about blasting that music in front of my house." A frowned appeared on her face. She walked over to the door and opened it for her brother.

"What's up?"

"Don't be what's upping me, nigga I done told you about blasting that shit in front of my house. You don't do it in front of mommy's house and you're not going to be doing over here. She followed her brother until he turned around with his hand raised in the air. "NIgga I wish you would." She stared at her brother.

"Happy now?" He squeezed a button on his key chain and the music turned off. "I'm in a rush." He walked up to Rodney, he pulled out a wad of money and handed it to Rodney,

"Is this everything?"

"You know it is." Boonie, looked at him he like he knew better than questioning his money."

"That's what I like."

"What's that?"

"It's all there money." They laughed along with each other.

"I'm out." He shook Rodney's, hand. Boonie, left te house and moved into his car then pulled off.

"Rodney, are you leaving?" Disappointment stained her face. "You're not going to smoke a blunt with me?" She stared at him hoping he didn't say no.

"Well I'm sort of busy. I got to get some more money." He lied. He sensed her need to spend time with someone other than herself.

"I'm." She thought for a second before saying another word. She looked at him hoping that he understood her needs. He did, but pretended not to. She reached out and grabbed his hand. "I just need somebody right now." Her eyes fell to the floor. He closed the front door and followed her to the couch.

"I guess I could shave a few seconds off a few minutes." He sat down. Tiffany, rolled two blunts quickly and lit one of them. She smoked all of the weed. Rodney, inhaled the weed smoke, but held it inside his mouth for a few short seconds then blew it out.

A little while later she was sitting on the couch looking devastated by the powerful marijuana. Her eyes hung low and contained a look of drowsiness and scooted across the couch and leaned over onto Rodney's, shoulder.

"Rodney, do you think that I'm an ugly chick?" She spoke low softly.

"No." He said flatly, but his true response was hell no.

"Tezo, seems to think so." She leaned over on him. She wrapped her arm around him. She pulled him closer to her. He allowed his body to be pulled into hers. "He just keeps shitting on me. Why do men do shit like that?" She never raised her head up to face him. She spoke her mind without thinking.

"What do they do?" He asked her rubbing a soft caress down her back.

"Play games." The seriousness of her words came out in her statement.

"I can't answer for him or no other dude, but." His words never came, he finalized his sentence with the word but.

"He asked me did I love him, then said prove it, and left calling me childish." She cried and began rubbing his stomach. "Do you know I have been with this mutha fucka since I was eighteen." Her voice cracked a little and came out in broken sobs. "I was faithful to his sorry ass and gave him my all."

"That could be hard to deal with." Rodney, rubbed on her back and massaged her scalp. He stroked her hair and rubbed down her body. She leaned over and pressed her hands into his lap. She touched his private parts through his jeans. His eyes lit up with surprise, he held her tightly in his arms, and felt his zipper being pulled down. He felt her hands fumbling around inside of his pants until his dick came out of the slit in his boxers and stood up erect.

"Rodney," He heard his name after the first lick from her tongue touched his dick. She looked up at him to see if he was watching her. He was, but turned his head away when he felt her lifting up in his lap. He stared at the t.v. screen pretending to be unaffected by the sensitivity that tingled around the head of his penis.

"Rodney, did you feel that?" She asked him still holding his penis in her hand. He didn't answer her, kept his eyes focused straight ahead looking at the t.v. the second lick turned into a third one, a fourth one, fifth, and sixth which turned into a long lick that started at his balls, ran up his shaft, and stopped at his pee hole engulfing his meat into her mouth.

She sucked it with a vengeance, pulled on it, yanked it up and down. Rodney, felt pressure and force clenching down on his penis. He scooted downward on the couch and gave himself some room to stretch out so he could feel the pleasure all over.

She held his balls in her hand moving them along her hand. He let out a short moan. His excitement encouraged her gave her more of reason to suck harder. Tears fell from her eyes and landed on his lap. She ached and burned with the guilt of fucking another man. She was cheating on her no good ass husband, and feeling the pain of watching all of her years invested in a relationship go down to drain because of some ugly ass black chick.

Images of Tezo, screwing his ugly side dish angered her. She took it out on Rodney's, penis. She squeezed it hard while pulling down the base of it, and squeezed it harder as she pulled it up. Her tongue moved around like she was forming sentences and cursing her husband out as she sucked on him.

Rodney, reached around her back and rubbed on her breast. Frustrated and upset she pulled her shirt up furiously. Her breast fell down and touched his leg. Her head moved up and down fast. Her mouth flopped down hard on his penis she took it in her mouth and squeezed her jaws tight as she could. She wanted to hurt Tezo, and satisfy the hunger in between her legs. The fire that desperately needed to be put out, but could only be distinguished by a man's touch.

She pulled Rodney's, pants down and dropped down in front of him bobbing her mouth side to side up and down pausing and sliding it all the way down to the base of his balls. She felt a choking sensation gagging in her throat. She relaxed and rose up pulling his shirt over his head.

She laid down on the floor and he leaned closer to her. He wanted to grab his condom out of his pocket, but the moment was hurried, his mind was clouded with the desire of finally getting Tiffany, after all of these years. He lowered down on top of her and pushed his meatiness inside of her.

"Ooh." A soft murmur escaped her lips. The moan was one of sincerity. It came from being stretched apart by his size and the need to feel him move around inside of her.

He climbed on his toes, held her in place, and jack hammered her pussy. He drilled her into the floor, moving wildly, and crazy. He felt her hands touching his back and digging into his skin. He got off her and turned her around. Her head fell into the middle cushion on the couch and rested against the softness of the pillow.

He gripped her hips and pulled her into him. He pushed into her body savagely. She pushed backward banging into him. The newness of his size stretched her out and made her wince in pain. It was a good pain one that she loved and felt good feeling. She loved it and moaned out. She reached backward and dug her nails into his thighs.'

"Rodney, oh oh Rodney, oh." She pushed her hands backward to slow down his speed and force. He pushed her hands out the way and smacked her across the ass. That was his way of telling her to get her hands out of the way. He smacked her ass again. "Oh." She moaned out.

He climbed up along her body until his balls were swinging underneath her body touching her inner thighs. He grabbed a handful of her pony tail and held it, used it as a rein to keep her in place and pounded her from the back. Her eyes winced in pain. He hit harder and kept hitting it.

"Fuck me, fuck me!" She wailed out in pleasure and kept moaning. He held her ass in front of him and lined it up with his penis and jammed it inside of her hard as he could. He pumped into her until he was moving his hips hard as he could. He rocked the couch causing it to knock lightly on the wall. A little girl's face rattled around inside the picture on the wall. He pumped until he was spilling his juice inside of her body.

He backed up pulling his penis out of her. He looked down at it and felt that it was slicked up with gooey and sticky female spunk. He reached between her legs and felt the same goo, except in between her legs it was scorching hot. He stood up and put his clothes on. He helped her up and held her hand while she got dressed.

When she stood up face to face with him, tears stung her eyes. She looked at him with sadness, then smiled at him happy that he was the one that let give her what she was missing. She hugged him tight as she could.

"Don't be a stranger." She held onto him.

"I won't." He looked at her and watched the tears roll down her face and fall into her hands. He squeezed her tighter to comfort her, but it had the reverse affect. She became sadder. Her tears ran down her face and fell harder.

After comforting her and assuring her that he would be available when she needed to talk and whenever she wanted to talk. He got in his car and drove until he reached his house. Ebony, was on the couch sleep. Janet, was the other end of the couch sleep. He got in the shower and washed off his creep move.

Rodney, woke up entangled around Ebony, he pried her hands from his body and got out the bed. He pulled his clothes on and left the house. His mind was racing and deciphering a dream that he had last night. The dream troubled him, it gave him the chills, and made him question his need for Christopher,

Rodney, got out of his car and walked up to Christopher's, house. He raced up the stairs and beat his fist into the door nonstop until Christopher, opened it. The boy looked at Rodney, stretched out, and yawned wide as he could. Rodney, looked away contemplating slapping him across the face, but decided against it.

"Yo, we about to make a power move." Rodney, looked at Christopher, and maintained a steady look.

"One like what?" Curiosity lingered around the boy's eyes.

"Lie we about to get all of this paper. I need you, get dressed." He shoved the boy back into his apartment. "I'll be back in ten minutes."

Rodney, drove home and called Dooski, he sat around replaying the dream over in his head. The dream was fuzzy, gave no real clarity or meaning, but it left him in a deep state of paranoia. He looked over at Ebony, rubbed his hand over her leg, rose his hand up higher, and ran it smoothly across her butt. She opened her eyes, smiled, and moved closer to Rodney, He thought about her, his mother, his life, and how he wasn't going to allow anyone to ever take his freedom from him, fuck jail, fuck probation, and fuck other people's opinion about his life. He was in charge of it. He looked over at Ebony, his stare promoted love, admiration, and a need to keep his feelings private.

The telephone rung, he snatched it up, and held it pressed it tightly against his cheek.

"Dooski," Need spilled over the phone.

"What's up B?" Dooski, answered smoothly.

"Can you see that?" He asked referring to the number he pressed into his pager.

"Right now?" Dooski's, answer contained traces of unwillingness. He didn't want to sell the rest of the drugs, he was extremely close to sleeping with Tasha, again and selling Rodney, the rest of his inventory would send him right back on the road to get some more product.

Dooski, thought about Tasha, and the conversation that he had with her the night before. He was thinking with his dick and unaware that his love interest was merely a puppet connected to the string dangling around Rodney's, finger.

"Right now?" Dooski, questioned.

"Right now." Rodney, confirmed. There was a short silence between the two friends then they hung up.

Ten minutes later Rodney, was pulling up at the hotel and getting out of his car. He knocked on the door and waited for it to open. Once it opened Samantha, stared at him.

"Its Rodney!" She yelled behind her stepping aside allowing him entry into the room. Liar." She whispered in his ear as he walked pass her.

"I was tired, but we can get into something later tonight." He winked at her and moved his eye brows up and down then smiled.

"May not be able to." She turned her head to the side and walked away. Rodney, walked up behind her and grabbed both of her ass cheeks into his hands and squeezed them. He tried to pick her up by her butt. She patted at his arms and let out a small chuckle.

Dooski, was in the bathroom pulling the tape off of the drugs. He wiped sweat off of his face and thought about taking out some of the product and shorting Rodney, on the weight of the drugs.

Samantha, sat on the arm of the chair nearest the front door. She held up her shirt flashing her breast at Rodney, He looked at her nipples and made a funny face. He started squeezing his nipples indicating what he wanted her to do. Her hands roamed generously around her breasts then flickered around her nipples.

"Stick your tongue out." Rodney, whispered to her. She smiled and stuck her tongue out. She flipped and rolled it around. "Let me see your pussy." He spoke to her using a low voice that was designed for her and only her to hear. She stood up, unzipped her pants, and pulled them partially down revealing the top layer of pubic hairs.

The sound of the bathroom door opening caused her to pull her shirt down. She didn't have time to fasten her pants. She plopped down on the chair quickly and stared straight ahead.

"Yo, this is everything right here for a couple of days." Dooski, said handing the drugs to Rodney,

"Well I need more I need at least twelve." He opened up his bag and pulled out stacks of money. He placed the each across the dresser top. Samantha, looked at him, then over at the money, and developed a plan to make him her man.

"Damn Rodney," Dooski, spoke out in disappointment, but greed took over his lust for Tasha, He reasoned that by going to get twelve more bricks for Rodney, he would have more time to be with Tasha, who he was on the verge of stealing from Rodney, right up under his nose. He thought about it then looked over at Samantha, "Yo, get ready we leaving in a few minutes." He turned and walked back into the bathroom.

"Not tonight either." She held her hands up in the air.

"Soon though." Rodney, reached in between her legs. She closed her legs trapping his hand in between her thighs. He squeezed her leg through her jean material.

Rodney, left the room, got into his car, and drove home. He put the drugs up, drove over to his Audi, and switched cars. Twenty minutes later he was two blocks away from Christopher's, house. He didn't want people to mark him as the one driving the car. He stood on the porch knocking on the door. Christopher, came out the door, shook Rodney's, hand, and together they moved sneakily to his car.

"Whose car is this?" Christopher, asked admirably.

"I rented it." He looked ahead as he drove out toward the hotel. "Yo, duck your head down in between your legs." Rodney, didn't smile.

"What?" Christopher, asked in disbelief. One second later his head was jerking backward. Rodney, pulled his hand back to his side. He wiped the blood from the side of his hand. Christopher, cleaned his nose, then lowered his head in between his legs.

Rodney, sat inside the parking lot of the hotel. He waited for a few hours until Dooski, pulled out and took off. Rodney, let a few cars get in between them and took off in pursuit of Dooski,

Several hours later he was back in front of the familiar building watching Dooski, move around and talk to his connect while his people hid the drugs in the trunk of the car. Dooski, walked down the block to kill some time. Rodney, tapped Christopher, on the shoulder.

"Go steal that car, drive it around the block, and wait for me."

"Now?" Christopher, asked unsure.

"Yeah nigga get the fuck out." Rodney, frowned at him. Christopher, walked across the street, got in the car, hot wired it in two seconds flat, and pulled off. Rodney, watched as he drove the car off. He waited for Dooski, to come back to the building.

Dooski, came up the block until he got to the front of the building. He looked around for the car, threw his soda on the ground, and ran into the building. Two minutes later five Spanish guys along with Dooski, came out the building looking around baffled. Frustration covered Dooski's, face, he walked around a few feet and looked at the guy. They started arguing and pointing in each other face. A fat man with a long pony tail hobbled back into the building and Dooski, and everyone else followed him. Rodney, started up his car and pulled off.

Rodney, found Christopher, sitting in the car. He hopped out of his car, broke into the trunk, took the drugs, put them in his trunk, and pulled off. Christopher, looked at him.

"How much is it?"

"I don't know, but I need you." He drove at a normal speed while looking in the rearview mirror. He drove and kept driving until his phone vibrated against his leg. He looked at the number. "Yo, I need you to get up with your Rochester, connect and tell him that you need two bricks." Rodney, looked over at Christopher,

"I can do that."

"You got to do that." He looked at him. "Then we can be partners." He thought about his next words before speaking them. "I treat you rough only to toughen you up. I can't have no soft ass nigga watching my back." He looked at him and remained silent until he dropped him off. He drove to the storage and switched back into his car.

Twenty minutes later he was at the park talking to Pookie,

"Yo, Pookie, I don't know how to say this, but I saw the nigga Christopher, over there copping work from those Rochester, niggas. He's probably the one pushing his own shit out here in the park."

"How do you know?"

"I saw him when I was over that way with one of my bitches." Pookie, looked at him and stared ahead.

"When will he be there again?"

"How do I know?" Rodney, looked at him seriously. "Yo, I got to go." He pulled his phone out of his pocket answered it, shook Pookie's, hand, and walked over to his Accura.

Twenty minutes later he was at Tasha's, house fucking her hard from the back. He banged her head into the pillow. He spread her ass cheeks far as they could go and stuck his finger in her anal cavity. He fucked her violently his intentions were to fuck her loyalty out of her. He lied to her and promised her shit that was only meant to sound good and keep her on his side.

When he finished her held her close to his body. He whispered sweet lies into her earlobes. He caressed her body, held her tight, and did the unthinkable. He kissed her in the mouth. He wanted to give her the impression that he was becoming soft on her. He wanted her to think that he was falling in love. He kissed her again, this time it was a deep and passionately kiss that stole her breath.

She smiled at him delicately and looked into his eyes revealing portions of love. He looked at her and returned her loving gaze. He turned to leave the house.

"Are you coming back?"

"I don't know." He made a face like it hurt him to not be able to be with her. She looked at him understanding his position.

He left the house, got into his car, and drove home. He sat in his house until night fell upon the street. He got in his car and drove over and picked up his Audi. He called Christopher, and told him where to meet him.

Christopher, stood at the corner waiting for Rodney, who circled around the block five times making sure Christopher, wasn't being followed by Loop, or Pookie, Rodney, pulled up on his and let him in the car. He pulled off soon as his butt touched the seat. Rodney, drove him over to the street where his Rochester, connect had a spot. He handed him the money and looked at him while his eyes widened with shock while he view the money. He looked at Rodney,

"Yo, once you get that give me one and you take the other one. That's your cut." He stared straight ahead. He waited in the car until Christopher, returned. "You got it?"

"Hell yeah." Christopher, said excited about coming up over night. He finally had become a certified brick layer. Now all of his dreams were coming true. All he had to do now was keep mixing his own drugs up in the bunch with Pookie's, drugs and he would be paid like a mutha fucka. He smiled at his thoughts and drifted off into his mind envisioning a future lifestyle filled with big booty bitches and street fame.

Rodney, drove Christopher, home. He made sure to be seen in all the exclusive areas. He wanted people to see his new car. The baige Audi, with limo tints, so dark you can't see in, but he could see out. He dropped Christopher, off in front of his house and pulled away.

He drove the Audi back to the storage, stashed it, and jumped in his Accura Legend. He backed up and drove until he was parked in front of his house. He got out the car and went into the house. He moved quietly around his bedroom. He unlocked his safe, added the other brick to the twelve that he had stolen, and the two he brought from Dooski, before following him to his connect. He looked at the fifteen bricks and over at the money in his safe. He had nineteen thousand dollars in cash.

Rodney's, phone vibrated against his leg. He pulled it out and checked the number. He looked at it. It was an unfamiliar number with a 212 area code. He answered it.

"Yo B, niggas is trying to kill me!" He was breathing heavy like he had been running. "Yo, shit went haywire. Niggas think that I got on some shit."

"Where are you?"

"I'm in the city B!"

"Where is Samantha?"

"Fuck that bitch B, niggas is after me." Fear took over his voice. "Niggas want me dead. I'm fucking broke. All man this shit is fucked up!" He yelled over the phone.

"Get back here and I got you." Rodney, assured him.

"B, I don't have shit I'm twisted." His voice broke down in defeat.

"Yo, I'm going to wire you some money, hop on a plane, and I got you." Rodney, hung up the phone and went to Western union.

The next time Rodney, walked in his front door it was two o'clock in the morning. He walked upstairs and laid across his bed and fell into a deep sleep.

His mind drifted off into the same dream that he had been having all along. He couldn't make sense of it. All he saw was faces, heard shots, a few screams, then saw himself fucking a girl who he didn't know. He rolled around inside his bed barely sleeping. He sat up and looked around. He was alone. He got out the bed and took a shower attempting to lessen the stress that he was feeling. It had to be stressed how else could he explain the feeling of paranoia while he slept?

Rodney, checked his phone and saw Tiffany's, number. He called her back.

"Yo,"

"My brother wants to see you again." She spoke seductively.

"I'm on my way." He hung up the phone and made his way down to his car. He drove over to her side of town and stopped in front of her house.

He stepped out the car and walked up on the porch. He knocked at the door. Tiffany, answered it in a tight fitting shirt that looked like it could of belonged to a sailor. She even wore a white sailor's hat. He stared at her, felt blood gushing downward racing for his groin area. The bulge in his pants stuck out and aimed outward in Tiffany's, direction.

"I was just about to get dressed." She pulled on a pair of sweat pants. He watched her wiggled her body around in the clothes. Boonie, pulled up with his music blasting. "What did I tell you about that disrespectful shit?" She looked at her brother angrily.

"Yo my bad." He kissed his sister on the cheek and handed her a few hundred dollars.

"This doesn't buy me." She put the money in her pocket.

"No, but it makes me feel better knowing that you have it." Boonie, looked at his sister than walked over to Rodney, He handed him his money.

"This is a half of joint. I'm going to be away for a couple of days and that should hold you over." Rodney, handed him the drugs. "You can give me the rest later." The two boys shook hands and parted ways.

"What about me?" Tiffany, asked looking at him.

"I'm wrapped up right now, but I got you the first chance I get." He backed away and moved out her front door. He pulled off until he was at his spot giving Darius, and Freddie, a half of a brick to split. He gave them the price, left the spot, and ended up at home looking in the auto trader staring at his Audi, the one he put up for sale soon as he had the dream about screaming, funny faces, gun shots, and fucking a strange girl. He got in his bed and fell asleep.

When he woke up he was still tired, though he wanted to get up, his body refused to compromise. When he woke up it was two days later. He got up, showered, get dressed, and checked his phone for missed calls. He saw Tasha's, number five times in a row. He dialed the number back.

"Dooski, is here." She said soon as he answered the phone.

"Let me talk to him." He looked at his face in the mirror.

"What's up B? I'm here." His words sounded fake and forced.

"I got you like you had me when we were younger." Rodney, lied.

"Alright B, that's real." He laughed and made a statement about getting it on with Tasha,

"That's my broad chill out and take it easy." Rodney, said for no other reason other than saying it.

"I'm fucking around B, you know how I be." He laughed then hung up the phone. Rodney, laid down in his bed and thought about his next move. He saw himself in the near future counting three hundred thousand dollars. He got up and went to his safe and pulled out all of his money. All nineteen thousand dollars of it and counted it. He kept looking at it. He pulled out the cocaine and lost himself in his mind as he imagined all of the cocaine sold and the money piled up.

Twenty minutes later he was riding up to Tasha's, house. He walked into the house. Upon seeing him Dooski, sprang up off the couch and shook his hand. He handed Dooski, two thousand dollars.

"I will hook you up with some more after I make a few moves. That's just to keep you use to the feel of money." Dooski, looked unsatisfied with the money. Rodney, watched his reaction closely. He looked in his pupils and didn't break his stare until he observed all the emotions in his face. He saw the jealousy, the anger, the resentment, and the greed along with the willingness to get rid of him in the process of taking over his enterprise and for unlimited access to Tasha's, pretty ass.

"Good looking B, I need that, but yo I need some coke." He looked over at Tasha, "I need to make my own moves." He strutted around like he was a king.

"Yeah, but first we got to get you a place to rest your head." He watched as disappointment formed in Dooski's, face.

"I'm saying B, I could stay here." Tasha, looked over at Rodney, and shook her head no. Dooski, caught her head shaking through the corner of his eye. He frowned and walked out the house. "Take me to a room." He said on his way out the door. Rodney, watched Dooski, climb into his car then he walked over to Tasha,

"Listen I want you to allow this nigga to get close to you, get up into his mind, and tell me every thought running around in his mind." He grabbed her and kissed her and dug his tongue around her mouth. She held him close to her and embraced him tighter when he tried to walk away.

"I miss you." Her eyes displayed every drop of emotion inside of her body.

"I like to hear that." He said referring to her falling deep into his trap. He raised his hand up her shirt and fondled her breast. He focused his gaze on her eyes and watched the twinkle sparkle in them. Love spiraled around her face as she looked back at Rodney, She reached down and massaged his penis through his pants. "We can't do that now."

"Make it quick." He closed his eyes and shook his head side to side. When he opened his eyes he was staring at the wall. He looked down toward the ground where Tasha, kneeled on her knees, untangled his pants, and pulled out his penis. The area inside her mouth warmed up like a pussy on the verge of heating up. Her lips formed circles around his penis, slid up, and touched the base of his penis. She wiggled her head around and pulled her head back slowly and then forward slowly dragging her tongue against the bottom of his shaft. His eyes darted toward the front door which was still open. He looked at Dooski, sitting in his car playing with radio.

"Rodney, will you fuck me please?" Her words came out slurping and smacking catching the saliva inside her mouth. "Mmm." Soft moans escaped her mouths she grabbed hold of his hips and moved her face into and away from his groin. "Please Rodney," More slurping and smacking accompanied the sound of her talking with her mouth full.

"That's what you want?" Rodney, maintained his emotions. He had to stay in control regardless how powerful her jaws were as they pulled the meat of his penis into her mouth. He held her head in place and humped into her face. She moved her head in tune with his movement. Every time he pulled back her mouth came backward. When he thrust her mouth came forward moving up his dick nice and smooth.

Before long Rodney, was hard as he could get. He looked at Tasha, with her hand down in front of her panties playing with her clit. Rodney, pulled her up and took her to the couch. He laid her down on the couch and pushed her legs up to her shoulders. He reached around his pocket for a condom. He felt the material of the condom, pulled it out, and ripped it open.

His dick slid into her with no resistance, her juices lubed her pussy, and made it easy for him to ease into her. Rodney, mowed away at her pussy like a lawn mower cutting through patches of unkempt grass. He didn't have a style, a pattern, a technique, all he had was the urge to get some pussy. He banged away at her filling her up with all of his penis. He held her in place, she bucked her hips, spread her legs wider only to have them pushed further toward the back of the couch.

Ten minutes later Rodney, was moving faster, he held his bottom lips with his top teeth and humped harder. He moaned out soft moans that sounded like painful grunts. He pushed into her and kept pushing until his stomach felt relieved. He slowed down, got off her, and pulled his jeans up. He stepped away from Tasha, she lifted up and stared at him.

"Bye." She looked at him with so much emotion that it caused him to smile and contemplate fucking her again.

"Bye, girl." He kissed her in the mouth. He looked down at her naked form the waist down. He walked away and left the house. He jumped in his car and pulled off. He drove until he was a motel. He paid for the room, gave Dooski, the room key, and got back into his car and went home.

His phone vibrated, he reached into his pocket, and pulled it out. It was Ebony, he pushed it back into his pocket and drove until he was home. He got into the shower and washed his body. He got dressed and sat down on his bed then dialed a few numbers.

"Hey baby daddy." She said playfully.

"What?" He asked wondering what the hell she was talking about."

"Syke I was with my cousin and I heard her say that and I thought it was cute."

"Oh."

"I think that it's corny when she does it, but I wanted to see how you would act to it."

"I would say hey baby momma." He smiled at himself while he looked in the mirror.

"What are you doing?"

"Why?"

"I want to spend some time with you tonight." Her words reeked with truth. Rodney, looked at his face and turned his head side to side checking his face.

"I will come and get you later."

"Why?"

"I need time to think and sort some shit out."

"I can be there with you while you think." She was disappointed.

"No you will only distract me."

"Alright." She finally agreed to hang up.

Rodney, lay in his bed thinking about his next move. He was fucking Tiffany, Tasha, and Ebony, and all three of them had some good pussy. No matter how many times he fucked them he would fuck like it was his first time getting introduced into the sweetness of good pussy. He didn't mind getting all of their attention, but realistically he didn't know how effective his sex would be. If he fucked all day, everyday.

His mind raced forward thinking into the future where he was spending time with the girls getting them attached to him and his personality instead of his dick and money. He figured out away to save up his sex and distribute it out evenly with all three girls and still maintain a hold on them.

He came up with a plan to use the next four months to build up his money and establish his spots. He would use this time to spend a week with each girl and get further into their minds and hearts.

Rodney, spent the first week with Ebony, he walked her around the art museum. He held her hand. He listened as she pointed out paintings and explained the artist's life and struggle. He pretended to listen and care. They talked and fed each other. He took her home and spent time with her in her bedroom watching cheesy movies and listening to her talk.

The second week he spent with Tiffany, all she wanted to do was smoke weed and sit on her front porch and watch what everyone else was doing. She talked about her husband, asked Rodney, why would he do what he did, and asked him how does it feel for a man when he's in love. He looked at her and shook his head then looked away.

She asked questions and kissed him and he kissed her back. They kissed and kept kissing more often until he was tired of kissing all the got damn time, but it was all part of his overall goal and he had to keep his plan in order.

The third week he spent with Tasha, she was the most fun to him. She was feminine, everything about her was womanly. The way she moved, the way she talked, the way she attempted to seduce him. The thing he like the most about her was her realness. She kept it real, explained her life, talked about her pain, and told him how important he made her feel. She told him about being a stupid and weak bitch who didn't know shit until she got turned out on the street. Her words rung true and they touched his heart because they were close to his own reality except he didn't suck dick, smoke crack, or do most of the shit she did.

She held his arms around her and leaned her head against his chest as she talked. She told him about the first nigga that she ever loved or at least thought that she loved. She told him about her mother and uncle. Her uncle raped her and when she told her mother she beat her for lying on her brother. She broke down told him her entire life story. The interesting part about the whole thing was that she was able to hold his attention.

She asked him questions that he answered with nods, head shakes, shoulder shrugs, and silence. He looked at her and thought about how hard it must have been for her. He listened as she told about getting evicted after she couldn't pay her rent. Then she told him about being broke and fucking damn near all the little boys in the hood for a blast of cocaine. Tears of shame fell from her eyes. She told him about her educational background and how she now had the strength to be strong since meeting him. He smiled at her words. When it came time to leave he didn't budge he lay there holding onto her.

Rodney, continued his routine while selling out all of his drugs, finding a new connect, and getting his money in order. After all the drugs were sold he had three hundred and forty eight thousand dollars. He took out two hundred thousand to flip and stashed the rest in a new hiding place.

Ebony, got a job at the hospital working as a nurse. Tiffany, sat on her ass looking pretty, getting money from Boonie, and her husband when he stopped by and fucked her. Tasha, went to work writing for a local newspaper. She became full of life and started feeling good about being alive.

Rodney, turned seventeen and didn't bother celebrating his birthday. To him it was just another day. Ebony, and Janet, baked him a cake, sung happy birthday, and took pictures of him all of which had him pulling his fitted cap over his face.

"Boy stop being corny." Ebony, said aiming the camera at him.

"I don't do pictures." He stood up. "I'll be right back." He ran upstairs and got something out of his closet. He came back down stairs and handed his mother and Ebony, both a pair of diamond earrings.

"How are you buying people stuff on your birthday?"

"I can." He walked over to the table and ate a piece of cake.

Later that night Rodney, lay in bed next to Ebony, who lay flat on her back exhausted from being fucked into a noiseless sleep. Rodney, lay in bed looking up at the ceiling wondering what Tasha, was doing?

His phone vibrated in his pocket and rattled against the floor. He got out the bed and picked up his pants. He pulled his phone out and checked the number. It was Tasha, he dialed the number back.

"Hello." He spoke softly.

"Are you asleep?" Her voice was weak and timid.

"Why?" He asked.

"I'm sort of lonely and I wanted you to come over here." Tasha, spoke into the phone sincerely.

"Here I come." He looked at Ebony, got dressed, and left the house. He got into his car and drove around to the park, he had to do it, something inside of him lured him in that direction.

He rolled pass the park and saw Christopher, leaning over the driver's side window of an undercover narcotics car. He looked around staring backward peeking over his shoulder. He shook his head and stared at the people and backed away from the car. Rodney, felt a tight feeling gripping at his stomach.

He made a u-turn and went home, dressed in all black, especially the hooded sweater, and got his pistol. He parked his car a few blocks away from his house and walked back over to the park.

Forty minutes later Christopher, was walking and looking over his shoulder. He paused before taking a few steps. Rodney, walked behind while pulling his hooded sweat shirt over his head. He moved swiftly increasing his pace until a car pulled up in front of him. Rodney, slowed down. Loop, came out the passenger side aiming a pistol. The first shot caused him to run in the direction that Rodney, was in. Rodney, backed up and hid in the shadows as gunshots fired. He saw Loop, running after him shooting wildly, but not really aiming at him. It was that or either he was just a lousy fucking shot.

Two more men emerged out of the car running after Christopher, he ran and shook them. He ran around the park, hid in some bushes, and ran out when the coast was clear. He ran across the street, into a back yard, and through another one until he was walking down the ally looking over his shoulder.

Rodney, moved quickly following each of Christopher's, moves until he walked through a yard that led him into the ally. Rodney, walked out of the shadows.

"Oh shit you scared me." Christopher, gripped his heart through his chest. "Damn Rodney, these niggas are trying to kill me. They know about our deal. You got to help me." He spoke softly afraid that someone would hear him. He looked around then back to face Rodney, he saw the barrel of the gun, felt the burn in his chest, then his neck, and finally it stopped hurting when he took his last breath.

Rodney, walked out of the ally looking around while moving along the street. He went home, showered, got dressed, and went to get rid of the gun.

Shortly after doing what he had to do to secure himself. He wound up naked in bed with Tasha, He lay on his back watching her head bob up and down in his lap moving faster than a comet racing toward the earth, any other time cum would have shot out of him, but he was thinking of a way to make someone else look guilty and eventually get sentence for the crime of killing Christopher, He also thought about where the hell was Christopher, keeping his money at? Tasha, sucked, slurped, stroked, jerked, and tasted pre-cum that dabbled against her tongue.

She climbed on top of his thighs and waited for him to put the condom on. He slipped it on and let her ride him. She bounced her ass around dancing on top of his dick. He reached up and squeezed her nipples. They fucked for two hours she came the most. Rodney, came once. He smiled at her and laughed at her body as it lay trembling and curled up in a fetal position. She had her hands in between her thighs holding her legs. Sweat trickled down the side of her face while she rocked side to side.

He rubbed her back and kissed the back of her neck. She rocked on her side not answering any of his questions. She just rocked, stared ahead at blank space, and breathed slowly regaining her breath. She was in love and it showed in her face and ran down her legs in puddles, after exploding out of her coochie lips.

Rodney, got up and got dressed. He kissed her all over her face, neck, and breast. He prepared to leave.

"Can you stay the night with me?"

"Alright." He laid back down and held her until the morning light came creeping inside the bedroom window. He got up, put his clothes on, kissed her, and left. When he got home Ebony, had already gone to work. Janet, gave him the message that she left for him. He listened to it then went upstairs to his bedroom. He looked in his closet prepared to check his safe. He shook his head as he remembered that he had moved it to the other house. He walked over to one of his sneaker boxes and counted out ten thousand dollars which he kept on hand just in case. He put the money back in the shoe box. He pulled out the wad of cash that was in his pocket and looked at it until his mind had envisioned that he was holding onto fifty thousand dollars.

He pocketed the money, got in the shower, put the same clothes back on, and drove over to the park to investigate what was happening. He saw Pookie, bend over the hood of a police car. He parked his car and stepped out and listened to the police harass him, Loop, and the rest of his crew.

"So you kill poor old little Christopher?" the white cop said looking at Pookie,

"Killing a little kid Pookie, that's low even for a no good piece of shit like you." A fat cop said staring at him.

"You killed that boy, had him out setting people up." Pookie, stared back at the cop.

"Where is the murder weapon?" The white cop checked him, got to his nuts, and squeezed them hard as he could. "What the fuck did you say?" He asked leaning in close to him, whispering in his ear. "When I find that murder weapon your ass is going away for a long time, join Turtle, you piece of shit." The cop turned to face Loop, "It was you. Did you shoot and kill that young boy?" He looked at Loop,

"If you referring to my dick I stay shooting it in white bitches mouths." Loop, smiled until the cop punched him in the face. "Book that son of a bitch for obstruction. Are you on parole?' He asked looking down at Loop,

"Maxed out bitch." Loop, laughed from the ground.

"Fuck him he'll just bail out." He kicked Loop, and walked away. The rest of the cops followed behind him. "You'll slip up and then we will arrest your ass. Have a good day monkey, I mean Pookie,"

"Fuck you." Loop, added while getting up from the ground.

"Shut the fuck up." The cop stomped down on him shoving him back into the ground.

"Rodney, pulled off after seeing what he needed to see. He learned what he wanted to know. The police were all over Loop, and Pookie, for the killing. His name never came up, well at least he didn't it did. He made up his mind that he was going to hang out in Tiffany's, neighborhood and sell drugs around her way.

Rodney, pulled up in front of Tiffany's, house, but kept going and pulled over six houses down. He got out the car and walked up on someone else's porch. He knocked on the door, not knowing who lived at the house. He only wanted to see who was at Tiffany's, house.

He watched her husband walk out the house. He yelled at her and shoved her as she tried to hold him.

"Tezo, why are you acting like that?" She wondered.

"Your always fucking up a good thing. I can't come home and love my wife. Your always fucking something up." He snatched away from her and jumped in his car and sped away.

"Tezo!" She yelled standing in the middle of the street. He r eyes welled up with tears. She looked around in pain and shame then walked back into her house. Rodney, got back in his car and backed up and parked in front of her house. He got out the car and knocked on the door.

"Who is it?"

"Rodney,"

"Who?" her voice gained some of its luster. She approached the door and looked at him. "Hey Rodney, how are you doing?" She came out on the porch and sat down with him. "Do you got some weed?" She looked at him.

"Not right now, but I can get you some." He looked at her.

"Good a bitch is stressed the fuck out." She looked at him and attempted to smile, but depression was in her chest and wouldn't ease up or give her a happy moment.

Rodney, got into his car and rode away to get some weed. He pulled up at the spot and ran in and talked to Darius,

"What's up?" He asked looking at Darius,

"What's good?"

"Give me some weed."

"How much?"

"Something for this broad."

"Here ." Darius, handed him a quarter ounce of weed. "That's that purple, guaranteed to get you some pussy." He smiled and nodded his head up and down. "I'm almost done too."

"I'm waiting on you to call." He shook his hand and pulled off. He stopped by the store and picked up some blunts. When he pulled up at Tiffany's, house Boonie, was sitting on the porch with his sister. They were smoking a blunt and talking to each other.

"What's up?" Boonie, yelled soon as Rodney, stepped out of the car.

"Chilling. What's up?" He responded to him. He walked up on the porch and handed Tiffany, the weed.

"Man she don't deserve no purple." Boonie, said reaching for the weed.

"Excuse you." She looked at her brother like he knew better than to get in her business.

Ten minutes after they rolled up a few blunts, lit one up and smoked blowing purple clouds in the air. Tezo, pulled up in front of the house and got out of his car. He walked up on the porch and looked at Tiffany, then Boonie, and finally at Rodney,

"Who is this?" Jealousy crowded his face.

"This is Rodney, one of Boonie's, friends." Tiffany, looked submissively at her husband. He walked into the house, she hurried inside after him. There was a brief shouting match, before he emerged out of the house. He slammed the door and got into his car and pulled off.

"Yo, we need to step this shit up right quick."

"I was just thinking the same thing." Boonie, inhaled more weed. "Yo, let me go check on my sister." He got up and attempted to open the door, but it was locked. He knocked on the door and called out his sister's name, but she didn't respond to him. He knocked on the door until it opened. Tiffany, walked away from the door quickly before Rodney, could see her face.

Twenty minutes later she was back on the porch smoking another blunt. Ten minutes later Boonie, was gone, an additional ten minutes Rodney, and Tiffany, were in the house on their way to her bedroom.

Tiffany, loved sucking dick or at least the thought of kissing her husband after gobbling down on another man's dick. She was on her knees moving her head quickly in between his legs. A skilled performer Tiffany, could do it without using any hands. She used a lot of neck movement, lip suction, jaw muscles, and the area in the back of her throat that relaxed as she inserted all of his penis.

Rodney, couldn't do anything, but get caught up in her movements. He felt her tugging at his body with force. She wanted to use his body to bang out the kinks that frustration gave her body. She didn't know any other way to dissolve her feelings, but through sex, and she sexed the hell out of Rodney, she sexed him harder and better than she ever loved her own husband. She didn't' mean to. It just happened like that. Her husband's dick was a little bit bigger than a thumb. Rodney's, was a little bit smaller than a foot long ruler. He touched places that she didn't know existed. He crushed her pussy, hurt it, beat the shit out of it, and treated it like it was made for punishment.

She couldn't love her husband like that because he couldn't last. A few moves and a couple of squeezes and he was coming all over her and falling asleep. He didn't do for her want Rodney, did for her, but still in all she loved Tezo, and wanted to have a family with him.

Rodney, shot his load in her filing her with the warm fluid of sperm. He got off her and listened to her. She pressed her finger to her lips and walked over to her bedroom window and looked out a tiny slit in the blinds.

"Tezo, is still out there." She looked at Rodney, with a look of satisfaction on her face. She was in her bedroom loving Rodney, while her husband rung the doorbell.

"What are you going to do?" He asked getting dressed.

"Nothing." She looked at the street from behind the blind. "He will leave in a minute." She waited for him to leave then walked with Rodney, to the door. He left her house and got into his car. He drove over to Tasha's, house. He got out and walked up to the front door. He knocked on the door although he had a key to the house.

No one answered Rodney, got back into his car and prepared to leave, but turned his car off. Tasha, came walking up the street. She noticed his car from the middle of the block and smiled wide and hard.

He stepped out of his car and walked to meet her half way down the block. He met up with her and grabbed her hand. He took her to his car and held the door open for her. Once he got in the car he pulled off.

"Where were you coming from?" He asked never taking his eyes off the road.

"I told you that I have a job now."

"I know, but why are you walking?"

"I don't have a car." She looked at him sensing he wasn't happy with her answer. "Plus I don't mind walking." Rodney, pulled over a few blocks away from where he had his Tahoe, stored. He got out the car.

"Where are you going?" Tasha, asked looking at him strangely.

"I'll meet you at your house." He shut the door and walked away from the car. Tasha, did as he asked and drove off in the car. Rodney, went and got his truck and drove over to Tasha's, house.

Rodney, knocked on the door while calling her name. She opened the door and stared at him.

"How did you get here?" She stood in his face, but backed up every time he took a step forward.

"I got another car." She sat down on the couch.

"Dooski, keeps calling here." She sounded annoyed.

"What is he talking about?" Rodney, stood up and pulled her down on top of him. Before kissing her meant nothing, it was part of the plan, but now it came natural, even felt good, and made his dick hard. He backed away from her emotionally.

"What's wrong?" She was on the go and approaching him. He stared at her. She focused on his eyes while he smiled at her.

"I don't know if I could afford to fall in love." He said still lying although he told a half truth.

"It comes natural you just have to go with the flow." She smiled at him. He looked at her and smiled her naïve appearance made her appear to be innocent although she was a far cry from it. Her vulnerability made his dick hard. He rubbed on each of her ass cheeks and felt the roundness that resembled the softness of bubbles.

"Let me up." Rodney, patted on her leg. He reached into his pocket and pulled out his phone. The number was new, he didn't recognize it, but he did answer it.

"Hello."

"Yo, B," Dooski, yelled over the phone. Rodney, knew what his call meant and hung up the phone. He drove over to Patty's house. She was a cute older broad who Dooski, met, ran game on, fooled into loving him, and moved in with her. He sold drugs to people in her neighborhood, sold it to her brothers, and whoever else wanted big eights and stuff that he could handle.

Thirty minutes later Rodney, pulled up in front of the house.

"Hi Rodney," A fast ass little girl who couldn't have been no more than fourteen said looking at him.

"What's up? He replied. "Where is Dooski?" He asked then walked pass her.

"I'll get him." She brushed up against him sticking her booty out and smushed it into his crotch. He looked at her. The look in her eyes belonged to her and every other hoe in the world. He smiled at her. "Dooski, Rodney, is here!" Her voice contained the willingness to fuck right there in front of whoever and that wasn't even the half of it.

"What's up my dude?" Dooski, pulled out a bag of money and handed it to Rodney,

"This two bricks." He took the money.

"Oh check out my new shit." Dooski, walked out the front door and pointed a red Lexus that was sitting across the street.

"Nice." Rodney, said without feeling.

"Oh that's you?" Dooski, said walking up to the truck.

"Yeah."

"When did you get this?"

"Not too long ago." Rodney, shook Dooski's, hand and got inside his truck and drove around waiting for someone to call him.

Rodney, saw some activity that caught his attention. He looked at the two boys. One with dreads and other was bald headed.

Rodney, rolled slowly by the two men posting up on the street corner. He looked at the chain that hung off the bald headed boy's neck, then over at the long haired boy's watch and bracelet. He pulled over and searched his glove compartment pretending to be looking for something.

His real motive was monitoring the boy's activity. One of the boy's spoke on a cell phone as if he owned the world. He moved around importantly, his eyes lit up watching people move in, and out, and around the house a few feet behind him.

The bald headed boy stood close to him posing like a body guard. Rodney, watched the boys then looked around the spot checking to see if there were any more people affiliated with them standing around on either side of the street.

One second later Boonie's, car pulled up. His music blasted the beat of some hardcore rap music. Rodney, watched Boonie, hop out of his car, slam the door, and strut over to where the two boys stood.

Boonie, held his own cell phone pressed against his ear. He looked around while he moved pass the two men and into the house. One second later the boy with the dread locks disappeared inside the house. The baldheaded one remained posted outside peering around as he looked up and down the street.

Rodney's, eyes followed his movement up and down the street. He took in the two little kids, a boy and a girl. They stood around holding the handle bars of their bicycles. He noticed an elderly lady bent over holding something against her leg, then reach down, and pick something up from the grass. He saw a car with both doors open, the trunk was up, and people were coming out of a house removing groceries from the car.

Rodney's, eyes went back over to the house. Boonie, came walking out the house carrying a bag. He looked around, tossed it in his front seat, got in his car, and pulled off. Rodney, pulled off slowly following Boonie,

When they reached the stop light Rodney, blew his horn. Boonie, looked in his rearview mirror, didn't recognize the truck, and reached for his pistol. Rodney, rolled his window down.

"Boonie, it's your man!" He waited to see if he recognized his voice.

"Rodney?" Boonie, looked out the window. He laughed then pulled over. Rodney, pulled up alongside him and rolled his other window down.

"What's up with you?" He looked at Boonie, "I saw you with those two cats and I pulled over thought you needed my help." He patted his gun that rested beneath his shirt.

"Them niggas need the help. They keep fucking up my money." Boonie, looked aggravated.

"It be like that sometimes." Rodney, laughed and pulled off. Boonie, blew his horn and pulled off in another direction.

Chapter 26
Stay scheming and looking hard

Rodney, sat in his house counting up all of his money. He counted six hundred and ten thousand dollars and exhaled deeply. He wanted more money and fast. He needed something to do with his money, but had the slightest idea as to what, but he had to do something with it. He thought about Ebony, and her life wondering was there something that she was into that he could put his money into. He wasn't sure he had to talk to her soon as he could. His phone vibrated against his leg. He reached for it and read the number.

Ten minutes later he was on the phone with Tiffany,

"Where is your brother?"

"I don't know somewhere." She said annoyed by something.

"Are you alright?" His eyes averted directly in the mirror going over every detail in his face. He watched his eye brow slant in when he frowned, looked at how his dimples caved in when he smiled, and admired his face structure while he listened to Tiffany, talk about Tezo,

"This nigga Tezo, is something else." She let out a strong sigh.

"Why, what did he do?" He didn't care, but he wanted to appear to be her friend for obvious reasons.

"He came over here today, packed all of his shit, and told me when I'm done playing with my new nigga he'll come home." Rodney, sat on the phone listening to her talk her mind. He didn't interrupt her, just listened. He looked over at the clock on his dresser and realized that forty minutes had passed by.

"Yo do you want to smoke some weed?' He asked soon as she paused from her point of view.

"I do, but I don't have any money, Boonie, was suppose to come by and drop something off to me, but I haven't seen him all day.

"Whose at your house?"

"Who lives here?" She answered unaware that her frustration was spilling into her conversation with Rodney,

"Excuse me."

"No, not like that." Laughter cooled her mood and softened her heart. She apologized. "It's not you, it's this nigga over here."

"He's there now?" Rodney, asked teasing her.

"You know what I mean." Her smile was visible through the phone.

"Well I'm coming over then." He hung up the phone. He stepped back from the mirror and walked out of the house.

He pulled up in front of Tiffany's, house. She came off the porch to meet him. He handed her the weed.

"Roll up. I'm about to make a quick run." He maintained a straight face while he lied in hers. He wasn't going to the store. He was going wherever Pookie's, Range Rover, went. This was the second time he saw Pookie, on this side of town and he wanted to know why.

"Hurry back." She gave him a seductive look. He nodded his head up and down then pulled off. He kept his distance while he trailed behind the man who he once hero worshipped until he was too old to be hero worshipping.

Rodney, pulled up behind three cars and watched Pookie, get out of his car, look around, and walk up the steps to a huge brick house. He knocked on the door and was instantly let inside the house. Rodney, sat around waiting for him to come back out. Three hours later Pookie, walked out the house looking around nervously. He got in his car and pulled off.

Rodney, got out of his car, and walked up on the porch. He looked at the name on the mail box, stored it to his memory, and hurried off the porch. He got in his car and pulled off. He was going to stop by and pay her a visit soon enough.

He pulled up in front of Tiffany's, house. She sat on the porch with a bright skin girl. She was than Tiffany, much shorter, and a little prettier. She carried most of her weight in her thighs. Rodney, looked at her as he approached the house.

"Don't tell me you smoked up all the weed." He said shaking his head side to side.

"Boy you was gone for like two days, but I save you some." She pulled out the weed and a few blunts. At least she was considerate he thought to himself.

"I was playing anyway I brought it for you."

"Why didn't you come right back?" She looked disappointed.

"People won't leave me alone." He sounded like a little kid who had gotten suspended for fighting in the cafeteria.

"Whatever." She laughed.

"I'm Mindy," the girl said looking all over Rodney, absorbing his facial features, the area behind his zipper, then over at the bulge in his front pocket. She looked at his other pocket and noticed another bulge at that point she made her mind up. "You not going to tell me your name?" Her eyes sparkled with interest.

"Mindy, bitch don't nobody want your fat ass." Tiffany, spoke up immediately dismissing her sister's attempt.

"I'm talking to him."

"Fire this up." She handed her sister a blunt and a lighter. A few minutes went by, the blunt burned, and went out. Another one was sparked up in its place. Rodney, pretended to smoke, but passed the blunt quickly as he got it.

"You're not even smoking for real." Mindy, looked at Rodney,

"I need a clear head I can't smoke all like that." He concentrated his eyes on hers.

"Do you got a girlfriend?" Rodney, looked at Mindy,

"Why?" He kept his focus on her.

"I'm just saying." She leaned over in her chair, rocked a little, and exaggerated her voice until it was sounding ghetto and broken down. "You could have me." She laughed then looked at him. "I'm saying I'm a big girl I go after what I want." Her approach was bold. Her life was in shambles, her use in his life wasn't needed, but her ass, soft thighs, and the way her pussy print pressed against the front of her jeans; made him consider wasting a couple of days out of his life fucking her until he satisfied his vanity.

"Mindy, chill!" Tiffany, spoke firmly giving her sister the impression that she had better let that man alone.

"Bitch aint you married?" Her sister faced Tiffany,

"Mindy," Tiffany, said her name with such force that her sister decided to let it go.

"Well I'm about to go." She stood up. "And will call you tomorrow." She walked off the porch. "Since you hating real hard today, with your jealous ass. You aint giving up no pussy, got it put up for Tezo," Mindy, looked at Rodney, smiled and walked away.

"Don't fuck my sister." Tiffany, waited for her to get out of hearing distance. She stood with her arms folded over her breasts. She stared at Rodney, seriously. "I mean it Rodney, anybody, but my sister." She stood in front of him waiting for him to agree with her and adopt her principals as his own.

"You do know it's a difference between fucking and making love." He smiled at her playfully. She didn't smile, budge, or find his attempt at humor amusing. "I won't fuck your sister." She stood up. "But if she was riding me technically she would be fucking me and."

"Shut up." She let out a short laugh and passed him the blunt.

Rodney, wound up in Tiffany's, house in the living room sprawled across the couch. He lay on his side as did she, but in front of him. One of her legs hung over his while they rocked against each other trying to push the other to a place of completion.

Rodney, slid his tongue up and down her neck. She enjoyed every minute of it. He sucked on her shoulder, rubbed on her breast, and gave her nipples a tight squeeze. He ran his hand smoothly over her belly. She ground her butt cheeks into his body. She reached behind her and pulled his dick out of her and massaged the tip of it. She continued to roll his tool around the palm of her hand.

He moved her around until her hairy mouth was lowering down over his face. He flickered his tongue moving it greedily around her clit, then delved his tongue inside her pussy, and licked over her sugary walls. He felt the tip of his dick slip in between her parted lips as they lay across each other sixty nine style.

She held his penis inside her hand and slowly licked the base of it, then inserted it in her mouth. He head bobbed up and down as she focused on the feat of swallowing him whole.

Her mouth relaxed, widened around him, and eased down his shaft slowly. She was careful not to gag herself. She moved until the end of his penis rested on her lips while the rest of it filled her mouth. She grabbed his balls and began rubbing roughly over them.

Rodney, moved his tongue around viciously creating whirlwinds of pleasure that tingled across her body. She pulled him out her mouth and nibbled on the head of his meaty member and toyed with his balls.

She shuddered and quivered as her juices slid down her thighs and stained his face. He didn't stop, he kept licking and sucking until her second dose of pussy juice dripped down into his mouth. He rolled her off of him and stood up over her. He grabbed his dick and aimed it at her mouth, but she turned around ready to receive him from the back.

One hour later Rodney, sat on the edge of the bed drying his face off with a towel. His phone vibrated in his pocket. He got his phone, looked at the number, and over at Tiffany, He got dressed.

"Yo, I have to bounce this is some important shit." He looked at her, smiled, and left her house smelling like two hours of adulterous sex.

Inside his truck he maneuvered around traffic wondering what the hell was so urgent. He drove over to Sissy's, house. He hopped out the truck, but got right back in it and pulled off. He drove down the street while searching his rearview mirror. He saw the police leading Sissy, Bernie, and Freddie, out the front door. He wasn't sure, but it looked like Freddie, was crying.

Rodney, turned the corner and ran a stop sign in the process of getting far away from the scene as possible. He drove to his house, grabbed is other two guns, took them next door to Terry's, house, and handed them to his old neighbor. He gave him three hundred dollars to hold a kilo of cocaine and two guns for him.

"Hold that for me until I come back for it." He looked at Terry, without smiling.

"Hell boy, bad as I needed some money I would have been holding this shit for you." He sipped on the can of beer he held onto.

"I'll be back." Rodney, jumped in his truck and drove over to Tasha's, house.

Chapter 27
You use to be my homie, you use to be my ace, now I got to empty out your safe

When he walked into her house she sat upright and smiled cheerfully. Her smiled disappeared when she saw the look on his face.

"What's wrong?"

Freddie, went to jail today." He looked over at her.

"Is he in big trouble or drug court trouble?" She asked looking at him.

"I'm not sure, but it look like he was crying."

"He was?" She looked around the phonebook and used the rest of the day researching lawyers to get Freddie, out of jail.

He made a few calls, dropped a few dollars, and paid a bail bondsman. He drove over to the spot and picked up Darius, then drove over to the lawyer's office to see if Freddie, was cooperating. The lawyer told them that Freddie, was scared, but willing to take his bumps and bruises.

Rodney, sat inside his truck waiting for Freddie, to get released from the jail house. Freddie, walked down the stairs to the building. He looked happy to be out of there. He walked across the parking lot. He searched for Rodney's, Accura, but didn't see it. He put his hand over his eyes and scanned the parking lot.

"Over here!" Darius, yelled from the passenger's window. Freddie, ran over to the truck and climbed in the backseat.

"Yo, they raided the spot today, bagged a nigga with seven grams." He shook his head in disbelief attempting to deny his fear. "Yo, they took most of my money." He looked at Rodney, waiting for his reaction.

"It happens, all we got to do is make sure you hold it down and keep your mouth shut." Rodney, looked at him seriously.

"Come on now." Freddie, looked offended.

"People do all sorts of shit when the pressure is on." Rodney, pulled off.

Later that night Rodney, gave Freddie, and Darius, nine ounces a piece, got back in his truck, and pulled off. He drove over to Ebony's, house.

He knocked on the front door. She answered it smiling and talking over her shoulder to her mother and father.

"Hey boy." She kissed him on the cheek, turned around, and went back into the house. He walked in behind her. "I was thinking more like you helping me pay for a brand new car." She looked at her mother and father.

"What's wrong with a use car Ebby?" Her mother asked.

"Ma," Her eyes went upward in disgust. "What if I put up like two or three thousand dollars?"

"And where would you get this money?" Her father asked getting in the conversation.

"Never mind forget it." She looked over at Rodney, and smiled. "Do you see how they treat me?" She shook her head side to side. "Are we still going out?" She looked at Rodney, who nodded his head up and down backing up her lie.

"Ready when you are." He stood up.

"Let me get my jacket." She walked away from her parents.

"We can talk some more when you come home." Her mother looked at her compassionately.

"Alright." She closed the door behind her. Rodney, climbed in the truck and started it up.

"Why didn't you ask me to buy you a car?" He looked straight ahead.

"It's not your responsibility."

"What?" He reached over and grabbed her arm. "Now Ebby, don't be taking your frustrations out on innocent people." He sounded like her father intentionally.

"I know right, but I'm mad because they brought my brother a car, a house, and paid for his wedding." She crossed her arms over her chest.

"If you want you can have this truck."

"This is something that a man would drive." She frowned up her face. "An Audi, a Nissan Altima, or something that would be cute for a girl to drive." She looked truly sad.

"How about a PT cruiser?" He asked playing with her.

"How about no." She rolled her eyes.

"I got you." He turned up his radio ending the conversation.

Two days later Rodney, brought two more cars. A black Escalade and a black Nissan Altima, for Ebony, He put her car in the shop and fixed it up for her while he stashed his new truck in his storage garage.

Two weeks later Rodney, was sitting in his Tahoe, when his phone rang.

"Hello."

"What are you doing?" Ebony, asked sucking her teeth.

"Still mad at your daddy?" He was being sarcastic and playing with her.

"A little bit." She let out a short sigh. "But that's not why I called you."

"Why did you call me?" His voice was filed with silliness.

"I need a ride home from work, truth be told I want to spend some time with you." She wanted to relieve some stress.

"When do you get off?"

"Now."

"Well here I come."

"Bye."

"Peace."

"Oh Rodney, stop being." He hung up on her before she could finish her sentence.

Ebony, walked out of the hospital and stood in front of the building waiting for Rodney, to pull up. He was having fun and watching her look for him. He blew the horn. She looked in the direction where the sound came from and saw Rodney, waving out the window signaling for her to come to him.

She smiled, covered her face to hide her happiness, and walked quickly across the street. Rodney, stepped out the car and opened his arms. She walked into them and buried her head into his chest.

"Thank you." He barely heard her due to her speaking softly into his chest.

"I gotta keep that good pussy in my life." He lowered his mouth and kissed her on top of the head. She heard his comment, but ignored it.

"Rodney," The way she said his name made him aware of her position in his life.

"Here." He handed the car keys to her. He got in and buckled his seatbelt.

"I can drive." She looked at him offended that he would assume otherwise.

"I know." He pulled on the seatbelt making sure it was secure.

"Whatever." She laughed and pulled off.

After riding around and blowing her horn to every damn person that she thought she knew she stopped by Dena's, house to show her friend her new car. Dena, stood in front of her house looking at the car. Her face revealed a secret disappointment. Rodney, liked her, was suppose to be her man, and that was supposed to be her mutha fucking car.

"Ebony, your car is cute." Dena, smiled concealing her true emotions. She walked around the car admiring it. "Hey Rodney," She said his name casually.

"What's up Dena?" He gave a weak wave.

One minute later they were pulling off from the curb and driving over to her parents house.

"Bye Dena," Ebony, called behind her and blew the horn.

"I'll see you at work tonight."

"I already did my shift this morning." Ebony, told her friend.

"Yo, take me to my truck." Rodney, looked at her.

"Why I want you to come by my parents house with me." She pleaded with him already knowing that he wasn't going with her.

"I have to handle something."

Ten minutes later Rodney, was climbing into his truck. He drove over to the house that he followed Pookie, too. He got out of the car and knocked on the door. No one answered, he knocked again, but paused, and leaned closer to the door. He heard music playing and wanted to make sure that's what he was listening to.

He went around to the back of the house. He wedged open a back window and crawled into the apartment. He landed on his feet in the kitchen. He walked through the house softly. He pulled out his gun and cocked it. He moved stealthy against the wall careful not to alert people if there was any sitting in the living room. He walked into the living room.

Music played on the stereo. He quietly snuck upstairs. He moved slowly doing his best not to cause the stairs to squeak underneath his feet. He got half way up the stairs, turned his head to the right, and saw a woman. Her back was to him. She stood in front of her mirror fully nude brushing hair, she flung her hair to the left, a little over her shoulder and brushed it. Rodney, looked at her and admired her ass, the roundness of her fluffy ass cheeks sat upright waiting to be squeezed and held tightly. Her legs were thick and meaty. The meatiest that he ever had seen on a woman. He saw her titties, round, juicy, and poking outward as he looked in the mirror.

Rodney, was lost in his own fantasy staring at the woman from behind until her phone rang. He moved down a couple of stairs to lower his head out of the way. She grabbed the phone.

"Hey pookie, how are you baby?" She laughed and giggled. "I'm looking forward to tonight too." She giggled and laughed some more before hanging up the phone.

Rodney, looked up over the railing and saw something that made him blink, he did a double take, and looked again. He saw in between her legs a short and stubby black ass penis with a brown tip. What the fuck? He thought as he backed away moving down the stairs.

"What type of shit is Pookie, on." He asked himself in disbelief as he left the house the same way he entered through the window, but not before unlocking three more windows.

Rodney, drove over to Tiffanys', house. Mindy, answered the door.

"Hey Rodney," She smiled from ear to ear. She looked at him staring at his dick through his pants.

"Mindy, who is it?" Tiffany, called out from the kitchen.

"It's your boo. I mean dude or the boy who you don't plan on fucking, but all up in my way." She said while staring deeply into his eyes.

"Move girl." Tiffany, pushed her sister aside. "Come in Rodney," She let him in.

"Yo, do you got one of those phones with the camera on it?"

" Yeah." She looked puzzled.

"Let me get that and I'll get you another one." She looked at him. "I'll bring you another one right back. I only need to take a picture." She handed him her phone. He smiled and turned to leave. He ran to his truck and pulled off.

Rodney, sat outside the house in the same spot until darkness covered the street. He sat in the truck a few more hours and waited for Pookie, to pull up. When Pookei, pulled up he got out of his Range Rover, looked around, and made his way to the house. The woman met him at the door, wrapped his arms around him, and they kissed each other.

Rodney, waited a few minutes before walking up into the yard and walking around to the back of the house. He looked around before climbing through the window. His feet touched the floor softly. He moved along the wall as he did earlier. He crept up the stairs and sat outside the bedroom door. He aimed the phone at the bed where Pookie, sat up across the bed. His shirt was rolled up and held underneath his chin, the woman was down in between his legs, with hers spread apart, her skirt was hiked above her waist, her lips were busy sucking his penis, while rapidly jerking her own fast as she could.

Rodney, positioned the phone until he had Pookie's, face, his dick in the woman's mouth, and the woman using her free hand to jerk her own dick. Once everything was in place he pressed the button. He frowned up his face watching someone who he looked up to get his pleasure from a man.

When Pookie, was hunched over the woman's back pumping hard as he could. Rodney, frowned up his nose and snapped picture after picture of what he saw taking place. He took more pictures of the person riding Pookie, and the two of them in various other positions. He backed away and snuck out the house the same way he snuck into it.

Rodney, got into his truck , and took the phone over to Ebony's, house. He had her download it to her computer and make copies of them.

"Rodney, why are you looking at stuff like this?" She asked fearful that she would lose her man to another man.

"You see two gay niggas. I see three hundred thousand dollars." He took the pictures, kissed her on the cheek, and left the house.

Three days later Rodney, pulled up at the park. He walked over to where Loop, and Pookie, sat. He sat down beside them.

"Savage," Loop, stuck his hand out and shook Rodney's,

"Loop," He shook his hand and turned to Pookie, "I need to holler at you it's about some real shit. Some real get money shit." His eyes lit up as he stared at Pookie,

"Make it quick." Pookie, said walking behind Rodney, They both climbed into the truck. Rodney, turned on the music.

"See my stereo?" Rodney, played with the radio wondering how he was going to lay it on him.

"What's up nigga I don't have all day?" Pookie's, tone was enough incentive for Rodney,

"This is what it is Faggot." Rodney, tossed a square envelope in his lap.

"What the fuck did you call me?" Pookie, was on the verge of being angry.

"Look at the fucking pictures." Pookie, took the pictures out of the envelope, turned ash gray, and damn near passed out.

"Who gave you this?"

"Don't matter, but three hundred thousand and four bricks will buy you all of those and the backup flicks." He looked at Pookie, "I was there all night and saw everything." Rodney, lied, but the look in Pookie's, eyes revealed that he didn't want anyone to know about that night.

"Who put you up to this?"

"Deal or no deal?"

"I was good to you."

"I'm better to me." He unlocked his door. "You can get a couple of days to decide what you want to do. Oh yeah Pookie, if something happens to me before you decide to pay, a few of these flicks will be sent up to Turtle, up north." He fanned a second set of the pictures around in his hand.

"You'll get your money, and you'll get the fuck out of town." Pookie, slammed his truck's door hard as he could.

Rodney, thought about Pookie, and almost felt a tinge of guilt, but drowned it out with the reality of remembering that he was too old to be hero worshipping another nigga, when he had the capabilities to make it happen for himself.

Rodney, pulled off and went home. He walked in the house and called Tasha,

"Hello."

"Hey Rodney,"

"What's up?" He asked feeling his penis stiffen in his pants.

"Nothing." She said cheerful and carefree.

"I'm coming over tonight?" He asked her.

"I don't know are you?"

"See you then."

Rodney, rode around until his phone vibrated inside his pocket. He pulled it out and read the number. He dialed it back.

"Hello." Rodney, said looking around the street watching his back.

"Where do you want the money dropped off at?"

"I can come and get it."

"I don't want to see your face." Pookie, sighed hard and loud.

"It's not personal its business." Rodney, said ready for whatever was due to him.

"For me it is, trust me on that. It's very fucking personal." The phone slammed down in Rodney's, ear. He smirked at the phone then placed it back in his pocket. He looked around and felt his waist for his gun, got in his car, and pulled off.

Rodney, rode over to the park and pulled up at the curb. He stepped out of his car. Before he could take a step forward Loop, approached him.

"What's up Rodney?" Disappointment seeped out of his eyes. "Whatever you did, you got Pookie, tight with you. He's ready to hurt you."

"I've been hurt before."

"Take my advice and run Rodney, don't look back." Loop, handed him the money and drugs then turned and walked away from him. Rodney, hopped in his car and drove home. He circled the block making sure no one followed him then he went in the house and called Tasha.

Chapter 28
Real niggas do real things, but treachery takes the crown from the King

Rodney, sat on the edge of his bed talking to Tasha, killing time. If someone was watching him they would assume that he was fucking Tasha, and probably bragging to her about what he had did. He stood in front of her taping stacks of money to her body. She stood patiently in front of him allowing him to stick money all of her body.

"Rodney, this is a lot of money." Nervousness made her feel uneasy. She stared at him wondering what he was up to.

"Trust me and do like I say and everything will go smooth." He planted a fat kiss on her lips. "When you get home call me." She kissed him again and pressed her lips into his mouth like it would be the last time that they would ever see each other again.

Soon as she left out the front door Rodney, snuck out the backdoor using the night as a shield. He ran through a few yards and hopped a few fences, and ran until he was in the backseat of a taxi cab on his way to Tasha's,

He met Tasha, at her house, snuck out, and used more of his tactics until he reached his real stash house. He went inside and put the money up with the rest of his money then vanished in the night.

Back at the house next door to Terry, Rodney, sat on the couch waiting for Dooski, to call, but he was taking too long. Rodney, called him.

"Hello."

"Yup." Antonette's, fast ass said speaking sassily into the phone.

"Let me talk to Dooski,"

"I will give you all of this pussy you just don't know."

"What?"

"You heard me." There was a rustling sound then Dooski, got on the phone.

"What's up?"

"What are you up to?"

"I was just about to call you." Dooski, said with excitement in his voice.

"I'll be there." Rodney, hung up the phone, got in his truck, and pressed his foot into the gas pedal and didn't stop pressing it until he was at Dooski's, house.

When he walked into the house Dooski, wasn't there. No one was except for Antonette, she lay sprawled across the couch watching television.

"Dooski, said he will be right back. He had to run and grab something." Rodney's, eyes flinched. He hated waiting for people, he didn't like moving in situations that he didn't' plan. He sat down and waited. He needed Dooski, and a couple more people to run interference by fighting with Pookie, while he made a few more moves and sold his drugs and planned his next move.

Rodney, sat down on the arm of the couch. Antonette, stared at him licking her lips. She opened her legs and rubbed her hands in between her legs.

"Rodney, look." She pulled her shorts to the side revealing two puffy pussy lips, a single slit, and a patch of nappy pubic hair. Rodney's, dick stiffened.

"How old are you?"

"Grown." She looked at him. The look in her eyes asked for permission to take off her clothes.

"Really."

Fifteen." Rodney, walked over to her, unzipped his pants, and pulled out his dick through the zipper of his pants.

"Get that." He commanded like the word no wasn't an option. She lifted up and opened her mouth. The head of his dick pierced through her lips, danced against her tongue, and dangled in her mouth. She licked all over it and grabbed his balls like he told her too. She opened her mouth to insert more meat into her mouth and spilled a ton of slob. She pulled back in a long stride and slid all the way up his dick until she gagged. She backed up and coughed, wiped her mouth, and went right back to it.

Rodney, grabbed her face and pulled it feverishly into his lap. She gagged, but didn't let up. Rodney, was a baller and she wasn't about to fuck up her chance to get one. If he wanted his dick sucked hard and nasty well then she was going to step up to the plate and allow him to punish her face.

Rodney, liked Antonette, not her personality, but her whorish ass nature. He used his hand to ram her face into his lap. He held the sides of her face with both hands, while she held each of his ass cheeks in her hands pulling him forward.

The house was empty and all that could be heard was the sound of something being sucked really hard. Rodney, pulled out his condom, slid it on, and turned her over. He slipped inside of her and fucked her ruthlessly. Her moans could have been mistaken for cries and his lovemaking could have passed as a violent assault. He held her shoulders and pulled her down into him so hard that he was grunting and cursing her out under his breath.

"Bitch you want to play games, you not going to be able to use this pussy for the rest of this week, is you bitch? Huh?" He sounded angry while he spoke. He mashed into her fifteen year old body doing his best to damage her insides.

"Oh..oh..oh!" She moaned sinking deeper into the couch from the force that Rodney, applied while fucking her. She tried to grab his waist and keep him from digging to deep in her. "You're hurting me." She whispered in his ear and found out that he didn't give a fuck. He pumped on her harder. He kept pumping until he shot a load into the condom.

When he lifted up off of her, she rolled of the couch, grabbed her clothes, and tried to flee. Rodney, grabbed her and pressed her into the wall. Her titties touched the wall while her head hung backward. Rodney, had her hair bunched up in his hand and sucking on her neck.

"Rodney, my mother is coming home." She pulled her pants up and snapped them shut. Rodney, fucked her like she had never been done in her life, ever."Rodney, please." Her eyes begged for mercy. "I want to stop now. I won't play with you no more." She looked at him seriously. The sound of Dooski, made Rodney, let go of her. She ran upstairs. Rodney, turned and walked up to Dooski,

"What's up B?" Dooski, shook his hand.

"Chilling."

"Yo, I got some bitches in the car, bad bitches, come on B," Dooski, turned around and jogged down the steps. Rodney, followed him out to the car. Rodney, got in the car. Two girls were sitting in the backseat smiling.

"What's up?" Rodney, looked at the girls. He didn't want either of them. He just wanted to get Dooski ,wrapped up in his plan.

"Dooski, my mother wants you." Antonette, stood in the doorway.

"Her mother?" Rodney, looked at him. "How old is that girl?"

"Fourteen probably fifteen, but more like fourteen." Dooski, got out the car. One second later Rodney, stepped out the car. A mini- van turned the corner and shots rang out. Rodney, ran only to be shot in the leg. He stumbled, got up, and backed up seeking shelter. He grabbed his pistol and aimed at the van and shot. He shot out the front windshield, he ran toward the house, but saw Dooski, aiming a pistol at him. The first bullet hit his stomach, the second one hit his thigh. Rodney, turned and ran for his car, but bullets tore his truck up, and flattened his tires.

Scared for his life Rodney, ran. Dooski, chased behind him shooting. Rodney, felt a bullet hit his back. That didn't' stop him from running he ran until he outran his attackers. When he looked behind him he was alone, but when he looked down at his body he was bloody, so fucking bloody, too damn bloody he passed out.

Chapter 29
Touch one of mine and I will destroy everything you love; play the game nigga

Rodney, lay face down on the ground, blood ran from underneath his body.

"Yo, kid be strong the ambulance is on the way." A dark skin kid no more fourteen said. He stood over Rodney, he stood down and searched Rodney's, pockets. He felt a wad of cash and took it out of the man's pocket.

"Naji!" His sister's friend said while watching him steal from a dying man. The boy ignored her and reached down and picked up the gun that lay a few feet away from the fallen boy's hand. Naji, stuck the gun in his pocket and took it in Cocoa's, house.

Ten minutes later the ambulance arrived. The workers went directly into action. They placed him on a gurney, then pushed him in the back of the ambulance, and sped away.

Rodney, lost a lot of blood and needed a blood transfusion. He underwent five hours of surgery and lay in ICU waiting to recuperate. Days went by without him waking up. He was oblivious to how many times Ebony, was there by his side crying her eyes out, hugging onto his body, and praying that he would wake up.

Janet, came to see him once and never came back. Her heart wasn't strong enough to watch her only child lay dying in a hospital one week before his eighteenth birthday. She left the hospital tempted to calm her nerves with a few cheap beers, but didn't.

Rodney, lay in bed appearing to be dead, his body lay unable to move, yet his mind raced rapidly. He burned with vengeance, a desire so urgent and powerful it gave him a purpose to live. He had the will to survive. He ached with pain from being shot, but felt worst about being caught sleeping.

His mind rolled over and over, he saw the young girl. He heard the gunshots, and felt the same burn. Then his dream replayed in his mind, sex with a strange woman, gunshots, and screams. He knew it was coming, but failed to prepare for it, had ample time to prevent it from catching him, yet he ignored his dream. Now he lay in bed cursed for his negligence.

He saw a kid, a young dark skin boy sitting at his bedside. He tried to focus on his facial features, he needed to remember him, was he sent here to finish the job, or was he Ebony's, brother or what he didn't know, hell he didn't know if the boy was really there or if he was suffering from delusion.

Three weeks later Rodney, woke up. His eyes blinked as he looked around. He sat up pulling the tubes out of his body. He winced at the pain associated with being shot, recuperation, and pulling the needles and other devices out of your skin. Rodney, sat up in time to see the dark skin boy walking into his room. Instinctively Rodney, reached for his gun, but it wasn't there. He was naked covered by a thin hospital gown. He sat up bracing himself to be hit again.

"Yo, my name is Naji, I found you shot up outside my people's house." He looked at Rodney, and maintained his gaze on him. "I heard a lot of gunshots, then I saw you stumbling around the corner, and I knew it was on." He looked at Rodney,

Rodney, stared at the young boy wondering what angle he was coming from. He didn't speak just listened.

"Yo, I took you money and your gun. I didn't want you to get caught with it." He looked at Rodney, "I didn't count it or nothing." Rodney, looked at his face and realized that the boy wasn't a threat and rose to silence him.

"Good looking out." He looked away embarrassed that he was caught slipping. He looked at the boy.

"I got your gun in the car if you need it."

"You got a car?"

"No, but my brother do. He's at work I just took his car."

"How old are you?"

"I'm fourteen, but I'm almost fifteen. I put that work in." Rodney, smiled sincerely looking at the young boy.

"Yo, I'm about to get the fuck out of here." He sat up in the bed, felt tremendous pain, and had to brace himself by holding onto the side of the bed. "Yo, I need your help, I got something for you when I get this situated."

"Yo, I'm a gangster I do this out of love." Rodney, recognized the hunger and drive glowing inside the younger boy's face. He smiled at him. Rodney, looked around for his clothes, but didn't 'find them . The nurses threw them in the garbage they were torn to shreds and extremely bloody. Rodney, looked at the boy. "I can go get something out of my brother's closet."

"Fuck that we don't got time." Rodney, tied another hospital gown around the back of his body to cover his ass. He walked away moving slowly as he moved out the hospital room. Naji, walked slowly with him.

"Hey excuse me sir you need to be in bed." A concerned white woman stared at Rodney, He ignored her and kept walking. Naji, was in the process of helping Rodney, into the elevator when the nurse picked up the phone and dialed some numbers.

Ten minutes later they were in the front of the lobby moving along the corridor.

"Rodney," Dena, called out to him. She walked behind him. "You have to sign out, but I wouldn't recommend it."

"Back up bitch!" Naji, scolded reaching under his shirt.

"Chill-chill." He winced in pain. "Dena, niggas will kill me if they know that I'm still alive. I got to get out of here." She looked at him and decided to help him move quickly into the car.

Naji, started the car and drove off.

"Where do you want me to take you?"

"I need time to think." Rodney, looked disappointed in the face.

"We can go to my crib, my mom's aint never home." The boy looked ahead as he drove. Rodney, decided to let the boy take him to his house.

When they pulled up in front of the house. He helped Rodney, into the house and led him into the living room.

"Naji, what the fuck are you doing nigga!" Nathan, walked out of the kitchen and into the living room.

"The nigga need our help."

"What are you trying to do get us all fucking killed!" Nathan, was scared and it showed.

"Fuck Pookie, that nigga aint shit." Naji, looked at his brother.

"Nigga that boy's money is long he can kill us like that." He snapped his finger. Naji, pulled out his gun.

"I can kill him like this." His face frowned up as he aimed his pistol at an imaginary target.

"I'm telling you now."

"He'll be alright." Rodney, sat down on the couch.

"Yo, your name Savage?" A little boy no more than seven years old asked sitting down next to Savage, The little boy looked at Rodney, looking for an answer.

"Yeah."

"You're a G kid." The little boy stuck his hand out to shake Rodney's, Rodney, smiled and took the little kids hand and shook it. "We about to come up like that too." The boy's eyes contained sincerity.

"What's your name?"

"I'm K.K. that's Naji, that's Nathan, and my cousin Gotta, didn't get here yet, but he's a G too, that nigga is serious." Rodney, couldn't help, but laugh. He never saw anything like this in his life. A whole family on some gangster shit. He looked up and smiled at the boys.

"Yo, I'm going to put yall boys on the map, just fuck with me for a minute." Rodney, looked over at Naji, studied his dark features and saw his own reflection. "What did you say about Pookie?"

"He put a hit out on you." Naji, looked at him. "He paid some niggas from over here to get at you. They fuck with Dooski, he be hitting them niggas."

"That nigga was probably there too." K.K. said standing with his arms crossed over his chest. He looked at his brothers.

"Yo, can I trust yall boys?" Rodney, asked already knowing the answer.

"What?" They all asked in union. Rodney, smiled and looked away. "Yo, I got a plan. Rodney, stood up.

Rodney, sent Naji, to his house to get his drugs. He taught Naji, how to lay on people, spy on them, watch their movement, and how to determine who had the money. He taught him tactics to go out and take the money after putting together a well thought out plot.

Rodney, lost a lot of weight sitting up in the hospital. He lifted weights in the basement with Nathan, and Gotta, Once he regained his strength he sent Nathan, to buy him another truck. He told him how he wanted it. Rodney, gave Naji, one of his cars that he had an storage.

After sitting back for three months Rodney, was ready to strike back. He sat in his passenger seat while Naji, drove the truck.

"Pull up over there." Rodney, pointed at the curb behind a cream colored Benz. He sat back in the passenger seat looking over the street. He waited until he saw Antonette, come walking out the school. "There she is." He looked at her with ill intentions.

She walked with a few of her friends. Her hair weave was longer than before. It was bright red and twisted around in curls. Her chest poked out further due to her pushing it out. The two girls that walked with her were ugly, but well shaped.

"I want you to get next to that bitch and fuck her."

"What if she don't like me?" Naji, stared ahead taking in every detail about the girl.

"She will she loves a baller." Rodney, sat up in his seat looking harder. He saw Dooski, pulled up in a cream colored Benz. He sat back relaxing his seat. "Yeah muth fucka." His words were low and steady. "Follow that car."

Antonette, smiled and looked at her friends then waved bye. She ducked into the car and Dooski, whisked away dipping into traffic. Naji, started the truck and followed his car.

"Slow down, don't' get right up on him. He may see us following him." Naji, slowed down and let a few cars get in between them. Rodney, sat in the truck with his eyes on the back of the Benz.

Dooski, pulled up at a hotel. He got out the car and walked toward a room. Antonette, followed him.

"Come on." Rodney, opened his door and climbed out of the truck. Naji, was close on his heels as they walked to the room.

"Do you want to shoot him or do you want me to shoot him?"

"Were not going to kill him now, first were going to rob him." Rodney, leaned close to the door and listened. He looked around and walked a door away for the one that Dooski, walked into. He knocked on the door no one answered. He knocked again, waited for an answer, when he didn't get one; he shoved his shoulder quickly into the door and went through it. Naji, looked around before walking in behind him.

Rodney, walked up to the dresser, moved it aside, and stuck his ear to the wall. He listened as he heard the headboard rocking against the wall in the next room. He smiled to himself. He heard Dooski, telling the young girl to say his name. She pretended to be in back breaking pain. Rodney, turned to leave forgetting that Naji, was with him until he looked at the boy.

They got into the car and waited for Dooski, to finish fucking his girlfriend's daughter. Ten minutes later Dooski emerged out of the room walking smoothly as Antonette, followed behind him.

"Yeah nigga." Rodney, spoke out in anger. He waited until the Benz turned out the parking lot. "Follow him." Naji, pulled out after the car. Rodney, sat in the passenger seat as Dooski, pulled up at the same house that he shot him up at.

Dooski, and the girl got out the car and walked into the house.

"Do you think it's in there?" Naji, asked wondering if Dooski, kept all of his shit in this house.

"Knowing Dooski, it's at the hotel we just left."

"Let's go get that shit." Anxiousness filled Naji's, voice.

"When he re-up we going to take all of his shit." Rodney, sat patiently in his seat.

"You still want me to get the girl?"

"Yup."

"Shoot her too?"

"No you're going to break her heart and fuck her up forever." He wiped his hand across his forehead.

Chapter 30
Bullet wounds had him laid back, mad as hell, thinking about the payback

Three hours went by before Dooski, came out the house freshly dressed and carrying a bag. He tossed it in the backseat of his car and pulled off. Naji, started the truck up and drove away following after him. He drove until the Benz pulled over and waited in the darkness.

A few minutes later another car pulled up. Loop, hopped out the car, got into Dooski's, car, gave him something, and got out the car carrying the bag that originally belonged to Dooski, Rodney, sighed at the result of his double cross.

Dooski, pulled off Naji, followed him. He drove until he pulled up at the same hotel that he fucked his step daughter in. He got out of his car and went into the room.

Ten minutes later he came out the room checking his watch. He got into his car and pulled off. Naji, started the truck up.

"Chill." Rodney, said touching his wrist while he held onto the steering wheel. "Come on." Rodney, got out the car and Naji, followed him. Rodney, broke into the room, went into the bathroom, checked under the lid on the back of the toilet. He pulled out the drugs. He smirked as he looked at the three kilos taped under the lid. He pulled the drugs off the lid and left with them.

Rodney, fronted the drugs to Naji, who fronted them to his brother and cousin. Naji, didn't get a chance to sell much. Rodney, kept him busy following people, robbing them, and spending time with Antonette,

Rodney, arrived at Tasha's, house. He got out the truck and went up to her front door. He knocked on the door. He looked around watching the street. He felt for his gun making sure it was intact.

She opened the door, covered her mouth, stood in place for a few moments, finally she reached out for him. She wrapped her arms around him and squeezed. He pushed her backward into the house. He kissed her and fondled her ass cheeks. She grabbed his hands and took them off of her ass.

"Talk to me. I was so worried about you. I didn't know what to think." Tears fell from her eyes.

"I'm built to last." He smiled at her. She grabbed him and held onto him. He kissed her and she kissed him back.

"What are you going to do now?" She looked at him and waited for his response. "What about your family? People think that you are dead." She looked at him with sad eyes.

"It's going to work itself out." He unbuttoned her pants, pulled them down, put on a condom, and fucked her savagely.

Chapter 31
No more Pookie

Rodney, set back a couple more months earning more money, he schooled Naji, along the way, and listened to his progress with Antonette,

What's up with that girl?" Rodney, smiled.

"I fucked her like twelve or thirteen times now." Naji, said not really interested in the girl.

"How does she act when you fuck her?"

"She screams, cries, and whines like I'm hurting her."

"Do you fuck her rough like I told you too, do you pull her hair, and ram it up her ass?" Rodney, sat on the edge of the couch leaning over while listening to Naji, explain.

"I do everything that we talked about."

"Are you still buying her shit?"

"Yeah."

"Have you fucked one of her friends yet?"

"Michelle's, ugly ass." Rodney, smiled and felt good preparing to rip the emotional life out of the little bitch that distracted him long enough for him to get caught slipping.

"How is she acting?"

"I did what you said. I brought her clothes, I ate her pussy, and lie to her fucking her head up." Naji, smiled.

"What?" Rodney, asked picking up on the smile.

"I got enough naked pictures of her to start a porn magazine."

"Keep playing those bitches like I tell you." He looked at Naji, and shook his hand. "I gave your brother something for you." Rodney, stared at Naji's, back while he walked out the front door.

Naji sat inside of Antonette's, bedroom dipping his dick in her mouth. She sucked on it, while he pushed it down her throat. She held her hands his thighs attempting to regulate how much dick entered her mouth. Naji, slapped her hands out of the way and pushed hard as he could down her throat. She gagged as water filled her eyes.

Naji fucked her fast and hard. He fucked her like she was a blow up doll instead of a person with feelings. He fucked her crazily, pulled her hair, pinched her ass cheeks. He rolled her over and smacked on her butt.

"Open your asshole." She grabbed both of her cheeks and pulled them apart revealing her pussy slit and a tightly circled asshole. Naji, puckered up his lips and spit in her ass then fucked her like a dog until he came.

He got finished and gave her three hundred dollars.

"Go buy you some more shit."

"Where are you going?"

"I'll be back."

"Naji, you always tell me that you will be back." She pouted and gave him a sad look.

"You know what I do." He said walking out of her bedroom. She grabbed his arm and held onto it. He looked at her contemplating slapping a few shades of skin color off her face.

"I'm saying I want to be with you." Sincerity pierced her eyes.

"Yo, I might need some space if you're going to be acting like that." He walked out the room and down the stairs.

"Wait I'll get better." She didn't want to let her meal ticket cut her off.

"I'll be back." He walked through the living room.

"What's up Dooski?" He smiled at him like he liked him.

"What's up Naji, you need to stop playing B, come and get this real paper." He stood up. "I just got robbed for ten bricks and I'm back already. Naji, looked at him lying through his teeth. He knew it was only three bricks because he helped steal them.

"I'm saying I'll see what's up." Naji, memorized every word in the conversation so he could tell Rodney,

"Alright." Naji, walked out the house, he got in his truck, and drove over to Michelle's, house.

Rodney, was financially stronger, mentally stronger, and physically ready to go up against Pookie, he called Naji, and told him what to do.

Naji, called Antonette, but she didn't call back she couldn't. She was inside a hotel room underneath Dooski, thinking about Naji, while she wailed out in fake delight. Naji, called her again, waited for her to answer, but got her voice mail. Soon as Dooski, came she checked her messages. Instantly she wanted to call him back, but thought against it.

She snuck out of the room and walked a few blocks down and called him. Rodney, watched her walk out the room and pulled his mask down. Soon as she was out of sight Rodney, stepped out of the car and walked over to the room.

He came through it fast and silently. He aimed his pistol at Dooski,

"Oh shit B, chill all the money is in the bathroom." He sat up butt naked. Rodney, looked at his dick looking little and weak. He shook his head in disgust. Rodney, waved the gun toward the bathroom. He walked behind Dooski, took the drugs and money then made him walk back over to the bed. Dooski, got in the bed.

"Come on B, this aint no faggot shit is it?" His eyes fluttered around hoping he wasn't about to get raped.

"No this is personal shit." Rodney, lifted his ski mask over his face, but stopped it at his forehead.

"Rodney?"

"Don't say my name." He walked up on Dooski,

Antonette, sat on the phone crying.

"Please Naji, I love you don't be like that to me." She shook her head side to side. "No..no…nope your wrong I'm not fucking nobody." She shook her head no again.

"It's over bitch I hate you!" He slammed the phone down in her face. She screeched out and looked at the receiver wondering what happened. She called him back, but the phone just rung.

Inside the hotel room Rodney, smashed his gun across Dooski's, head. Blood splattered on the wall. Rodney, pulled out a long butcher knife and jammed it in Dooski's, throat. His eyes lit up in surprise that his life was finally over. Rodney, wasn't satisfied he wanted more violence. He stabbed him in his chest, then his face, his stomach, and finally slashed his throat. Rodney, left the hotel room, got in his car, and pulled off.

Antonette, walked into the hotel room and found Dooski, laying dead in a pool of blood. The bed was covered with blood. She backed out the room and walked away. She walked down the street and called a taxi cab.

Rodney, pulled up in front of Naji's, house. He went in the house and handed him the two kilos.

"It's been real kid." He shook his hand.

"Good looking out." Naji, smile at Rodney,

"Yo, keep fucking that bitch for another year and fuck her head up." He stopped and turned to face Naji, "Do that for me, keep it up, keep doing what you're doing, but don't love her, dump her ass, and break her heart." He smiled. "Yo, she'll be here in a minute is Michelle, here?"

"Upstairs." Rodney, laughed.

"Alright my nigga." Rodney, gave Naji, a handshake and left.

Ten minutes later Antonette, walked up to Naji's, house and knocked on the door. She had tears in her eyes.

"What's up?" K.K. smacked her on the ass.

"Stop playing K.K." She looked at him. "Where is your brother?"

"Which one?" The little boy said smiling.

"Is he in his room?"

"Yup." K.K. Smiled and sat back on the couch.

Antonette, walked upstairs and into his bedroom and screamed loud as she could. Rodney, rode around for the past two days keeping a close watch on Pookie, he followed him to his house, to the supermarket, and to his son's little league basket ball game.

Rodney, sat in the truck watching the kids run up and down the court. He saw people on the bleachers cheering and yelling, but the one person that stood out the most was Pookie, Rodney, watched his face fill with pride as his son scored point after point. When the game was over Rodney, trailed behind him, parked a few houses down from his house, and waited for him to come out.

Hours went by before Pookie, strolled out the house. He got into his car and drove over toward the park. He parked his Range Rover, got out, and walked over to the park.

Rodney, sat in his truck for three minutes. He got out and walked over to Pookie's, truck. He broke into it, got inside of it, sat there for a few minutes, and got out of it. He walked back to his truck feeling satisfied with himself. Rodney, got in his truck and dialed a few numbers, and said a few words. He started up his truck and headed toward the park.

Rodney, sat in his truck watching Pookie, sit on the bench looking like his normal self. Loop, sat next to him, then stood up, and yelled at some of his workers. He walked around giving out orders. He yelled warning everyone else about the swarm of police detectives coming. Loop, and everyone else walked away pretending not to be a part of the confusion.

"Pookie, Pookie, Pookie," The short stocky yellow haired narcotics officer stepped closer to him.

"What's up?" Pookie, looked away from the man.

"Umm." The cop had a smug look on his face. He smiled and looked away then directly at Pookie, "Murder, weapons possession, criminal possession of a controlled substance. Preferably A-1 weight and conspiracy." He smiled as he pulled out an arrest warrant for Pookie,

"I'll beat this like I do all of your weak ass charges." Pookie, smirked at the cop.

"Really?" The cop nodded his head up and down confidently. They cuffed Pookie, and put him the back of a squad car, they placed handcuffs on Loop,

Rodney, drove behind the police as they rode over to the street where the Range Rover, was parked.

"Whose car is this Pookie?" The same short cop asked. Pookie, looked at him and turned his head away. The cop opened the door and reached under the seat and pulled out a kilo of cocaine. He pulled out the murder weapon that was used to kill Christopher, and Dooski's, cell phone. He dug deeper and pulled out a bunch of pictures of Pookie, and his shemale friend.

"Pookie, who would have ever thought?" The cop laughed and passed the photos around. Pookie, sat in the backseat of the squad car feeling sad and fucked up.

Rodney, drove slowly pass the squad car. He moved slowly his window was half way down. He stopped directly beside the cop car. He looked over at Pookie, and let him take a good look at him. He pulled off.

Rodney, drove over to Pookie's, house and got out the truck. He placed copies of the photos in his mail box for his wife to find. Rodney, got back in his truck and pulled off. He stopped by Janet's, house and knocked on the door. She opened the door.

"Oh my god Rodney," She embraced him and held onto him tight as she could. He held her too.

"I'm leaving town. I just wanted you to know that I'm alive. I love you." He held his mother in his arms and expressed his love. He went to his truck and came back with a bag. He gave her the bag with one hundred thousand dollars in it. He hugged her again and left.

Rodney, arrived at Ebony's, house ten minutes after leaving his mother's. He knocked on the door. She opened it and her eyes lit up.

"Rodney!" She leapt into his arms and held onto him tightly. She held him for a few seconds, but let him go when she didn't feel his strong embrace. He pulled back from her.

"You were one of my favorite people. I don't want you to get caught up in my shit." He backed up away from her.

"I love you too." She said weakly. Her head dropped toward the ground.

"I got something for you." He turned and left the porch only to return carrying a bag full of stolen drug money."

"I don't want your money Rodney," She looked sad and heartbroken.

"Ebony, use it to go to college, but I need for you to take this money." She smiled at him. One second later her tears fell. He kissed her and walked away.

The next stop was to Tasha's, house. He walked in the door. She was in the kitchen in the process of cooking something to eat.

"Yo," He startled her.

"Where have you been?" She looked at him slyly.

"Preparing to leave."

"Where are you going?" She asked not expecting what she heard.

"Not sure, but far away from here." She looked at him. He looked at her meeting her glare with his own. For a few minutes no words were passed, but awareness bred a silent understanding.

"What about your houses and stuff?" She sounded like a little kid.

"I sold the ones that I didn't need, but I saved this one, the one my mother lives in, and three other ones so she could have some money." Tasha, turned around, shut the stove off, and rushed upstairs.

Rodney, shook his head not expecting her to take his leaving this hard. He walked upstairs behind her to give her some closure before he got the fuck out of dodge. He walked into the bedroom where she was stuffing her suitcases with clothes and other things that were important to her.

"What are you doing?"

"It's nothing else here for me, but a shadowy past that no one will ever let me live down." She walked toward Rodney, and stared in his eyes.

"I didn't plan on taking you with me."

"I didn't plan on falling in love with you either."

"Love what does it really amount too?" He said that not wanting to give her the last word. He walked out the bedroom door. She walked out behind him.

Outside she packed her suitcases into the back of the truck, got in, and fastened her seatbelt, and lay back willing to follow her man to the end of the world. Rodney, looked at her and smirked at his fate. An ex crack head, his bottom bitch, life couldn't have been anymore realer.

Made in the USA
Charleston, SC
09 January 2011